"I'll do my best. And how are you?"

"I'm okay." It was the second time she'd lied that morning.

"I know you'll be fine."

This time, when she reached for the handle, she opened the door. She turned to face Ryan again. She pressed her hand onto his cheek and brushed her lips against his. The kiss was over before it began and still, it stole her breath. How could it be that the wrong man appeared in her life at the right time?

"I need to get going," she said, her voice a hoarse whisper.

He gave her a wan smile. "I know."

There was nothing else to do or say. Easing out of the seat, she dropped to the pavement. After closing the door, she gave him a small wave. In that moment, she caught her reflection on the side window and stood taller. She didn't know what would happen next, but she was ready.

Dear Reader,

For me, every book is unique. While I love them all equally, it's for different reasons. Sometimes, I find it a challenge to explain what makes a certain book special. But that is not the case with *Texas Law: Lethal Encounter.*

I love the characters.

The heroine, Kathryn Glass, is the undersheriff in her small Texas town. She's good at her job and has the confidence of her department. She's a smart, strong woman who loves her family and her community. A widow for over six years, she's ready to put parts of the past behind her and see what the future holds. And that's when she finds Ryan Steele trespassing in her backyard...

Ryan has made some bad choices in his life. But now, he's ready to make up for his misdeeds. There's just one problem—he's not sure how a *good person* should act. What's more, he's attracted to beautiful Kathryn. The one thing he knows is that a woman like her will never want to be with a guy like him.

But when the neighboring towns of Mercy and Encantador are thrown into deadly chaos by the return of serial killer Decker Newcombe, Kathryn and Ryan have to work together.

This time, Decker's come back with a plan—and help.

No spoilers from me, but the outcome is unpredictable.

There is one other thing I love about this book and it's you, Dear Reader. Thank you for taking this journey with me and I hope you come to love these characters as much as I do!

All the best,
Jennifer D. Bokal

TEXAS LAW: LETHAL ENCOUNTER

Jennifer D. Bokal

H HARLEQUIN®
ROMANTIC SUSPENSE™

Recycling programs for this product may not exist in your area.

ISBN-13: 978-1-335-59392-4

Texas Law: Lethal Encounter

Copyright © 2024 by Jennifer D. Bokal

For questions and comments about the quality of this book, please contact us at CustomerService@Harlequin.com.

Harlequin Enterprises ULC
22 Adelaide St. West, 41st Floor
Toronto, Ontario M5H 4E3, Canada
www.Harlequin.com

Printed in U.S.A.

Jennifer D. Bokal is the author of several books, including the Harlequin Romantic Suspense series Rocky Mountain Justice, Wyoming Nights, Texas Law and several books that are part of the Colton continuity.

Happily married to her own alpha male for more than twenty-five years, she enjoys writing stories that explore the wonders of love. Jen and her manly husband have three beautiful grown daughters, two very spoiled dogs and a cat who runs the house.

Books by Jennifer D. Bokal

Harlequin Romantic Suspense

Texas Law

Texas Law: Undercover Justice
Texas Law: Serial Manhunt
Texas Law: Lethal Encounter

The Coltons of New York

Colton's Deadly Affair

The Coltons of Colorado

Colton's Rogue Investigation

Wyoming Nights

Under the Agent's Protection
Agent's Mountain Rescue
Agent's Wyoming Mission
The Agent's Deadly Liaison

Visit the Author Profile page at
Harlequin.com for more titles.

To John: My love, my life, my everything.

Chapter 1

The song of insects filtered through the open windows. Ryan Steele sat in the cab of his truck and stared into the night. A bead of sweat rolled down the side of his face, and he wiped it away with his shoulder. Old Blue, his dog, sat in the passenger seat and panted.

"Hell of a night," he said to the dog. "It's..." He glanced at his phone. It was 8:32 p.m. and it was still 81 degrees. "Well, it's too late to be this hot."

After slipping his phone into the cup holder, he shifted in his seat. Ryan didn't mind spending the night in the cab of his truck. In fact, he'd slept in worse places. Jail. A bare mattress on the floor of a house that smelled like stale beer, body odor, and worse. For most of his thirty-eight years, he'd wandered—avoiding anything that would tie him to one place for too long. Not for the first time, he contemplated how things would've been different if Decker Newcombe hadn't been a part of his life.

Decker had been born bad—plain and simple.

And Ryan? Well, his misdeeds were more of a choice.

He remembered how they'd started in elementary school. Both boys lived in the same neighborhood outside of Dallas. It began with a few sodas swiped from the convenience store next to their trailer park. Kid stuff, right? Then, by middle school, they were breaking into trailers. They kept some of their loot but quickly learned how to sell the stolen property for cash. The summer before high school, Decker was paid to beat up a classmate who'd flirted with the wrong girl.

To be honest, he imagined that his old compatriot would have done the crimes for free. But Ryan saw them mainly as a way to make bank. Money was the only way to escape the crappy life he'd been given.

For decades, he'd managed the business end while Decker committed offenses for hire—assault, robbery, arson, even assassinations Then they took a job that ended with a Wyoming DA dead, and both Decker and Ryan were wanted for the murder. Sure, Decker was the killer, but Ryan had accepted payment for the hit. That was enough to be considered an accessory to the murder.

Decker disappeared.

Ryan was arrested.

Corny as it sounded, even in his own mind, that was when he got a chance to start over. It all began when Isaac Patton visited him in jail. Ryan was waiting for trial— held without being given bail. Isaac had just opened a private security firm—Texas Law—and he had a plan to catch Decker. It was as simple as it was audacious.

In exchange for being used as bait to draw Decker out of hiding, Ryan would have his criminal record expunged.

It had taken nearly a year of watching and waiting for the killer to emerge. During that time, Ryan had been set up with several businesses to run in the town of Mercy, Texas—not far from where he now sat. For the first time in his life, he'd been legit. During the months he worked, his businesses made a profit. He took care of his employees. He was part of a community. Life wasn't perfect, especially since he was living a lie. But he'd been happy.

What's more, it gave him a glimpse of how things could be different.

As they all hoped, Decker had contacted Ryan. From there, things had gotten seriously messed up. Decker had gone on a killing spree—leaving four people dead and several more seriously wounded.

After a shootout, the killer had escaped into the desert. More than a year later, and Decker was still at large.

Since Ryan had kept up his end of the bargain with Isaac and his federal partners, his criminal record had been cleared.But even life without a criminal record hadn't been easy. Without his felonious history, he had no history at all. It turned him into a ghost, walking among the living but never really being seen or heard. Legit employers were leery of hiring him because they all knew he had a tale—and the ending wasn't happy. He'd thought about selling his story for profit. After all, he was one of the people who'd known Decker best. But if he was going to cash in on his former association, his past would follow him like a shadow forever.

Luckily, he'd found a general contractor who needed help and didn't ask too many questions. Ryan worked hard and got paid for his time. Now he had enough money in his pocket for a down payment on a small house. Or maybe there was a business for sale that he could turn over.

Anyway, after 15 months, he was back—and this time, he planned to stay.

Too bad there were no vacancies at the motel, in Encantador. It forced Ryan to find an out-of-the-way place to park his truck where he could spend the night. The vehicle sat at the edge of a gravel lot. It was bordered on one side by a canal. On the other side, there was a county route and endless Texas desert. In the distance sat a housing development that was filled with small homes.

Old Blue looked at him and whined. After turning in several circles on the passenger seat, he dropped into a ball. With a sigh, he placed his head on his paws.

"I know how you feel." Reaching over the center console, he scratched the top of the dog's head. "I didn't want to spend the night in the truck, either. Sorry, boy."

The heat leeched his energy, and he was ready for a rest. After folding his arms across his chest, he let his eyes drift closed. Old Blue sat up. The sound drew Ryan from the edge of sleep. He glanced at his canine companion. The dog's spine was ramrod straight. His ears were back. Peering into the darkness, Old Blue growled.

Something—or someone—was out there. Ryan was awake now. "What is it, boy?"

The dog growled louder. He followed Old Blue's gaze. A figure emerged from the canal's bank. The hair at the dog's nape stood on end. The person looked male, and they wore dark clothes. They crept along the trail, keeping to the shadows. After a moment, he lost sight of them in the darkness. But a moment was all he needed.

Ryan was sure he'd just caught a glimpse of Decker Newcombe.

For a moment, he tried to think rationally. He'd seen someone, sure. But it wasn't Decker. After all, he'd just been thinking about the killer, who was still at large. So of course, he imagined seeing him emerge from the shadows. But the killer was presumed to be dead, for Christ's sake.

Ryan settled back in the seat, his hand drifting to his side. The scar ran right under his ribs, still a raised weal. It was a reminder of the last time he'd seen Decker and the killer had stabbed him in the gut. Again, he looked out of the windshield. The man—whoever he was—was gone.

An upstanding citizen would call 911. Leaning forward, Ryan reached for his cell. The sheriff's personal information was still in his contacts. He placed the call.

Before it even rang on his end, voicemail answered. "You've reached Sheriff Parsons…"

He didn't want to leave a message, he wanted to talk to the man. With a curse, Ryan ended the call and threw the phone back in the cupholder.

"What do I do now?" he asked, although he knew the answer. He still had to call 911.

The dog glanced over his shoulder. Looking back to the open window, Old Blue sprang out of the truck.

"Boy." Ryan leaned across the center console and yelled through the window. "Get back here."

The dog paid no attention. Old Blue sprinted toward the trail until the only thing Ryan could see was the white tip of his tail. Soon, even that was gone.

He opened the door of his truck and stepped into the night. Somehow, it was hotter outside than in the cab. "Blue." He patted his thigh as he called out. "Get back here, boy." He held his breath and waited. The dog did not return. "Blue," he called again. "Come here."

Ryan wanted to curse. Instead, he jogged into the darkness, following the dog's path.

The housing development was less than five hundred yards from where he'd left his truck. The narrow dirt trail was bordered on one side by a tall, wooden fence that ran along the back side of the neighborhood. On the other side was a canal with concrete banks. A trickle of water ran down the center. Scraggly trees and bushes clung to life next to the waterway.

"Blue," he called out. "Where are you, boy?"

Ryan's chest was tight. Sweat dripped from his hairline. It soaked the collar of his T-shirt and burned his eyes. Earlier in the day, he'd tied a flannel shirt around his waist. Now, he used the hem to dry his face. He peered into the darkness and looked for any sign of the dog. The glint of his collar in the night. The rustle of bushes a moment before the dog emerged. The sound of a happy bark.

There was nothing.

Heart still pounding, he slowed his gait to a walk. The dog couldn't have gone far, right? Although, he knew that was wrong. If Old Blue started running, Ryan would never see him again. He'd gotten used to the canine's company. Was he on his own once again? A sour taste filled his mouth.

A bridge had been built across the canal, and the path rose to the berm. He climbed the hill and he sagged with relief. Sitting next to the fence was Old Blue. The dog looked up. His tail started to wag.

"You scared me, running off like that." He moved to the dog's side and rubbed behind his ears. *Damn.* He hadn't thought to grab the dog's leash from the truck. Now, he just had to hope that Old Blue would follow. "C'mon, let's go."

Old Blue whined and looked toward the fence.

Ryan gripped the dog's collar and tugged. Old Blue didn't budge.

"What's the matter?"

The dog sat next to a gap in the fencing. Between the slats, Ryan could see a flat backyard with a large tree. A concrete patio sat off the back door of a single-level home. There was a grill and patio furniture. It was all covered by a striped awning.

Then he saw it. Movement in the shadows next to the house. It was a person. A man. Holding his breath, he stood still and watched. The way the man moved—his posture, the tilt of his head—was familiar.

Ryan knew that it might not be Decker. But what if it was?

Over the years, he'd gotten used to minding his own business. He was good at looking the other way when trouble was near. But he also knew that if he wanted a different life, he had to be a different person.

It meant he had to warn someone.

Besides, he had a score to settle with Decker.

Slipping a hand into his pocket, he reached for his phone. *Damn it*. He'd left it in his vehicle. Still, he had to know if he'd really seen Decker.

Looking through the gap in the fence, he scanned the yard. The back of the house was visible, but the man was gone. Despite the heat, a chill ran down his spine.

"Where'd you go, you son of a bitch?" he asked, though nobody was around to hear his question.

Old Blue nudged his side. He looked down at the dog, who regarded him with brown eyes.

"Should we find out if Decker's in the neighborhood?"

Old Blue stood and stared into the yard.

Well, he supposed it was settled.

Ryan was a big guy, over six foot two. What's more, his broad shoulders had gotten more muscular from months of working construction. A few slats in the fence were missing, but the opening was narrow. Turning sideways, he slipped between the boards.

Old Blue followed.

With the dog at his side, he crept across the yard. Light spilled from a window where the curtains had yet to be drawn. Decker could've snuck into the house already. The family who lived there might not even know that their lives were in danger.

Ryan hadn't always done the right thing. But he had to stop his old associate—no matter the personal costs.

Undersheriff Kathryn Glass stood in her bedroom. It had been an especially long day. The sheriff, Mooky Parsons, was on vacation in Cancun for two weeks to celebrate his wedding anniversary. His absence left

Kathryn in charge. She didn't mind the responsibility that came with being the acting sheriff. But the Encantador Sheriff's Department was small to begin with. A missing set of hands made everyone's workload heavier.

It was almost 8:45 p.m. on a Saturday evening and Kathryn was still in her sweaty uniform. But she had been at a back-to-school fair hosted by the elementary school's parent–teacher group and had spent the evening talking about internet safety.

Her mind wandered, as it did often now, to her eldest child. Morgan was just beginning her senior year of high school. The past few years had been rough on her daughter. She'd experimented with drinking and some drugs and boys. Kathryn always struggled to find the right parental balance between discipline and understanding. Especially since she suspected that much of her daughter's behavior was a way of dealing with the death of her father and Kathryn's husband two years earlier.

Her son, Brock, a sophomore, was completely opposite to his sister. He was class treasurer and had recently made the varsity football team.

Working her wedding band up and down her finger, she wondered what her husband might think if he were still alive. But she knew. He'd be like Kathryn and love their kids so much that it hurt.

Staring at the golden band on her finger, her chest ached with loneliness. There were still times she picked up the phone, ready to call Edward. But now, those moments no longer ended with her in tears. A few months back, she'd even managed a wistful smile as she recalled how he'd greet everyone with a cheery "Yello!"

His own little joke, he used to say when she or the kids teased him.

She missed Edward, truly she did. Yet, recently, Kathryn wasn't so focused on the past. She was looking forward to the future—like Morgan's pending college applications and Brock's talent on the gridiron. She glanced at her ring once more, but movement behind her caught her eye.

Looking up, she scanned her room through a mirror atop her dresser.

Nothing was out of place.

The bed was made. A pile of clean clothes—folded, but yet to be put away—sat on a chair. A book lay on a nightstand.

She turned.

A face peered through the window.

Her blood turned cold as her heart started to race. Then her training kicked in. Kathryn's pulse thundered in her ears as she ran from her bedroom. She sprinted down the short hallway and dashed through the kitchen. Thank goodness both of her kids were out with their friends.

Kathryn fumbled with the handle on the kitchen door as she unlatched the locks. She jerked the door open. It hit the wall with a crack. She ran into the night, just in time to see the man as he sprinted around the side of her house.

"Stop!" she yelled as she ran after him. "Encantador Sheriff."

She skidded around the corner. The man was already running down the sidewalk. A large, brown dog loped at his side.

"Hold your hands up," she called again, "and turn to face me."

The man didn't stop.

Neither did Kathryn.

As she ran, porch lights turned on. Opening their curtains and front doors, her neighbors looked into the street, eager to see who or what the undersheriff was chasing.

The man veered to the left, sprinting across another lawn. He was headed toward the canal.

Kathryn had lived in the area her whole life. She knew the town better than she knew herself. If the man made it to the path and the canal, he could get away.

Unless...

She cut through a neighbor's yard. The grass was baked, brittle and brown, by the long Texas summer, and the blades crunched underfoot. Running through the backyard, she reached for the top of the fence and scaled the boards with her feet. Sweat trickled down her back and dampened her shirt. She had a clear view of the canal path and waited for the man to appear. He still ran at a full sprint, and his speed only gave her seconds to react. She came down, landing hard. The impact sent a shock wave through her knees. She turned, just as she and the man collided. He slammed into her, knocking her down. Lying on the ground. she had a sense of having been hit by a brick wall, and white dots floated in her vision.

Rolling to her hands and knees, she watched the man as he sprinted away. The dog sniffed her as he passed. Once again, she was driven more by instinct than thought. Reaching for the dog, her fingers looped through the collar. She pulled him to a stop.

The canine yelped. The sound was one part terror, one part fury. He bared his teeth at Kathryn. She quickly rose to her feet and straddled the dog near his front legs. She wasn't exactly sure what she'd do with the mutt. Hopefully, the pet had a rabies tag that linked him to his owner.

"You're coming with me," she said to the canine. Her breath came in short gasps. "Let's go."

She tugged on the dog. He snarled, lunging at her. She jerked her hand back, barely avoiding the sharp teeth.

"Old Blue," a male voice called from the darkness. "It's okay. It'll be okay."

She looked up. The man was standing on the trail, less than ten yards from where Kathryn held his dog. From where she stood, she could see that he was tall. He had dark hair. A five-o'clock shadow covered his cheeks and chin.

It occurred to her that the guy could've gotten away. Instead, he'd come back for his companion. She admired that kind of loyalty—even in a person who looked through windows.

"You stay where you are," Kathryn ordered the man.

Holding up his hands in surrender, he said, "I won't move, so long as you let go of my dog."

Old Blue whimpered and wagged his tail.

"I don't think so," said Kathryn. With the dog calm, she commanded, "Sit."

The canine dropped to his haunches. Still holding his collar, she scratched the back of his neck.

"Traitor," the guy muttered.

She refused to smile. "You want your dog back? Come to my office and answer some questions."

"I really don't think that's necessary, do you?"

This time, she gave a quick laugh. "Buddy, I caught you looking through my bedroom window. You want your dog, you come to my office." Did she feel bad using the dog as a bargaining chip? Maybe a little.

Still, she had a job to do. She needed to find out if the guy had any outstanding arrest warrants. She might have to charge him with trespassing or stalking. Mostly, she wanted him out of her town—because Kathryn knew one thing. "You aren't from these parts, are you?"

"Well…" he scratched his chin "…not exactly."

Not exactly? "What's that supposed to mean?"

"I lived in Mercy for a year a while back."

She recognized the voice. Kathryn's heartbeat raced. She swallowed. "Take a few steps closer. Let me get a look at you."

The man took three steps in her direction. He cut the distance between them by half.

"That's enough. Keep your hands up." She rested a palm on the gun at her hip, a not-too-subtle warning.

With her eyes adjusted to the darkness and the man standing closer, she saw him clearly. The last time she'd seen him, his hair had been shorter. He'd been stockier but was now all muscle. But still, it was him.

"Talk about a bad penny turning up again. Ryan Steele. What in the hell are you doing?" She paused a beat. The dog, whose collar she held, must've been the canine who survived the Decker Newcombe massacre. She'd heard that Ryan had adopted the mutt. "Why were you in my backyard?"

"I didn't realize it was your yard, Undersheriff. Honest," he said.

"What were you doing in someone's backyard at all? Trespassing is a crime." She'd also heard that for helping the feds, Ryan's criminal history had been erased. That didn't save him from being charged with something now.

"I thought I saw something. Someone." His voice was barely above a whisper. She had to strain to hear what was said. "They were in your backyard. I was worried."

Despite the heat, gooseflesh covered her arms.

"Then why were you running from me?"

He lifted one large shoulder and let it drop. "Old habits, I guess."

She didn't really like his answer, which brought up more questions. "Who did you see?"

He shook his head.

The law-enforcement officer inside her had to consider that Ryan was lying. He hadn't seen anyone lurking in the shadows. The only reason he'd been in her yard—or anyone else's—was to find an easy house to rob.

Yet, there was another part that believed Ryan had seen someone else. But why? Maybe it was because he'd come back to save his dog. Or maybe there was something sincere in his tone of voice.

She tried once more. "You aren't giving me much to go on, Ryan. Who was it that you saw?"

He stared at her. Their gazes met and held. "I saw…" he swallowed "…I thought I saw him."

Him. A hard knot formed in her gut. She could already guess the answer. Yet, she had to ask, "Him who?"

"Decker Newcombe," he said, his voice still a whisper. "He's back."

Chapter 2

"You saw who?" Kathryn choked on the last word. Decker Newcombe was worse than the boogeyman to those who lived in Encantador and the neighboring town of Mercy.

Her hearing was fine. But Ryan's words were unbelievable.

"Decker," he said again. This time his voice was louder. "I only caught a glimpse of the guy, but the way he moved was just the same." With an exhale, he continued, "Anyway, I saw someone. I followed him—whoever it was—into your backyard."

Kathryn had been first on the scene when one of Decker's victims had been found. The one-time assassin—killing only for money—had switched his modus operandi to become a serial killer. The image of the woman—bloody and bruised—still haunted her dreams. Past trauma aside, she had to think. She was the undersheriff, after all. While running her fingers through the dog's fur, she said, "Your story doesn't make sense." She paused a beat to let him comment. He didn't. "If you thought you saw a serial killer, you should've called 9-1-1. Why go after him yourself?"

"It wasn't exactly my plan." He nodded toward the dog that sat at her feet. "Old Blue jumped out of my truck window."

He answered some of her questions and created others. "Your truck?"

"I was parked at the end of this trail." He hooked his finger over his shoulder.

Parking in the middle of nowhere was suspicious. "Why?"

"Just getting some rest."

"In your truck?"

Even in the dark, she could see Ryan stiffen. "That's not against the law. What do you call camping?"

"Camping usually includes someplace nicer than the end of the canal trail." She nodded toward the dog. "You got a leash for him?"

"In the truck," said Ryan.

"Not a problem." Still holding the dog's collar, Kathryn used her other hand to loosen the belt that was around her waist. After pulling it free of the loops on her uniform pants, she secured the end to the dog's collar. It wasn't a long lead, but at least Old Blue could be walked.

Then to Ryan, she said, "Step toward me. Spread your feet and put your arms out at your side." He followed her order. "You got any weapons? Anything I should know about?"

He gave a quick shake of his head. "Nothing."

She patted him down quickly. His pockets were empty and there was nothing hidden in his clothes. "Let's go," she said.

"You talking to me or the dog?" Ryan asked.

"Both. You've got some questions to answer. And you're going to do that in my office. If I buy what you have to say, I'll give you a ride back to your truck." She didn't want to get ambushed from behind and gestured for him to pass. "You go first." Ryan walked by, and Kathryn followed.

Tongue lolling from his mouth, Old Blue seemed content to go on a walk.

As they walked, Kathryn couldn't help but ask, "You saw someone in the dark and you thought it might be Decker. Why's that?"

Raising his large shoulders, he let them drop with a sigh. "Like I said, it was just the way he moved, I guess. I tried to call Mooky but he didn't answer. Before I had the chance to call 9-1-1, Old Blue took off. I went after him, and we ended up in your yard." He paused. "Maybe we should call the sheriff now. He could meet us at your office."

She shouldn't be surprised that Ryan wanted to speak to her boss. The two men had worked together to find the killer months before. Yet, his suggestion stung, like a slap to the cheek. "He's on vacation, so you're stuck dealing with me." She tried to keep the snark out of her voice, but it was a losing battle.

Ten years earlier, Kathryn had been hired as a sheriff's deputy. It didn't take long for her to be promoted to undersheriff. Since Mooky had a decade's more experience in law enforcement, she'd never get the top job. What's more, he was a popular figure in the community. But she worked hard every day, too. So, it always left a bad taste in her mouth when she was overlooked by those who only wanted the sheriff. Right now, with Mooky out of the country, Kathryn was the first line of defense in protecting her town.

"There's a gap in the fencing, just ahead." A storm had pulled slats off her fence months earlier, and Kathryn had yet to repair all the damage. Until she did, it provided a passage from her yard to the canal trail.

After ducking and turning sideways, Ryan barely squeezed through the narrow opening. It made it impossible for her to miss his toned physique. His T-shirt hugged the muscles in his pecs. The cuff on his short sleeve was snug around his biceps. She really shouldn't be noticing the handsome ex-con—especially since she didn't trust him at all.

Drawing in a shaky breath, Kathryn shoved aside all thoughts of hard arms and tight abs. She followed Ryan. The dog was the last to squeeze through the gap. Using her free hand, she pointed to the side of her house. "My cruiser is parked at the curb."

"Your place looks nice," said Ryan, while walking through her backyard.

On the back patio, she'd created an outdoor-living space. "Thanks," she mumbled.

"You eat out here often?" he asked.

She understood that Ryan was just making small talk. But the patio had been a year-long project for her, the first after Edward's death. It was a place that brought a sense of accomplishment and peace. What's more, she served dinner alfresco whenever she could. Not that her kids were around much for meals. It meant she ate alone most nights. Still, she said, "Actually, we use the patio a lot."

"I don't blame you."

"Go around the house to the right. You can't miss my car."

She followed Ryan. Old Blue, still on his makeshift leash, trotted happily at her side. Kathryn's house was like many in South Texas. Sitting on a square foundation, the one-story residence had adobe walls and a tile roof. Everything was built to keep out the heat. From her front yard, she could see several open doors along her street. People stood on stoops and watched the road.

When she stepped onto the curb, the elderly woman who lived across the road called out. "What's happening, Undersheriff? We all saw you chasing that man. What'd he do?"

She hadn't expected to be questioned by her neighbors. Working her jaw back and forth, she thought through her answer before speaking. "I've got it under control, Gladys. You can go back into your house."

Gladys wasn't ready to give up. "Who is he?"

"I can't comment on anything right now," she said, trying to strike a balance between in-control and amiable. "Y'all go back inside."

Another neighbor called out, "Is that the guy who used to own the bar in Mercy?"

And another, "Where'd you get the dog?"

Another neighbor, named Joe, said, "I thought I saw someone slinking through my backyard."

The last comment caught her attention. Ryan had certainly been in her yard. It didn't matter that he swore that he was following a man he thought could be Decker. From the beginning, she suspected that he was lying to her. Was this witness going to give her proof?

She stopped and turned to the man who'd spoken. Joe was in his late fifties and had two grown children. "Was this the man you saw?" She pointed at Ryan with her free hand.

Joe stood on the sidewalk, next to his driveway. He slowly shook his head. "I don't think so. The guy I saw was shorter. Thinner. He was dressed in all-black—like a ninja with a hoodie."

If Ryan had been telling Kathryn the truth, then someone else was roaming through her neighborhood. Someone who had an uncanny resemblance to Decker Newcombe.

Was the killer back?

The metallic taste of panic coated her tongue. She inhaled. Exhaled. "Y'all get back inside. Lock your doors. There's nothing to see here. But if anything turns up on a doorbell camera, text me the footage right away." Her car keys were still in the pocket of her uniform pants. Using the fob, she unlocked the doors. She opened the back door for Ryan. The man got into her cruiser. Old Blue pulled on his lead. She let the dog follow his owner. After shutting the back door, she rounded to the driver's side and slipped behind the steering wheel. The air in the car was hot and stale. She turned on the engine and set the air-conditioning on high.

A wall of mesh wire separated the backseat from the front. "Let me know if you get enough cool air back there," she said.

Old Blue sat next to Ryan and panted. For his part, Ryan scratched the back of the dog's shoulders and stared out the side window. "We're good."

"Can you hand me my belt?" She didn't exactly need the belt to hold up her pants, but she didn't want to give Ryan anything that he could turn into a weapon, either. He'd been compliant so far. But she'd be naive to think that his mood was guaranteed to stay so friendly.

He passed the leather belt through the wall of wire that separated the back seat from the front. "Here you go."

She took the strap and shoved it into the console. "Thanks." The car's interior was starting to cool. After pulling the door closed, she placed the gearshift into Drive and eased away from the curb.

"What now?" Ryan raised his voice to be heard over the engine.

Kathryn had to focus on the facts as she knew them. Right now, she didn't know a lot. If Ryan was right, then a dangerous and deranged man was in her town once again. And it was her job to bring the elusive serial killer to justice.

Ryan sat in the back seat of the cruiser. It wasn't the first time he'd been in the back of a police car. Still, he had hoped that those days were behind him. Scratching Old Blue's ears, he watched the undersheriff.

At least his situation had improved in one way. Kathryn Glass was better-looking than any other cop he'd met over his lifetime. Hell, she was an attractive woman. Full stop. She wore her long brown hair in a ponytail that skimmed the back of her neck. Her skin was tanned by the Texas sun. Her eyes were the same blue as the sky on a summer's day.

Blue as the sky?

When did he get so poetic?

Still, there was more about Kathryn to admire beyond her looks. He'd heard her life's story more than once, though she was never the one to tell him. A widow with two kids, she worked hard to keep her family together. She was smart, good at her job, and dedicated to her community. In short, she was the ideal partner for any guy with half a brain.

Despite his lack of formal education, Ryan wasn't stupid.

He knew that the beautiful undersheriff would never want a guy with a past like his.

She glanced at him through the rearview mirror. "Come on. You don't expect me to believe that you saw Decker tonight."

He'd spent a lifetime of lying, so telling the truth never came easy. Yet, he was determined to be candid with the cop. "It was dark. I can't be sure," he said. "But it surely resembled him."

Kathryn said nothing. After a moment, she reached for a mic on a radio that was set into her console. Pressing down on the talk button, she said, "Todd, you there?"

A moment later a male voice came from the radio. "I'm here. What do you need?"

"I want you to increase patrols tonight," she said, speaking into the mic. "Someone's sneaking around the neighborhood by the canal trail. From the description I've gotten, it's a male. Not too tall. Dressed in dark clothes."

There was a burst of static. It was followed by the deputy's voice. "That doesn't give me a lot to work with."

"You see anyone out of place, stop them. Check their ID," said Kathryn.

"Will do," Todd replied.

She set the mic back in its cradle.

Old Blue laid his head on Ryan's lap. "So you believe me?"

"I didn't say that, either. There are several possibilities." She held up a single finger. "One. You weren't out chasing some shadowy figure, like you said. Rather you and the other guy are working together. Since you got picked up, you needed an excuse. Telling me you saw Decker Newcombe is just a way to redirect my attention."

He sighed. If he were a cop, he'd probably have the same suspicions. "It's not a lie. I'm not working with anyone to break into houses. I'm not stupid enough to do anything like that, anyway." He paused a beat. "Not anymore, at least."

Looking out the window, he knew there was nothing more he could say. He'd been a criminal his entire life. No cop would trust him.

"What are you doing back in town?" Her question drew him from his reverie.

Ryan didn't know how to answer her. How was he supposed to tell her that Mercy had been the closest thing to a home he'd ever had in his life? This was the first place he'd felt a sense of community. But his belonging had been a result of the cover story. The words didn't come to him, so he remained silent.

"You awake back there?" Kathryn glanced in the rearview mirror once again. She waited a moment for him to answer. Ryan remained mute, not sure what to say next. "Everything okay?"

"I'm fine," he said with a sigh.

"But you didn't answer my question," the undersheriff pressed.

He looked back out the window. They were in downtown Encantador. There was the grocery store. The small hospital. Phil's, the barbecue restaurant, was permanently closed. Then again, who'd want to eat in a place where Decker had killed one person and seriously wounded another—even if it was more than a year past?

She continued, "Why did you come back? What is it that you want?"

Ryan wasn't ready to tell anyone what he wanted—not yet at least. But he'd gain nothing from lying to Undersheriff Glass.

"Well," he said, turning to her with a grin that he hoped covered the loneliness beneath, "I guess I'm looking for a place to call home."

Tessa Wray stood on her front lawn. Less than five minutes had passed since the undersheriff had driven away. Kathryn had told everyone to go inside and lock their doors, but hardly anyone had listened. The neighbors, gathered into a tight knot on the sidewalk, were discussing the recent events.

Joe, at fiftysomething, was the eldest of the group. Plus, he'd lived in the development the longest. He had lots to say. "People walk up and down the canal trail all the time."

Tessa jogged the mile-long trail every morning. She gave a slow nod. "That's true. We all use it."

Joe continued, "Since that big storm a few months ago, I've noticed that people use the undersheriff's yard to pass through to the development. If she wanted to keep strange people out of the neighborhood, she'd fix her fence."

"Yeah," said Tessa. "But she's really busy. She's got a full-time job and two kids."

Tessa was the branch manager for one of the local banks. Her work hours were set. Monday through Friday, 8:30 a.m. to 5:30 p.m. Even with her evenings free, she didn't have all the time needed for the upkeep her home required. What's more, she saw how often the undersheriff came and went. It surprised Tessa that Kathryn had any time for property maintenance at all.

"Her kids are older," snapped Joe. "She could get them working on the fence. Look at me. I got kids and a job. My fence is fine."

Joe also had a wife who worked from home and children who were grown and gone from the area. Yet, Tessa knew enough not to argue. Joe did his banking at Tessa's branch for both his personal account and the engineering firm where he worked as the accountant.

"All's I'm saying," Joe continued, "is that I expected more concern for security from the second-in-command of local our law-enforcement."

"Anyone know when Mooky's getting back?" another neighbor asked.

Joe sniffed, as if he could catch the sheriff's scent

on the air. "Can't be too soon." He paused a moment. "Who was that guy she arrested? He looked familiar."

"I know who he is," another neighbor offered. "Ryan Steele. He's the fella who owned House of Steele. The bar in Mercy."

"Of course, you'd know all about that bar in Mercy," Joe said with a laugh. Then again, everyone knew about the bar—even if they never frequented the establishment. House of Steele had been shown on the TV news constantly for weeks. And not just regional stations, either. The national and cable-news networks had covered the story of Decker Newcombe. "But I wonder why Ryan's back in town."

Tessa hadn't lived in Encantador when Decker Newcombe had terrorized this community. At the time, she'd been an assistant branch manager at a bank in the Panhandle. But she'd heard about the killer. Shoot, everyone in the country had heard about Decker Newcombe. It was said that he was a descendant of Jack the Ripper—the infamous Victorian era killer.

Was he back?

The possibility left her light-headed.

"You saw the prowler," said Tessa to Joe. "Was it Decker Newcombe?"

"Don't think so."

"Are you sure?" she pressed.

Joe exhaled loudly. "I've seen pictures of that bastard."

Tessa breathed deeply. Humid air filled her lungs, and she felt like she was drowning. For an instant, her body sizzled with alarm. But it wasn't just the suffocating air that filled her with panic. It was this place. She hadn't wanted the job here—which was part of the problem. Nobody had wanted the position because of what happened with Decker. But Tessa had been offered a promotion into the corporate level, so long as she stayed in Encantador for a few years. At least her neighbors were nice—or nice enough. She exhaled and turned to Joe. "So long as you're sure."

Gladys shuffled out onto her porch. "Y'all heard what the undersheriff said. Get back inside. Go to bed. It's late."

It wasn't too late—only 9:54 p.m. Still, Tessa wanted to watch an episode of her latest bingeworthy show before going to bed. "Well," she said, thankful that Gladys had shooed everyone back to their own homes, "good night."

Joe said, "Good night, y'all. Holler if you see anything."

Tessa strode up her walkway and opened her front door. After pulling it closed, she engaged the lock. Pressing her forehead into the jamb, she had to admit one thing. She didn't like the idea of a night spent alone.

While standing on the street, she'd felt exposed. But here, in her own house, she was truly isolated. Maybe she should go and visit Gladys. Or she could stop by and chat with Joe and his wife.

No. She refused to be afraid of her own shadow.

Tessa was a grown woman. She could take care of herself. Yet, she'd sleep better knowing all her doors and windows were locked. Moving through her living room, she turned on the hallway light. There were four doors off the corridor. Three bedrooms and a bathroom. All the doors stood ajar, and each room beyond was black as pitch.

A killer could be hiding in one of those rooms.

The thought came to her, unbidden. Pushing the notion away, she reminded herself that nobody had seen Decker Newcombe in months. The arrival of Ryan Steele meant nothing. As much as she tried to convince herself there was nothing to fear, her body betrayed her brain. Her stomach started to churn. After wiping her damp palms on the seat of her shorts, she pushed the door open with her toe.

A wedge of light stretched across the floor. There wasn't much furniture in her home office. A desk with a chair. Two metal filing cabinets and a bookshelf filled with manuals from work.

From where she stood, the room looked empty. But the corners were lost in the gloom. Inching her hand along the wall, her fingertips brushed the cool plastic of the switch plate. Her finger darted to the switch, turning on the light.

With the room fully illuminated, it was easy to tell nobody was hidden in the corner. She laughed. *Way to freak yourself out.* Crossing the room, she tugged on the window. It was also locked.

She turned to the closed closet door. Her mouth went dry. It had been decades since she'd feared monsters in the wardrobe. Standing alone, she knew even the worst things were possible. Still, she had to check.

Jerking the door open, she stepped back. Several coats that she'd never need this far south hung on a metal bar. Other than that, the closet was empty.

Tessa spent the next few minutes searching the rooms

along the hallway. With each empty room, her anxiety evaporated like a puddle in the sun.

At the end of the hall, she walked through her living room and turned to the left. The kitchen was dark, but Tessa could see well enough. This time, she didn't bother turning on the overhead light. There was a window over the sink and a back door, which she headed for, and her flip-flops slapped the linoleum floor with each step.

Reaching for the handle, she twisted. The door opened. *Strange.*

She didn't recall having left the back door unlocked. She closed it and engaged the dead bolt. "There," she said out loud. Talking to herself was a habit born of years of living alone. "Safe and sound."

There was a soft click a moment before a bright light shone on her from behind. Her heart ceased to beat. She spun around quickly, blinded by the glare. An illuminated ring light stood atop a tripod. A phone—it was hers—was secured in the holder.

Tessa felt as if the floor was tilting and she was sliding into a void. Nothing made sense. But then, she saw him. Standing in the corner, near the refrigerator, was the shadowy outline of a man. She gasped, and her heart began to race. Tessa tried to think, but her mind went blank. Her hands and feet felt like lead—cold, hard, and too heavy to move.

"I doubt that," the man said, taking a step toward her. He held a knife. The blade glinted in the brightness of the ring light. He moved to the phone and turned on the camera. Her own terrified face filled the screen.

Now that he was closer, she could see his features.

His long hair. His thin face. His silver-blue eyes, icy and cold. A chill shot through her body as recognition hit her hard.

Swallowing, she found her voice. "You doubt what?"

"I heard what you just said, 'safe and sound.' You might be sound," said Decker, his voice low, "but you definitely aren't safe."

Chapter 3

Kathryn flipped on the blinker a moment before letting her foot off the gas. Her exterior control covered up her runaway pulse and racing mind. She couldn't tell if Ryan's story was legit or not. Obviously, her life would be so much easier if the guy she had in the back of her cruiser was working with another crook to break into houses.

A little grand larceny she could handle. But a serial killer? Well, that was a whole different level of dangerous.

True, she was dedicated to her job. But she was a mother first and worried about her kids. Kathryn made a mental note to text Morgan and Brock as soon as she could.

Guiding her cruiser into the parking lot, she pulled into a spot at the back of the sheriff's office. Turning in her seat, she faced Ryan. He regarded her with his bright blue eyes.

Damn. He was too good looking for his own good. Just the sight of him left her with a thirst. She turned off her libido before images began to fill her mind.

Fighting to keep her gaze locked with his, she said, "I'm going to open your door. Don't run." She wasn't sure if he had committed any crimes, but she still had to be prudent.

"I wasn't going to run."

Old Blue sat up. His tail thumped against the back seat, the sound like a bass drum. Kathryn wondered if he understood the word *run*.

She couldn't help but smile. After putting the gearshift into Park, she turned off the ignition. After opening her door and exiting the car, she opened the back door for Ryan.

Holding onto Old Blue's collar, Ryan led the dog from the vehicle as he got out himself. Standing on the pavement, he waited as she closed and locked the car doors. She scratched Old Blue behind the ear. "Good boy," she said.

"Thanks," said Ryan. "I'm trying to behave."

Despite herself, she gave a quiet chuckle. "Come with me."

The sheriff's office was a one-story building made of red brick. Kathryn climbed the four steps leading to the back door. There, she entered a passcode into an electronic keypad. A light on the side of the device turned from red to green as the lock disengaged. After turning the handle, she opened the door.

Kathryn let Ryan and his dog pass. An automatic

light in the ceiling turned on, illuminating a long hall-way. Doors lined each side of the corridor.

As undersheriff, Kathryn had an office of her own. "Second door on the left," she said. While walking, she sent a quick text to the family group chat she shared with her kids.

Checking in to see how you're both doing.

Brock replied immediately.

Still at Lazaro's. He has a new game and his parents ordered pizza.

She smiled. At least her son was having a nice eve-ning. She sent another message.

I'd like both of you to stay in tonight. No going to par-ties, even if your friends' parents say it's okay.

Brock sent a thumbs-up emoji.

Morgan had yet to reply.

Kathryn tamped down her emotions, a mixture of annoyance and anxiety, and slipped her phone into her pocket.

Ryan stopped next to her office and waited. She used a key to unlock the door. Another automatic light turned on. Her windowless office was as large as Mooky's. Against one wall sat a sofa, covered in blue fabric. Next to the couch was an oval-shaped coffee table. A single-serve coffeemaker sat atop a three-drawer filing cabi-net in the corner. On her walls were framed pictures of her kids alongside Kathryn's work commendations and awards.

A leather chair had been pushed under her desk. She pulled it free before taking a seat. Gesturing to the sofa, she said, "Make yourself comfortable."

Ryan sat. Old Blue lay on the floor, next to his owner's feet, and panted.

"Can I get you anything? Coffee? Tea?"

"Is there any way my dog could get some water? I don't want him to get dehydrated."

It didn't matter that Ryan's record had been cleared; to her he'd always be a criminal. Still, he was good to his dog. Without comment, she swiveled in her chair. Behind her desk was a coffee station. Packets of sugar and creamer sat in a ceramic bowl. After dumping the packets onto her desk, she wiped out the bowl with a paper towel. Using the reservoir from her coffeemaker, she poured water into the dish. Rising from her seat, she set the bowl on the floor next to Old Blue. "How's that, boy?"

The dog rose to his feet and lapped at the water. Within a minute, he'd licked the dish dry.

"Looks like he was thirsty." She bent to the floor, reaching for the bowl.

At the same moment, Ryan reached for the bowl as well.

Her fingers grazed the back of his hand. An electric current ran up her arm. Her heart skipped a beat. It'd been more than six years since a man's touch had done much of anything for her. Ryan raised his eyes. Their gazes met, and her palms turned damp. The pulse at the base of his neck thrummed.

So he'd felt the connection, too?

Kathryn licked her lips. She wondered what it would feel like to kiss him—but she knew that there'd be hell to pay if she ever found out. Lifting the bowl from the floor, she stood. "I'll get Old Blue more water. You want some, too?"

He shrugged. "Sure."

She walked across the room. Wrapped in plastic, a case of water bottles sat in the corner. She peeled two away from the pack and set both on the coffee table, not sure what would happen if they accidentally touched again.

"Thank you very much," he said.

She nodded and returned to her desk. Jiggling the mouse for the computer, she woke her desktop. The monitor winked to life. The screen was filled with the seal of the sheriff's office, along with two fields. One was for Kathryn's username and the other was for her password. She entered both. Next, she opened a search engine for outstanding warrants. After typing in Ryan's name, she glanced up at him.

"Birthdate? Social Security number?"

He gave her both, and she entered them into the search engine as well. A colorful ball twirled in the middle of her screen. "This might take a minute," she commented.

The phone in her pocket shimmied. She pulled it out and read the caller ID.

It was Morgan.

Without a thought, Kathryn swiped the call open.

"Hey, sweetheart. What's up?"

"Don't give me that *sweetheart* crap—especially since you are literally trying to ruin my life."

Oh Lord, save her from the disrespect. "Do not take that tone with me," she began.

She bit the inside of her cheek, keenly aware that Ryan could hear every word she said. Hell, her office was so small, he could probably hear Morgan, too. It brought up an interesting question. What did she do with him? She couldn't leave him in her office while she stepped into the hallway to take the call. Nor could she ask him to be the one to wait in the hallway. There was no guarantee that he'd be there when she hung up. Calling Morgan back later was out of the question.

Turning in her seat, she kept Ryan in her periphery. It wasn't much. Still, it gave the illusion of privacy. "Do not take that tone with me," she hissed again. "I am your mother."

"Then, as my *mother*—" the last word was filled with a heavy amount of sass "—you should know how important tonight is to me."

Kathryn didn't know what made tonight more special than any other. Had she missed something big? She knew that it wasn't Homecoming.

"Omigod," Morgan whined. "It's Elliot's eighteenth birthday. He's having a midnight party at his house. He has a pool. Everyone in the senior class will be there. If you make me stay home, then I'll be a worse freak than I already am."

"You aren't a freak," Kathryn said, aiming to soothe.

"Who else, aside from Brock the Perfect, has a dead dad and a mom who's a cop?"

A hard kernel stuck in her throat. She did recall agreeing to let Morgan go to an all-night party a few weeks back. Could she really go back on her word? "Which one is Elliot?" she asked. "Is he the kid who constantly smells like marijuana?"

"I told you, Mom. A family of skunks live under his back deck. It's not weed."

"Is this back deck with all the skunks near the pool? Are you sure you want to go?"

Morgan huffed. "I called you instead of texting because I'm trying to work this out with you like an adult. Ashley's going to the party whether I go or not. So if I can't go anywhere, then I'll have to come home."

Kathryn wasn't sure how late she'd be working. If there was a stalker in their neighborhood, then her daughter was safer at a large party than home and alone. "Fine," she sighed. "You can go. I expect you home early tomorrow, though."

"Thanks, Mom." Morgan's tone was suddenly sunny. "Love you."

"Love you, too."

The call ended, and she exhaled. *Now, what was she doing?* Oh yeah. Swiveling her chair to face the front, she glanced at her computer. The report had been run. *No warrants found. No prior arrests.*

She turned her gaze to Ryan. Certainly, he'd heard every word of her exchange. At least he had the good manners to pretend he hadn't been interested in what was said. Currently, he watched his dog, who remained on the floor.

"Looks like you're good," she said.

"You know," he said, raising his gaze to meet hers, "my record was cleared after I left Mercy."

"I didn't expect to see anything from years ago," she said. "Who knows what you've been up to since you left the area?" She sat back in her chair and flicked her fingers at the screen. "But you aren't wanted for anything right now."

"Am I free to go?" he asked.

"Not yet," she said. "I really need to know what—and who—you saw tonight. If Decker's come back to town, that's a problem. A big problem." *What an understatement.* The specter of Decker Newcombe haunted every person in Encantador and Mercy both. "So let's go over this one more time—"

Her words were cut off by the ping of an incoming text. Her phone sat on her desk. She glanced at the screen. It was from one of her neighbors, Stan Vargasky.

A short video clip and a picture were attached to a two-word message.

Mystery solved.

The video was taken from a home-security camera. It was ten seconds of a male, clad in black, approaching the back of a house. A photo had been taken from the video and enlarged to show his face. She recognized him at once. He was a classmate of her son's.

Kathryn opened the video and rose from her desk. Handing the phone to Ryan, she asked, "Is this who you saw?"

Looking at her phone, he drew his eyebrows together. "Could be," he said, sounding uncertain. "I mean, I only saw a guy dressed in black." He paused a beat. "Who is he?"

"That's Romeo Rogers. He's a sophomore and plays football with my son. He's a charming kid who has probably dated half the girls at the high school." She rolled her eyes. "His parents must've known something about him at birth to give him a name like Romeo." Ryan held out her phone. She grabbed it with the tips of her fingers, careful not to touch him again. "My guess is that Romeo was stopping by the Vargasky house to see one of their daughters. They have twins in ninth grade, and the older girl is in eleventh."

She typed out a text to Stan.

Where's Romeo now?

He replied, My wife invited him in for cake. He'd inserted a face-palm emoji.

Emelia was planning on sneaking out with him, I'm sure. She's still dressed and has on enough perfume to choke a horse.

She read his text out loud.

Ryan shook his head. "The would-be lovers sound sweet but stupid."

"That's a pretty apt description," she admitted.

Kathryn typed out a reply.

Good luck with your kids. Let me know if you need anything else, and thanks for sending the video.

She hit Send.

Stan replied with a thumbs-up emoji.

Kathryn slipped her phone into her pocket. "I'll admit, I'm glad that this story had a happy ending."

"Happy for everyone but Emelia and Romeo." Ryan rose to his feet. "I guess we really are done. Can I get a ride back to my truck?"

There was no reason—legal or otherwise—to keep him. "Give me a minute to close down my computer."

Standing at her desk, she clicked the cursor on the X to exit the database. Then, she signed out of her account. "Let's roll."

They walked out of her office, Ryan first, then Old Blue, Kathryn at the rear. She pulled the door to her office closed and turned the handle, making sure the automatic lock was engaged. She retraced her steps to the back door. When Ryan opened the door at the end of the corridor, heat rolled down the hallway like a tidal wave. Even before she stepped outside, she started to sweat.

"Wonder if this heat will ever break," he said.

Kathryn wasn't much for chitchat. She saw all the meaningless conversation as little more than noise. Still, she felt as if there was something she should say to Ryan. The weather was always a safe topic. "It won't," she said with a snort. "This is West Texas. It's always hot. Some days the temperature is less brutal."

He nodded slowly.

Using the fob, she unlocked the doors to her police cruiser. "Tonight's one of those brutal nights," she continued. "You can sit up front and get more cool air."

"That's kind of you."

There was more to her offer than simple kindness. When she'd asked him why he'd returned to Encantador, he told her that he was looking for a place to settle. She had a duty to protect her community. She intended to do her job, and that meant having a serious talk with Ryan.

After opening the passenger door, he snapped his fingers. Old Blue jumped onto the seat, and Ryan followed. She rounded past the front fender as dog and master got settled. Opening her own door, she slid behind the steering wheel and started the engine.

While backing out of the space, Kathryn pressed her lips together. She needed to talk with Ryan, but the words had to be just right. "I've lived in this area my whole life," she began. "The people are kind. They work hard. For the most part, everyone gets along."

"Until now, I never really cared about where I lived. To me, one bed was the same as any other. When I found out that I had to live in Mercy..." he shook his head "...well, I wasn't exactly happy to run a bar in the middle of nowhere. In the end, I liked it more than I imagined."

He watched her as she drove. She swore that she wouldn't look at Ryan, focusing instead on the road and the flying insects that were in the beams of her headlights. But she felt drawn to his gaze. She let her eyes meet his. God, he really was handsome. More than handsome—if that was even possible. It made what she had to say more difficult. Then again, he had given her the perfect segue. "You know, this isn't really in the middle of nowhere. Sure, we have a lot of land, but plenty of people call Encantador and Mercy home."

"I didn't mean to come off that way," he began.

She ignored his comment and continued. "Decker killing all those people has affected everyone. And not in a good way, either," she added. "I've seen it on the job. People are more mistrustful. They're quicker to quarrel with their neighbors. Decker Newcombe stole our sense of security." His gaze turned hard. She looked back at the road.

"Just say what you want to say." Ryan's tone was filled with flint.

For a minute, she drove. The businesses on Main Street were closed. The windows were dark. Streetlamps cast pools of yellow light onto the sidewalk.

"There are two things I value most," she said, her eyes still on the road. "My home and my family. Because of that, I don't blame you for wanting to put down roots and grow your own life, so to speak. This is not the place for you, though. For a year, you lied to us about why you came here. What's more, a killer came to town looking for you." Sure, her words sounded cruel. But Ryan Steele living in Encantador would cause more problems than he'd ever solve. "You might want a home, but it's not going to be here."

She glanced in his direction. He stared out the passenger window. Old Blue sat at his side. Tongue hanging out of his mouth, the dog smiled at Kathryn.

God, she felt like a heel. What else was she supposed to do? "Is there anything you want to say?"

He glanced at her. "Is there anything I could say that would make a difference?"

"Not really. But you know I'm right." She decided to give him some unsolicited advice. "There are lots of small towns like ours. Find a new one. Make it your own."

He made a sound. She couldn't tell if it was a snort, a grunt, or a guttural laugh. Then again, it didn't matter. She imagined they all meant the same thing. Ryan didn't care for her less-than-warm welcome.

Drawing in a sharp breath, he braced his hands on the dashboard. "Goddamn it!"

Instinctively, she dropped her foot on the break. Her heart slammed against her chest.

"You okay?" Obviously, he wasn't. "What's wrong?"

He turned to her. His eyes were wide. His pallor was ghostly. "On the sidewalk," he said, swallowing. "There's a body."

Her head snapped around. Ryan was right. A figure was sprawled across the concrete and covered in blood. Slamming the gearshift into Park, she sprinted from the car.

She recognized the victim. There was a tangle of blond hair. A pool of blood surrounded the lifeless form. The clothes were torn and stained red with gore.

Dropping to her knees, she lifted Tessa's arm. The flesh was cool, but still Kathryn pressed her fingers into the wrist, feeling for a pulse. There was none.

A flashlight was attached to her utility belt—Kathryn shone it up and down the street. There was no perp hiding in the shadows. No obvious clues, either. Using the mic attached to her shoulder, she sent out a call. "Todd, I need backup." She gave him the address while rising to her feet. "Contact Doctor Garcia." She was the medical examiner.

"What's going on?" the deputy asked.

How was she supposed to describe the scene? Kathryn didn't have the words. "Just get here as quick as you can and tell Doctor Garcia to hurry, too."

He exhaled. "I'll be there in a few minutes."

Ryan stood right behind Kathryn, and his breath washed over the back of her neck. Old Blue was still in the car. The engine was running, and the air-conditioning was on. The dog would be fine for a few minutes. "Tessa, what happened to you?" she asked, the last word morphed into a groan.

"You know this woman?" Ryan asked.

She nodded. "She is—was—Tessa Wray. She's the new bank manager and lives a few houses up from me."

While standing next to the body, she compartmentalized her feelings. There was no other way for her to do her job—especially since she'd known the victim. Tessa's throat had been sliced open. A ghoulish smile ran across her neck. Her torso had been cut open, too. "I haven't seen anything this bad since we found Trinity Jackson's body." Trinity was Decker's first victim who had lived in Mercy, less than twenty miles from Encantador.

"You know what this means?" he asked.

She didn't bother to look up. "What does this mean?"

"It means that Romeo Rogers wasn't the only person sneaking through backyards tonight."

She stood and faced Ryan. "You still think it was him, don't you?"

"Think?" He shook his head. "I know it. This was done by Decker Newcombe. The killer's back."

Like she'd been plunged into ice water, Kathryn went numb. Her hands shook. Folding her arms across her chest, she drew in a long breath. "You don't know anything," she challenged. Speaking as a law-enforcement officer, she was right. There was evidence that needed to be collected. So far, they had a murder victim—which was bad enough—but nothing connected Newcombe to the crime. "We're going to conduct this investigation professionally. We won't jump to conclusions—even though the injuries sustained by this victim look like the other woman's."

"We?"

"I," she corrected. She needed to remember certain facts. "I'm in charge of the investigation."

She returned to her car and opened the passenger door. Old Blue had been lying on the seat. He sat up, and she scratched him behind the ears. The interior of the car was cool. "You'll be okay in here for a bit." She opened her glove box and removed two pairs of latex gloves from a bag.

Returning to the body, she handed one set to Ryan.

"Put these on," she ordered, while slipping on her own. "I don't want any fingerprints to accidentally end up on the corpse."

She knelt next to the body again. Ryan knelt next to her.

The wounds were as gruesome as before. A long and bloody cut ran up the middle of Tessa's torso. Kathryn needed to wait for the autopsy, but she imagined that several of the victim's internal organs had been removed—just like last time. Decker might not be the killer, but whoever had done this was a definite copycat.

"If Decker's back," said Ryan, "he isn't done yet. More people will die."

"That is only—" she could hear the conviction in her own voice "—if we don't find him first."

Chapter 4

By Kathryn's accounting, the body of Tessa Wray had been discovered at 9:21 p.m. Slipping her phone from her pocket, she checked the time again: 10:57 p.m.

After replacing the phone, she rubbed her gritty eyes. Since finding the corpse, Kathryn had done several things. First, she'd ordered barricades on the road, set up two blocks apart. Tessa's body was in the middle of the cordoned off area. Even though the street was closed to the public, the road was filled with first responders. She'd also completed the heartbreaking task of notifying Tessa's family that their daughter was dead. Her parents were on their way from Oklahoma. It would take them a full night of driving to get to Encantador.

She'd sent her deputies to the victim's home to look for evidence. From what they reported, the murder most likely had taken place at the house. Until the body was taken away by the ME, she wanted to stay with Tessa out of respect. She'd also contacted her kids and made sure they were okay. Both were safely back at their respective parties. With a sigh, she slipped the phone back into her pocket.

"Rough night," said Ryan at her side.

She wasn't sure if it was a question or a statement. Still, there was no way to answer other than by saying, "Sure is." She exhaled. "When we first found Trinity Jackson, Mooky didn't want any outside help. He thought he could solve the murder all on his own." She shook her head, knowing she'd come dangerously close to criticizing her boss. "Sorry. I shouldn't have said anything. Mooky's a good sheriff."

"But he didn't realize who he was dealing with in Decker," he said. "He didn't ask for help right away but should have."

It was as if Ryan had read her mind. She looked at the street. A yellow tent had been erected over the victim's body. Lights atop emergency vehicles strobed blue and red. The voices of more than a dozen first responders filled the night. With the garish yellow tent, the whole scene resembled a sideshow more than a crime scene. "I had to call in help," she said, not sure if she'd made the right choice. With all the other agencies involved, Kathryn had little to do.

"You did," he agreed.

She glanced at Ryan and smiled. "Thanks for hanging around."

"Where else am I supposed to go? Besides, I'm not leaving without Old Blue."

After finding the body, Kathryn had ordered a deputy to take the dog to her office. The mutt had been given water, food, and a walk. So even if he wasn't happy to be separated from his master, he was at least safe.

A black SUV maneuvered through the crowd and pulled up behind her car. The back doors opened. Two men exited the vehicle. She recognized both of them.

Ryan smiled and stepped forward with his hand outstretched. "Jason Jones. Isaac Patton. It's great to see you two."

He shook hands with Special Agent Jason Jones, the Supervisory Special Agent from the San Antonio field office. Then, he shook hands with Isaac Patton, who was the owner of a private security firm, Texas Law. It was Isaac who Ryan worked with when they were trying to find Decker. She'd heard that the relationship between the men had been complicated—starting with enmity and ending with something close to friendship. "How goes it?" Ryan asked.

Isaac was almost as tall as Ryan and wore a black T-shirt and jeans. He pounded on Ryan's back. "Good to see you. Weird to be back here, though."

Agent Jones stepped toward Kathryn with his hand extended. He was six feet tall with blond hair, kept short. It was the middle of the night, but he was still dressed in a white shirt, dark suit, and no tie. He had a firm handshake. She respected anyone who knew how to shake hands properly. Gripping his palm she said, "Thanks for coming on such short notice. I know it's quite a drive from San Antonio."

Jason withdrew his hand and waved away her comment. "I wanted to come here personally, especially after I heard that you'd found another body."

Isaac stepped forward. "Nice to see you again." He offered his hand to shake. She slipped her palm into his. "Wish it was under different circumstances. I heard that Mooky was out of town. Is that right?"

Letting her hand slip from his grip, she gave a terse nod. "He's on an anniversary trip to Mexico for two weeks."

"Have you briefed the sheriff?" Jason asked.

Kathryn had expected the question. Still, a spark of annoyance burned at her chest. "Until I know what we're dealing with, I don't want to waste his time. Besides, what's he going to do from the beach other than worry and ruin his wife's vacation?" What she said was true. But she was also determined to do a good job on her own.

"What is it that you have?" Isaac asked.

"We found the body of a thirty-two-year-old female. Her throat's been cut. Her body cavity's been sliced open as well." She placed two fingers on her own abdomen. One just under the rib cage, and the other above the pelvis. "The gash is about this long." She tilted her head toward the tent that covered the body. "Sheila Garcia and Michael O'Brien are with the body now."

"Can we get a look?" Jason asked.

Kathryn had seen Tessa's corpse and Trinity Jackson's during Decker's last killing spree. Both murders had been brutal, and bloody. Still, she said, "Come with me."

She walked the short distance to the tent and pulled back the flap. A single spotlight on a stand stood in the corner. The beam was directed at the body. The bright light turned Tessa's skin to pure white. The blood was bright red—and black, where it was dry. The contrast between colors was stark. Kathryn missed a step as she crossed the threshold.

"Stop right there," Dr. Garcia warned. She wore a lab coat and surgical gloves. Her dark hair was wound into a bun atop her head. "You can't come in here without PPE."

One of the several CSI techs handed Kathryn a pair of blue gloves and paper booties. "Here you go," the man said. "To keep you from contaminating the evidence."

He handed the same gloves and booties to Isaac, Jason, and Ryan. It took them all only a moment to don their protective gear.

Forensic pathologist Michael O'Brien was already on the scene. Where Ryan was muscular, Michael O'Brien was tall and lanky. Stepping away from the body, he asked, "How's everyone holding up?"

"Okay, I guess," Isaac said with a smile. "But we gotta stop meeting like this."

"Are we done with the jokes?" Dr. Garcia snapped. "Because if we are, then there are some things I'd like to show you."

Ryan gave Kathryn a side-eye. She could imagine what he must be thinking about the doctor. *Was this woman for real?*

Sheila and Kathryn had been classmates beginning in elementary school. More than being in the same grade, they were friends. The thing was, Sheila didn't mean to be rude. It's just that she could get so focused on her task that she didn't care about being polite. She'd always been that way, even as a little kid.

Clearing her throat, Kathryn asked, "What do you have for us?"

"Michael and I agree these wounds look like the ones inflicted on Trinity Jackson."

Jason asked, "Can you say conclusively that Decker murdered this woman? Are you sure it's not a copycat killer?"

Sheila glanced at Michael. He shook his head. "We can't say conclusively that Decker killed Tessa Wray. But…"

Isaac said, "For now, it's safe to assume that he's the killer."

"Assume," Kathryn echoed. A knot of disbelief was stuck in her throat. She choked on the single word. One of the first tenets of law enforcement was never to assume anything. Assumptions tainted investigations. "We aren't going to assume anything. What I need are facts." She paused. "Do you know what kind of uproar it's going to cause if we tell folks that we assume—" she made air quotes "—Decker's back? Tessa being filleted like a fish is bad enough. We can't cause mass hysteria without proof." She drew in a breath, slowing her racing heart.

The tent was silent.

The FBI agent was the first to speak. "Even if this isn't Decker, people should be alerted. Another young woman's been murdered. Besides, we were briefed that Decker might've been sighted near the victim's home earlier this evening."

"I'm not going to cause a panic until I know who

actually committed this murder." Kathryn realized she was being stubborn. She might not have a fancy college degree or expensive gadgets, but she did know her community, and the FBI agent had been right. People needed to be informed. She could release a carefully worded statement to the press.

Before she got a chance to acquiesce, Isaac spoke. "You know," he said, his voice icy, "you're being unreasonable, Kathryn."

Oh hell no. She wasn't going to be bullied by the feds or some high-priced security operative, like Isaac Patton. "You know that you've been invited to my town by me. This is my investigation. I'm the one who makes the final decisions. Got it?"

Michael raised his palms and stepped between Isaac and Kathryn. "I have another solution. We've taken several samples of hair and fibers from the victim's clothing." A small table stood in the corner of the tent. Several clear plastic bags lay on the tabletop. To Kathryn, they looked empty. But she knew better: each bag contained evidence taken from the victim, and that evidence might be as small as a single hair. Michael continued. "My lab is in Mercy. I can run these samples overnight. By morning, we'll have an analysis. If the killer left behind DNA, we'll get an ID."

"Fair enough." She drew in a calming breath. "And speaking of DNA, the body was dumped here. We believe that the killing actually took place at her home." To Sheila, she said, "How much longer will you be here?"

"We're done," said the doctor. "I'm going to get the body to the morgue. The autopsy will be in the morning."

Since the body was being taken from the crime

scene, Kathryn had done her due diligence. Now she could move on to other parts of the investigation. She spoke to both Jason and Isaac. "We can head over to the victim's house now."

"Lead the way," said Jason.

Kathryn exited the tent. She pulled off the booties first and then the gloves. Standing on the sidewalk, she shook out her hands and took deep breaths.

"You okay?" Ryan asked.

"Yeah, I…" She looked back at the tent. Jason, Michael, and Isaac stood in a knot next to the flap and spoke to each other in hushed tones. Were those men discussing her case and how to keep her from being involved in the investigation? "Maybe Mooky was right to try and handle Decker in-house." Although, it was worse for her than it had been for him. At least he was actually the sheriff. She was just a stand-in.

He followed her gaze. "Everyone here wants the same thing. To discover the truth and to stop the killer."

"You're right," she said with a sigh.

"It sounds like you don't believe me."

How was she supposed to describe the feeling of living in her own skin? That the desire to please was more of a need than a want. The fact that she relied on Mooky's as a taskmaster first. Then, her own judgment. Despite her uncertainty, she knew that failure wasn't an option. She stood taller. "You're right. We're all on the same team."

She watched as the conversation ended. Jason pointed to the black SUV, and Michael nodded. The trio began to walk toward the vehicle.

"We'll follow you to the victim's house," Isaac said,

his voice raised to be heard from a distance. "Ryan, you want to ride with us?"

"Nah, man. I'm good. I'll go with the undersheriff." He turned to look at her quickly. "Hope that's okay with you?"

When had Ryan become her ally? Then again, it didn't matter. She needed someone on her team. A spark of gratitude glowed in her chest. Pulling the car keys from her pocket, she said, "That sounds good." She unlocked the doors. Then to Jason, Isaac, and Michael, she said, "Follow me."

Kathryn opened her door and slid behind the wheel. Ryan slipped into the passenger seat. She started the engine, and the air-conditioning began to blow. Holding her fingers in front of the vent, she let the stream of air swirl around her hand.

Placing the gearshift into Drive, she pulled away from the curb. The street was filled with emergency workers. She flipped a toggle switch on her console, and the siren gave a single whoop. People stepped aside to let her pass. In the rearview mirror, she could see the SUV following her car like a shadow.

At the end of the block, a deputy stood next to a pair of yellow sawhorses that blocked off the street. He saw her coming and pulled one aside.

A group of twenty people had gathered on the opposite side of the barricade. She recognized Alicia Sanchez, the editor and lead writer of the town's weekly newspaper. Prior to becoming the editor, Alicia had worked for a major media outlet in Dallas. She'd only come back to Encantador to care for her aging mother.

Since her arrival, Alicia had improved the paper with her writing, editing skills, and dogged reporting.

Stepping toward the car, the editor waved. "Kathryn." She raised her voice to be heard over the engine. "You got a minute?"

As the undersheriff, she often acted as the de facto media specialist for the department. Mooky always said that she was good with the press. It was true that she and Alicia got on well enough.

Easing her foot onto the brake, she lowered the window. "What can I do for you?"

"Mind telling me what's going on?" Alicia asked. Despite the fact that it was the middle of the night and still hot, she wore a button-up blouse and a pair of slacks. Neither were creased or stained with sweat.

Kathryn glanced down at her own wrinkled uniform. She looked back at the other woman. "I can't comment right now. There's an open investigation."

"Does it have anything to do with the bank's manager, Tessa Wray?" Alicia paused. "There's a CSI team at her home now." She held up her phone. The screen was filled with a social-media post. It was a picture of Tessa's house with crime-scene tape across the door, along with the caption *What happened this time? #toomuchcrimeinEncantador.*

Her shoulders pinched together with tension. Rubbing the back of her neck, she sighed. "I can't comment on anything right now."

"You'll want to get ahead of this story." Alicia tucked a lock of dark hair streaked with gray behind an ear.

She imagined that the reporter was right. She also knew that Alicia's advice wasn't exactly altruistic. The reporter was looking for something to put in the online edition of the paper.

"When there's something to say," she said, "you'll be the first person I call."

Alicia leaned her elbow on the windowsill. "Can I ask you another question?" She didn't give Kathryn a chance to answer. "What's Ryan Steele doing in your car? I heard you were chasing him down the street earlier this evening. Why? Does he have anything to do with this street being blocked off and a CSI team being at Ms. Wray's house?"

Wow. That was a lot more than one question.

She replied, "I can't comment on an open investigation. In fact, I can't even comment enough to say if there is an investigation." Easing her foot off the brake, she let the car roll forward. Alicia stood up and stepped back. "I have to get back to work."

Using the lever, she raised the window. The knot of onlookers stared at her car as she drove slowly past. They said nothing, but she could feel the tension in their gaze. Keeping her eyes on the beams of her headlights, she focused on driving. As she passed the corner, she dropped her foot onto the accelerator and exhaled loudly.

"That was uncomfortable," said Ryan.

"Hella awkward." Her shoulders sagged, weighed down by exhaustion and the gravity of the situation. "Here's what I hope." She glanced in the rearview mirror to make sure that the black SUV was still following her car. It was. "I hope that there are no more surprises, like Alicia Sanchez, or the gawkers on the corner. I'd like to get a look at the crime scene quietly and without a lot of fuss."

"Well, I hope you get your wish," he said.

She glanced at Ryan. He smiled.

She couldn't help herself and smiled back.

As she drove, she knew two things for certain. First, Ryan's insights might help her to find Decker Newcombe. After all, nobody knew the killer better. And second, if she was going to be working with him, then she was going to have a hell of a time keeping her libido in check. But if she wanted to find and capture the elusive killer, she needed to do both.

She flipped the switch for a left turn more than a hundred yards from the road that led to her housing development. The blinker ticked, like a clockwork heart. While turning onto the road, she'd almost convinced herself that she'd get what she wanted. The neighborhood would be quiet. Then, she'd have plenty of uninterrupted time to examine the crime scene. But as she drove up the road leading to her house, she knew her wish for a discreet investigation wasn't going to come true.

Every house was filled with light. Her neighbors stood on the sidewalk in groups. The energy of a hundred frightened and furious people filled the night, like a lightning strike. A TV news van was also parked at the curb.

People stopped talking and glared as she drove past.

"Looks like it's about to get hella awkward all over again," said Ryan.

He wasn't joking this time.

Kathryn's friends and neighbors might not know the specifics, but they'd seen enough to have an idea of what had happened. They were mad and scared and wanted information. She didn't blame them. But without Mooky around, they'd be looking to her for answers.

How could she tell them that Decker Newcombe had returned?

Chapter 5

The dark room smelled of death. The stench was so bad that Decker was certain something was rotting in the walls. The floor was covered with dust and rodent droppings. He'd spread out a blanket before sitting down. Using the wall as a back rest, he got as comfortable as possible. Then, he opened the lid of his laptop.

The screen glowed. It was the only light in the room.

Hell, it was the only light for miles.

He entered a complicated set of keystrokes. It was the address to a private server buried deep in the dark web. A bar with cycling lines filled the middle of his screen. It took only a moment for a face to appear. The hacker wore gloves and a birdlike plague-doctor mask and a black velvet drape behind them. Their voice was also electronically disguised.

Honestly, he found the theatrics annoying.

But Seraphim, as the hacker called themself, was a true genius.

Decker's own face filled a smaller square on the bottom right corner of his monitor. His hair was long and hung loose around his shoulders. He'd changed clothes after his latest killing. But still, the victim's blood was smeared across his chin. Using the hem of his shirt, he wiped it away.

As had been his habit for years, Decker used free computers to check what was being reported about him on the internet. Two months earlier, he'd been in a small coffee shop near Texarkana. Seraphim had taken over his computer and made Decker an offer he couldn't refuse.

"Work with me," they'd said, "and you'll be the most famous killer of all time."

He'd scoffed, but in that moment, he knew it was possible.

"You did what we discussed." Seraphim's voice was like fingernails on a chalkboard and drew him back to the dingy room.

He held up the phone. "I recorded everything."

"Connect the phone to the computer. Then you can upload the video. I'll tell you how."

"I got it covered," said Decker. True, he wasn't especially comfortable with computers. But he'd be damned before he let the hacker tell him what to do. Besides, he couldn't listen to the obnoxious voice for long. After several moments, the phone was connected.

Seraphim played the video without sound.

In a way, the silence was more terrifying than if it had been filled with screams.

Decker smiled.

"That was…" Seraphim said as the screen went black "…intense."

"Now's not the time to get squeamish," said Decker. "You and me made a deal."

"I'm not squeamish." In the mask, Seraphim's eyes gleamed. "And I'm not backing out of our deal." The hacker spent a few minutes rehashing what would happen next. Decker knew the plan but suspected that Seraphim liked the sound of their irritating voice and ended by asking, "Are you all set?"

He nodded slowly. "But first, tell me. What's in this for you?"

It was a question he'd asked more than once. Seraphim never answered. What's more, he knew next to nothing about the hacker. He didn't know their age. He didn't know their race, nationality, or ethnicity. He didn't even know their gender.

"Why do you keep asking the same question?"

"I'm trusting you and your plan. Seems like you can trust me a little, too."

Seraphim said, "Is that what this is? An exercise in trust?"

Decker imagined that the hacker was smiling behind the mask.

"I've been betrayed before," he began. "It makes me cautious."

"I know, by Ryan Steele."

He refused to feel anything other than ice in his veins. "And others." He paused. "I appreciate your help. I like your idea. But what do you get out of all this?"

Seraphim leaned toward the screen. "I get a front-row seat," they said, "to see the world burn."

Ryan looked out the window as Kathryn drove down the street. He'd seen more than one unfriendly crowd in his life. The people who stood on the sidewalk definitely counted as hostile. The body language said it all. Their spines were straight. Their shoulder blades were pinched together. Their gazes narrowed as the vehicle drove past. In short, they were ready for a fight.

Kathryn pulled next to the curb. A house sat at the end of a walkway. It would have been unremarkable, except for the X of crime-scene tape that was draped across the door. A CSI van was parked at the end of the block. After turning off the engine, she looked over her shoulder. He followed her gaze.

She was staring at her own home.

This was her neighborhood, so he imagined her feelings were complicated. Besides wanting to solve the murder, she must be worried about her own kids.

He turned his attention back to Kathryn. Holding onto the steering wheel, her knuckles were white. "It'll be okay." Without thinking, he placed his hand on her wrist. The energy from her skin danced along his palm.

She let go of the steering wheel, and her arm slipped away from his touch. "I'm not sure it'll be okay, but I appreciate you saying so."

After pulling the keys from the ignition, she opened the door. The outside was hot and sticky. A scent clung to the air, like vegetables left to rot in the garden.

He watched as Kathryn slid slowly from her seat. As she closed the door, he exited the car. The black SUV was already parked behind the cruiser. Jason, Isaac, and Michael exited the vehicle. They stood next to the front fender.

A middle-aged man with dark hair approached. "Undersheriff, I need a word."

She held up a hand, halting the man. "Not now, Joe."

"Not now?" he spluttered. "Something's going on, and you owe us all an explanation."

"Until I know exactly what happened, I'm not going to comment," she said.

Someone from the crowd called out, "Where's Tessa?"

"Yeah," said Joe. "She was with us earlier this evening." He glared at Ryan. "Right after you picked up this guy for trespassing."

"My deputies will be around to talk to everyone soon." She gestured to several people who wore the uniform of the sheriff's office. "We can and will get to the bottom of this suspicious incident—together, all of us—as a community."

Honestly, Ryan liked the way she handled the crowd.

"Suspicious, like what?" Joe asked, a challenge in his tone. "Suspicious like the undersheriff chasing a known felon down the street? Or suspicious like deputies showing up at Tessa's house? Then, a few minutes later, crime-scene investigators arrive. Or is it the kind of suspicious where the people who are in charge aren't willing to say exactly what in the hell is going on?"

"I'm not going to comment on a pending investigation," she said, an edge to her voice.

"So you admit that something happened to Tessa," said an elderly woman. "Is she okay, at least?"

Ryan knew this was not going well for the undersheriff. "Just let the lady do her job, okay?"

His comment wouldn't calm down Joe. But he hoped that at least it'd get the attention off Kathryn and onto him.

Joe turned slowly and took a step toward him. It was a bold move. Ryan was over a decade younger than the other man and more than a head taller. If punches were thrown, the fight wouldn't last long. What's more, it would go poorly for Joe. Still, the other man didn't back down. Ryan wasn't sure if he should be impressed by the dude's bravery or troubled by his stupidity.

Joe said, "Why don't you mind your own business? Or better yet, get the hell out of my town." Then he flipped his fingers toward the trio who stood next to the black SUV. "And speaking of people who don't belong, what are they doing in Encantador?"

"We all need to turn this down a notch." Kathryn stood between the two men. She placed a hand on Ryan's chest. Her touch did nothing to slow his racing pulse. "Joe, go home."

"You can't tell me what to do," he challenged.

"Actually, I can. Right now, I'm asking you friendly-like. Next time, it's going to be an order." Joe took a step back. Kathryn raised her voice so that her words carried up and down the street. "I need everyone to go back into their houses. I will make a statement, but only once I have something to say." She let her hand slip from Ryan's chest. He could still feel her touch on his body. "Go on and get home. It'd be a shame for my deputies to have to start writing out citations for folks disobeying a lawful order given to them by police."

Joe took another backward step. "You know this isn't how Mooky would handle things."

She stood taller. "Well, Mooky's not here."

"And it's a crying shame that he ain't," said Joe.

"Go home before you start trouble," said Kathryn.

The crowd grumbled, but they obeyed her order. People began to move slowly down the sidewalk toward their homes. Standing on the pavement, she watched Joe. "I think he's going to cause problems."

"What gives you that idea?" Ryan's words were filled with sarcasm. "He seems like a real easygoing guy."

She rolled her eyes at him. "Let's collect your friends and get a look at the crime scene."

By friends, she meant Jason, Isaac, and Michael. They all remained by their SUV. He assumed that they'd taken Kathryn at her word and were letting her run things her way. It was honorable of them. They were all honorable men. And Ryan, well, he couldn't keep his mouth shut when Joe gave Kathryn a little lip.

Not that she needed any help.

But still, he'd tried.

Who was he kidding? Ryan was nobody's idea of a hero.

As much as his life had been shaped by Decker Newcombe, he'd helped to create the killer as well. If he really wanted to atone—and then be able to start over—it meant that finding his former friend was his responsibility.

Kathryn waved to the men. They approached, forming a loose circle on the sidewalk.

"Looks like you have some upset citizens," said Jason. "Anything we can do to help?"

She said, "Yeah, find out who murdered Tessa Wray and put the bastard in jail." She trudged up the front walk. "Truly, thanks for coming down to help me. Let's go see this crime scene."

Across the street, the elderly lady held up her phone. "Y'all," she announced to the neighbors who were still heading to their houses. "It's okay. I just heard from Tessa. She sent me a text."

The street was filled with one ping after another. All the neighbors stared at their phones. "I heard from her, too," said Joe.

"And me."

"Me, too."

Kathryn's phone pinged. She looked up at Ryan. Her eyes were wide with disbelief. "She sent me a message, too."

"How did a corpse send all those texts?" he asked, his voice low.

She showed him the screen.

I thought you'd like to see this.

The message contained a link.

Jason, Isaac, and Michael stood close.

"Where's the link take you?" Jason asked.

Kathryn inhaled. She exhaled and then tapped her thumb on the link. That's when the first scream ripped through the night.

Kathryn wanted to watch the clip with an analytical eye. But with the video on her phone of Tessa's murder, it was damn near impossible.

Blood covered every surface.

An arc of blood covered the cabinets. There was a smear of blood across the floor. A bloody handprint was next to the back door. A dark pool, where the body lay, spread across the floor.

Decker Newcombe, covered in gore, looked at the camera and smiled.

Then, the screen went blank.

The street was filled with crying, cursing, and screams as all her neighbors watched the video. Her heartbeat thundered in her own ears, making her all but deaf to the chaos around her. At the same moment, Kathryn felt the enormity of the situation crash down. It pinned her in place, making it impossible to move.

Ryan placed his hand on her shoulder. "Your neighbors are scared. They need you. What are you going to do?"

He was right. But what could she do—or say—to make everything better? After all, everyone had been sent the same horrific video.

"Y'all," she yelled. "Calm down."

Nobody heard her. And even if they did, nobody listened. Then, she saw her car and knew what to do. Walking to the street, she unlocked the cruiser's doors. Ryan followed.

Kathryn slipped behind the steering wheel and started the ignition. She turned on the PA system and let out two long blasts from her siren. The street went quiet. Now that she had their attention, she lifted the mic from the console. Standing next to her car, she said, "Everyone, calm down." Her voice was carried by the PA system in her vehicle.

"Calm down?" Joe repeated. He wiped his eyes with the back of his hand. "You got the same message as the rest of us. Tessa was slaughtered." He gestured to Gladys. The older woman sat in a lawn chair and rocked back and forth. Joe's wife, at her side, patted the back of her hand. "She's never going to be the same. None of us will ever be okay. It's all his fault." He took two steps toward Ryan. "If you won't get him out of here, we'll take matters into our own hands."

Kathryn went cold. The last thing she needed was a vengeful mob. "You better back up, Joe. There won't be any vigilante justice in my town. If you get folks all riled up, it's going to be you in a jail cell. You understand?"

"I understand," he grumbled, "that you'd rather protect a criminal than your neighbors. What is it with this guy?"

Kathryn wanted to deny her attraction to Ryan, but she couldn't. "Ryan was with me when Tessa was attacked. He's not the killer." She scanned the crowd to make sure everyone heard what she said. A few heads nodded. She took the gesture as a win. "We've got the FBI here already. They're going to help us find Decker and stop him once and for all." She paused. "I want everyone to get back in their houses. Lock the doors. If you don't feel safe on your own, stay with a neighbor. Be watchful. Be smart." She knew it wasn't enough. These people had questions, and they deserved answers. "Tomorrow, I'll tell you what I can. For now, we know that Decker's close. We can't let the trail get cold this time."

"When tomorrow will you talk to us?" Joe asked. "And where?"

"I can let you into the high school," said another

neighbor, Armando Cruz, the school's assistant principal. "As for the time, well, that's up to the undersheriff."

Kathryn quickly calculated what needed to be done. Early in the morning, Tessa's parents would arrive. It was only right that she talked to them first. "I'll have a briefing ready at noon." She glanced at Special Agent Jones. He gave a quick nod. Thank goodness, he'd be there. "To say that video is upsetting is an understatement, but I need to get back to work. I'll speak to you all tomorrow."

"How's anyone supposed to know about the meeting?" Joe asked.

Honestly, it wasn't an unreasonable question.

"I'll share the information on the school's social-media account," Armando offered. "We can use the auditorium."

"Thanks, that'd be helpful," she said to Armando. Then to Joe, she asked, "Can you watch Gladys?"

He nodded. "Of course. She can stay with us."

Truly, he wasn't all bad. "I appreciate it."

Turning her full attention to the investigation, she stepped closer to Michael, Jason, and Isaac. "I need some cyber help with this case. My guess is that Decker stole Tessa's phone." Bile rose in the back of her throat as she recalled the first cut. It started out as pink flesh. A seam of red appeared before the wound began to weep blood. But that moment was just the beginning of the torture.

Jason saved Kathryn from having to say anything more. "Send me that link and all Tessa's information. We can get our cybersecurity experts to try to track the phone remotely."

Kathryn did what Jason asked.

"Got it." He glanced at the screen. "I can access the internet from my vehicle. I'll make some calls, and we can regroup in a minute."

Isaac and Michael followed the FBI agent, leaving Kathryn and Ryan. They truly were alone. All her neighbors had gone into their own homes. Despite the fact that it was after midnight, she doubted that anyone would get much sleep.

It meant that in twelve hours, she'd face a scared, angry, and exhausted crowd.

At least there was one thing she could do right now. She turned to Ryan. "I hate to kick you out of town in the middle of the night, but you have to go. This is for your own safety. I can drive you back to your truck and then…" She let the silence say the words she couldn't speak.

"Listen," Ryan began. She could tell he was ready with an argument. "I know Decker. I can help."

She nodded slowly. "You're right, but Joe tried to get a mob to attack you."

Ryan folded his arms across his chest. "I'm not afraid of Joe."

"If they're frightened and mad enough, the best people can turn ugly. I don't want that for you. Can you let me help you out?"

His shoulders sagged. He was going to surrender. "I need to get my dog."

Right. Old Blue was still in her office. "We'll get him first."

Standing next to the black SUV, Jason waved. Isaac stood outside as well.

Ryan nodded toward the FBI agent. "Looks like he has news for you."

Together, they walked to the SUV. "What have you got?" she asked.

"Nothing good," said Isaac.

"It looks like Decker not only sent the video to everyone on the victim's contact list, but he also posted it to her social-media accounts," said Jason. "We've got people working with the companies to take down the posts. But, really, a lot of damage has already been done."

"What are our options?"

"For now, there are people trying to find Tessa's phone," said Jason.

Isaac continued. "We're going to set up shop at the Center." Months earlier, Michael had opened the Center for Rural Law Enforcement in the neighboring town of Mercy. The title was a mouthful, and everyone affectionately called the labs *the Center.* "There are forensics labs and supercomputers we can use."

"I'll run the investigation out of my office," she said, happy to finally have a plan of sorts. "But first, I'm going to get Ryan out of town. Right now, everyone is looking for a scapegoat. If he's here, then he's the most likely candidate."

The other two men nodded in agreement.

Now there was nothing more for her to do. She needed to get Ryan away as quickly and quietly as possible. "Come with me," she said to him, while walking toward her car.

Without speaking, they got into her vehicle and drove to her office. Old Blue was collected. While Ryan took the dog for a short walk, she raided the office's snack closet. There were enough assorted chips, crackers, cookies. She got the case of water from her office and put together a bag.

He was waiting next to her car when she left the building. She handed him the food. It was the least she could do. "I hope this helps you get where you're going."

"Thanks." After settling the snacks onto the floorboard between his feet, he snapped his fingers. The dog joined him on the passenger seat.

Kathryn set her phone on the console before settling behind the steering wheel. After starting the engine, she drove. Her eyes were dry, and her muscles ached. She was exhausted, but there'd be no time for her to rest. Driving through the night, she knew she should say something. After seeing the video of Tessa's murder, she couldn't think of anything helpful.

Her phone's screen glowed, and the device shimmied. The caller ID read *Jason Jones, FBI.*

She swiped the call open before turning on the Speaker function. "What've you got for me?"

"We've found the bastard," said Jason, his tone jubilant. "Or at least, we've found Tessa's phone and it's still active." He gave her an address that she recognized at once.

"That's the McCoy place. Nobody's lived there for years." The ranch had sat empty since the family moved.

"Looks like we can be there in twenty minutes," said Jason.

Kathryn was less than ten minutes away from the old ranch. With grim determination, she stepped on the gas.

Chapter 6

Caught in the beams of headlights, a lone farmhouse sat at the end of a long dirt drive. At one time, the worn wooden planks of the structure had been white, but now only flecks of paint clung to the warped boards. The wide lawn was now filled with dead grass and a Realtor's faded For Sale sign that leaned drunkenly to one side.

During the day, Ryan thought the desolate homestead would've been inhospitable. At night it was downright unnerving.

Old Blue pulled back his ears and nervously licked the air. He rubbed the dog's shoulder.

Kathryn parked near the front porch. A cloud of dust billowed behind the car. Lifting the handset to her radio, she pressed down on the Talk button. "This is Undersheriff Glass," she said. "I need an ETA on the backup headed to McCoys' ranch."

"Backup is on the way. ETA, ten minutes."

"Ten minutes," she said with a muttered curse. "Seems like eternity." Pressing the button again, she spoke to dispatch. "Copy that. Ten minutes."

After setting the mic back on its hook, Kathryn turned off the ignition. The engine went still. The night was filled with silence. "What's your gut tell you?" She glanced at him before turning her gaze back to the house. "Is he here?"

Leaning forward in his seat, he peered out the windshield. The windows on the house were dark, like dead eyes staring across the barren landscape. "This is the exact kind of place that Decker would want. Remote. Abandoned. Creepy." But there was more. "He's not a fool, and he knows that the cell phone can be tracked. If he was here when he posted to the internet, my guess is that he left soon after. Right now, he's halfway to San Antonio or Mexico City or God knows where. The device is still here because he wants you to find it. He's using it as a distraction."

"We didn't exactly sneak up on this place. If he's inside now, he saw the car the minute it turned onto the drive." She paused. "I just don't want him to sneak out the back door while we're waiting out here." Rolling back her shoulders, Ryan could see the look of determination harden her features. "I *am* the undersheriff. I'm going to walk the perimeter."

He unfastened his seat belt. "I'll come with you."

She regarded him but said nothing.

Ryan understood the silence to mean one thing. Kathryn was trying to decide if he were trustworthy—or not.

"You don't know me well, but at least you know I've been honest with you all evening."

"You're right, I don't know you at all. I think it's best if you stay in the car."

"Finding Decker isn't just a job to me—all of this is personal." He paused. "Besides, I won't stay."

She glanced at him before looking out the window. With a curse, she said, "If you want to come with me, then you'll need this." Kathryn leaned across the console and opened the glove box. Her shoulder grazed his chest and a current buzzed through his veins. From the glove box, she removed a black handgun.

She sat upright in her seat and held the firearm. "I assume you know how to use one of these things?"

"I do."

She placed the gun in his hand. "It's loaded. Be careful."

"Always," said Ryan. The gun was a SIG Sauer P226. He pulled back on the slide and took a single bullet from the chamber. Next, he removed the magazine. It was filled with fifteen rounds. He replaced the magazine. Then, he chambered a round. Next, he removed the magazine once more and slid the final bullet back into place.

Kathryn gave him a wry smile. "You are careful. I'm impressed." Her compliment wasn't much, but his chest warmed. "Will the dog be okay if I lower the windows a bit?" she asked.

Ryan scratched Old Blue's head. "Let me put him in the back seat. That way he won't get into the food. This guy will eat anything."

Ryan opened the front and back passenger doors. He snapped his fingers and pointed. The dog understood the command and trotted into the back seat. Then, he closed both doors.

Using a switch, Kathryn lowered all four windows enough to allow in fresh air. Afterward, she exited the car. In the distance, a fork of lightning danced along the horizon. A breeze blew, rattling the branches of the nearby tree. The scent of ozone wafted on the air.

"Smells like rain," he said.

She grunted. "I hope so. We can take some rain," she said, while removing her own firearm from the holster she wore at her hip. "Let's check the doors and windows. See if anything's unlocked or open."

The front door was solid wood with a narrow window at the side. A lace curtain hung limply behind the glass. Ryan's shadowy form was caught in a reflection. With the tattered fabric, he looked every bit like a ghost.

A ghost?

When was the last time he'd been worried about an apparition?

Then again, he was still haunted by Decker, the specter of his past.

Kathryn turned the knob. It rattled, metal against wood, but the door didn't budge.

"It's locked," she said, though that much was obvious. "Feels like the dead bolt is engaged, too." She gave a loud exhale. "Check the windows."

There was a set of windows on each side of the door. Ryan moved to the left. With his back pressed into the grime-coated wood, he glanced into the room. Limiting his exposure, he only looked inside for an instant. But an instant was all he needed.

"What'd you see?" she asked, her voice a husky whisper.

He ignored the fact that her words seemed to stroke his neck on the way to his ear. "Looks like it used to be a dining room. There's an old table and a few chairs." He paused and brought the image of the room back to mind. "Everything's dusty, though. No sign that anyone's been in the house."

He exhaled. Tension he hadn't noticed before slipped from his shoulders. He peered into the window on the other side of the door. The room beyond was bare, the wooden planks of the floor covered in dust. "Nobody's been in that room for a while, either."

After slipping the SIG Sauer into the waistband of his jeans, he gripped the windowsill and lifted hard. It didn't budge. "Locked or swollen shut, I can't tell," he said. "But those windows haven't been open for years."

"Let's check around back, just to make sure." Kathryn gestured to the steps that led off the porch. "I think there's a door in the kitchen."

"Let's go." He removed his gun as he descended the stairs.

A clap of thunder rolled across the plains. A single raindrop hit the dusty ground, creating a tiny crater.

So far, there was no sign of Decker, but it'd be irresponsible to let his guard down now. Kathryn paused at the corner of the house. He glanced around the house. There was nothing and nobody.

But he had noticed a window on the second story. In his mind, he saw a person watching them from above. Ryan started to sweat.

He looked up again.

The window was empty, save for the reflection of the moon.

* * *

Decker stood in the dark and held his breath. From the side window, he watched Ryan Steele and a female cop. It had been over a year since he'd last seen his onetime business manager, former friend, constant rival, and current enemy.

A scabbard was looped through Decker's belt. The hunting knife he used to kill the last woman hung inside. It was easy to imagine hot blood washing over his hand as he plunged the knife between Ryan's ribs. There'd be a look of shock and horror as he realized that Decker had won the ultimate battle between them. He'd twist the knife and smile as the other man died in agony.

But even in the dark, he could see the outline of the gun in Ryan's hand. Since reemerging from a year of living off the grid, Decker had been shot twice. Neither wound had healed right, and he loathed the idea of taking another bullet. It left Decker with a question. Was he fast enough to stab Ryan before his nemesis got a chance to fire a round?

Then again, if he was asking the question, he already knew the answer.

Stepping back, he melted into the darkness once more. He had to get out of the house, especially since he wouldn't be able to hide much longer. The computer, his phone, and backpack all lay in the corner on his blanket. He collected his belongings and shoved them into the sack. Moving quietly and quickly, he descended the stairs.

Two days earlier, he'd broken into the house by jimmying the lock on the kitchen door. Since then, he'd been living on the old farmstead while waiting for tonight. On the main floor, freedom was only a few paces away. It was so close he could taste it.

Then again, he wanted Ryan to know that he'd stumbled into Decker's lair. He wanted to stay and fight. He needed to destroy his old friend, the one whose betrayal was a scar on his soul. But he wasn't a fool. He'd never stand a chance against two guns. Especially since he was armed with only a knife.

Besides, he'd heard the conversation and knew that backup was expected. There wasn't much time before the entire property would be crawling with cops.

Decker moved to the edge of the kitchen. The linoleum beneath his feet sagged. He glanced over his shoulder. A door led to a basement. It was filled from floor to ceiling with boxes of unknown junk the family never took when they moved. Could he hide among the debris now and later sneak away unnoticed?

Not damned likely.

Through a dirt-coated window, he watched Ryan and the woman deputy pass. He had only seconds before they discovered the broken lock on the kitchen door. Which meant he had to decide on his next move—and fast.

There was really only one thing he could do.

With a roar, he launched himself out the door. He caught the sheriff around the middle at the same moment she turned and lifted her gun. They tumbled back as the gun's muzzle erupted with a burst of fire. The stink of gunpowder filled the night. The bullet passed his cheek, missing him by an inch. The air around him crackled and burned.

He focused all his effort on the woman's hand, the

one that held the gun. Gripping her wrist with both his hands, he brought her arm down hard. She screamed. The gun tumbled from her grasp, skittering across the ground.

"Stop, Decker, or I'll shoot." He recognized Ryan's voice and felt the crosshairs of a gun aimed at the back of his head. Yet, he wasn't about to give up. If he thought that getting the deputy to drop her weapon would take the fight out of her, he was wrong. She brought up her knee, catching his inner thigh. She'd obviously been aiming for his crotch. She'd missed, but the impact filled his leg with a tight knot of white-hot pain.

He took the agony and turned it into fuel. Grabbing the woman's hair, he pulled back on her scalp. Then, he drove her head into the sunbaked earth. She went limp. Dazed, her eyes rolled into the back of her head.

His old acquaintance didn't fire his weapon.

Why?

Was it because he'd never get off a clean shot? Even if he did hit Decker with a bullet, it could pass through him and still strike the sheriff.

When had Ryan gotten so weak and spineless?

Or maybe there was another reason he hadn't yet fired.

Pulling the knife from his sheath, Decker drove the blade into the cop's side.

Blood dripped from Decker's blade and wept from Kathryn's side. The coppery stench of blood filled the night. Fat raindrops fell, and thunder echoed in the darkness.

Ryan watched both Kathryn's prone form and Decker,

who stood beside her body. His eyes burned with anger—
for knowing that he had yet again failed to act. And because of him, Kathryn might die at the hands of his old
partner.

His blood heated, the urge to contain this madness
overtaking him.

"You bastard." Lifting his gun, he aimed at Decker's
chest.

"I'm the bastard?" he echoed. Rain turned killer's
hair and clothes sodden. He wiped his hand across his
damp face. "I've never sold out my friend. And what'd
you get for helping the feds? A clean record? How long
do you think it'll be before you go back to being on the
wrong side of the law?"

He'd never admit it, but Decker was right. What Ryan
feared the most was that at his core, he was a bad per-
son. He worried that his life hadn't been corrupted by
Decker and that his former friend had only accelerated
his criminal proclivity. What if he stopped Decker now?
Would it be enough to compensate for all his misdeeds?
He knew what he was supposed to do. He knew what
Kathryn would have done. "Drop your knife."

"You want this blade?" Like a mother holding the
hand of her beloved child, Decker gazed at his blade.
"You'll have to take it from me."

He aimed at Decker's chest. "Stop effing around.
Drop the knife. I've got the gun, and backup is on the
way."

"I'll never surrender. You of all people should know
that."

On the ground, Kathryn moaned.

He looked in her direction. Her back rose and fell

with each breath. She was alive, but how long would she survive without help? He looked back at the killer and ground his teeth together. "What'd you do?"

Decker shrugged. "Looks like she's not as dead as you thought. Now you gotta ask yourself a question. You want to save her or take me down?"

Ryan blinked away the rain. In an instant, he knew that he'd been played. Decker hadn't meant to murder Kathryn. He only wanted to wound her badly enough that Ryan would be boxed into a corner. He could either save a life or let a killer go. Anger flowed like lava through his veins. His body vibrated with loathing for a man he used to love like a brother.

The past didn't matter anymore.

He had to live in the present, and that meant choosing.

For him, there really wasn't a decision to make.

Ryan lunged to the spot where Kathryn lay.

There was so much blood. It covered her clothes and turned the ground to black mud. He needed to get the bleeding stopped and now.

Holding onto her shoulders, he gently flipped Kathryn onto her back. He lifted her shirt. The wound into her abdomen wasn't long, but he guessed it was deep.

Ryan's chest burned as it filled with mixed emotions. But he'd have to parse out his feelings later. Or better yet, he could ignore them altogether. Right now, he had to save Kathryn, and that meant stanching the blood flow.

Without thought, he pulled the flannel shirt from his waist. He pressed the fabric to her injury.

Kathryn's eyelids fluttered. Her lips moved. He could feel her breath.

Those were all good signs, right?

"Don't." His voice was thick with emotions he didn't want to feel. "Don't talk. Don't move. I'll take care of you."

But how?

Slipping his arms under her knees and back, he gently lifted her from the ground. Then, he ran like hell to the front of the house. A fork of lightning turned the night bright as day. It made it easy for Ryan to see the truth. Kathryn's vehicle was gone. The cruiser had been stolen by Decker, obviously. If he'd taken the car, it meant that Old Blue was gone, too. His gut burned with anger and frustration. Thunder rumbled, and he could feel the echo in his chest. Then, the skies opened. Water sluiced down his shoulders as a spray of cold water hit him in the face.

The storm had arrived in full force.

Gripping the steering wheel with both hands, Decker pressed his foot to the accelerator. The wipers swished back and forth, clearing away the rain that now fell in sheets. He'd stolen the cop's car, but he knew it wouldn't get him far. Certainly, the vehicle had GPS tracking. It wouldn't take the other deputies long to find it.

Which meant he had to find another ride quick.

As he sped through the darkness, he had problems beyond finding and stealing another car.

How had the cops found him?

He assumed they'd tracked him via the internet. But how? Seraphim promised that his connection was secure. His backpack sat on the passenger seat. He reached for the bag with one hand and opened the zipper. After fishing out a phone, he opened the top of the flip phone. A single number was programmed into the memory. He placed the call.

"Decker?" Seraphim's voice was still the same raspy wheeze as before. "I assume you made it out alive."

He went cold with shock. Then, it morphed to a fiery fury. "You knew they were coming for me? How?"

"Easy. I never took the victim's phone off the internet."

Disbelief hit him, like a fist to his gut. "You *what*?"

"For rest of our plan to work, the authorities had to find you. Then you had to get away. Otherwise, they wouldn't believe."

Honestly, he saw the sense in what the hacker said. But still. "What if I hadn't escaped?"

"But you did. You're resourceful. You're careful and you plan. But you can also think on your feet." He paused. "You know what to do next."

Decker did, but he had a detour to make first. "I'll be in touch."

"I'll be waiting."

He ended the call and slipped the phone back into the bag. A growl came from the back seat. Decker swerved as he looked over his shoulder. Behind the metal grille sat a dog.

He looked back at the road before glancing into the back seat again.

It wasn't just any dog. "Old Blue? How the hell did you end up in this car?"

The dog barked, baring its teeth.

Decker had to admit, he'd been surprised more than once tonight. He hated not being in control. He hated seeing Ryan again. He hated the only way to end it between them would be with one of them in a body bag.

His old *friend* knew that, too.

Ryan could've shot him. He assumed that the hesitation was to protect the sheriff's deputy. But why?

Was the woman something more to Ryan?

He hoped so, because then he could use those feelings to his advantage.

Chapter 7

Ryan stood in the middle of the muddy driveway. Rain washed over him in a single sheet. He held Kathryn in his arms. Her face had turned milky white—not a good sign. He had no car. No phone. No way to call for or get help.

He cursed and ran up the sagging porch steps. At least, under the overhang, he could keep Kathryn drier. He found a spot to lay her on the wood porch. Her head drooped to the side. Her lips had turned purple.

His throat tightened, until it felt like he was being choked. "Are you still with me?" he croaked.

Kathryn said nothing.

He tapped her cheek. She moaned.

Sagging with relief, he said, "You have to listen to my voice."

He looked out into the night. There was nothing other

than darkness and the endlessly falling rain. Where was the damned backup? It'd been more than ten minutes since they'd called in. Or maybe not. Time no longer meant anything.

"Stay with me," he urged.

Kathryn's eyelids fluttered.

"I want you to pay attention to my voice," he said to her, hoping like hell she was still lucid enough to hear him. Reaching for her hand, he rubbed her palm. "Can you hear me? Squeeze my hand if you know I'm here."

Her fingers twitched.

Flashing red lights shone on the horizon. "It's them," he said. The first vehicle was followed by others. At the back of the line, he saw a large, white ambulance.

He bent close to Kathryn. "That's the backup. They're here. You'll be okay. I promise."

Her lips moved, but she made no sound. Or did she? Leaning closer still, he asked, "What'd you say?"

She swallowed, grimaced, and muttered a single word. "Decker?"

"He got away. He escaped when I saw that you were still alive." He expected the words to taste like ash and soil. They didn't. He didn't regret letting Decker go— not if it meant keeping Kathryn alive.

She gripped his hand. The strength in her fingers startled him. Her eyes were open. He met her gaze.

"Thank you," she whispered.

The emotion that had choked him before got tighter. He couldn't have spoken, even if he'd known what to say. He gave her a single nod and squeezed her hand. Her eyes drifted closed. Ryan stood. He ran into the rain, waving at the oncoming vehicles. The first car to stop was the black SUV. Isaac opened the driver's door. Ryan met him before he put his foot on the sodden ground.

"I need the ambulance," he said. "Kathryn was stabbed by Decker. She's on the porch and hurt bad."

He tried to run. Isaac gripped his shoulder. "Where's Decker now?"

"Hell if I know where he went. But after he stabbed Kathryn, he stole her cruiser." He shouldn't be worried about a mutt when so much was at stake. And yet, he said, "Old Blue was in the car. And now, he's gone, too."

Isaac opened the back door of the SUV. "Michael, the undersheriff's hurt."

The lanky physician stepped into the rain. Michael O'Brien was a forensic pathologist, but he'd also attended med school. With the physician working with a set of the EMTs, Ryan hoped that Kathryn would get the care she needed.

The doctor said to Isaac, "Get the paramedics up here." Then to Ryan, "Take me to the undersheriff."

Sprinting through the deluge, he bounded up the steps of the porch. Michael followed. It was impossible to miss Kathryn's supine form. The doctor knelt next to her. "Tell me what happened."

He gave a quick rundown of the encounter with Decker.

At length, Michael said, "The good news is I don't think any internal organs are damaged. But she shouldn't lose consciousness with an abdominal wound. I suspect she has a concussion, too." Before he could say anything else, a pair of EMTs approached. One carried a folded stretcher and the other a medical kit. Ryan moved to the side to let the medical professionals do their job.

An EMT knelt next to Kathryn. "Undersheriff," he said, "it's me. Chase Martinez. I'm here to take care of you."

It took only minutes for the paramedics to get Kathryn into the back of the ambulance. Once the back doors closed, the vehicle turned on the muddy yard. Ryan stood on the porch, suddenly exhausted, and watched the ambulance drive away. As the taillights were swallowed by the darkness, he didn't know what to do next.

The desire to be with Kathryn was akin to the hunger of a starving man. He wanted to go to her. Did he have the right to make any demands?

He knew the answer. He couldn't ask for anything where she was concerned.

Jason and Isaac jogged through the rain. They climbed the steps. With Ryan and Michael, the four men formed a loose circle on the sagging porch.

Jason wiped a damp sleeve across his wet face. "Tell me what happened."

His story began with the call where Kathryn was told that the murder victim's phone had been found. He ended with Decker exploding like a cannonball from the back door and the attack that had left Kathryn unconscious and bleeding.

"How'd you know it was Decker?" Isaac asked.

Honestly, he didn't like that he was being questioned instead of everyone looking for the killer. Still, he didn't have a reason to lie. "It's been a while since I saw him last, but I still know what he looks like. After he stabbed Kathryn, I mean the undersheriff, we spoke. Honestly, I thought she was dead." He swallowed. "Once I realized that the undersheriff was alive, I started giving her first aid. That's when Decker took off."

"And you didn't think to chase him?" the FBI agent asked, his tone more an accusation than a question.

Working his jaw back and forth, Ryan spit out his next words. "Kathryn was hurt. There was blood everywhere. I couldn't exactly go after Decker because the undersheriff needed help."

Taking a step forward, Jason said, "Let me get this straight. You think that Decker attacked the undersheriff and wounded her just so he could escape. Is that what I'm supposed to believe?"

"I don't care what you believe. And I don't know how Decker thinks," said Ryan, although the last part wasn't true. "You asked me what happened, and I've told you."

"You know," Isaac said and raised his hands, as if surrendering, "Ryan's probably right. Decker threw Clare from a moving car. It wasn't meant to kill her but to hurt her enough that I had to stop chasing him."

Clare Chamberlain had been on the run from her ex-husband when she'd stopped at the bar in Mercy. Ryan had been working undercover with Isaac at the time. Clare had gotten caught up in the Decker Newcombe case. It ended with her being kidnapped and Ryan being stabbed. Well, since Decker was back, he supposed that the story hadn't really ended—not yet.

Jason and Isaac exchanged a glance that was impossible to miss. The look was a punch to Ryan's gut. "Stop throwing side-eyes at each other and just say what you want to say. Or ask what you want to ask."

Isaac shifted from one foot to the next. "I'm only going to ask you once, and I trust you'll be honest with me. Did you know that Decker was going to be in the area tonight? Are you working with him again?"

Ryan had never been a cop, but he knew how they thought. Decker and Ryan returning to Encantador and Mercy on the same night was too much of a coincidence to be an accident. "I'm not working with him—not anymore."

"Can you prove there's not a connection between you and Decker?" the FBI agent asked, a definite edge in his tone.

"Can you prove that there *is* one?" he shot back.

Jason didn't seem to have an answer to the question, which meant he had no proof.

Isaac was the next one to speak. "Why are you in the area anyway?"

Crap. Now what was he supposed to say? He definitely didn't want to tell them the truth, but he'd gain nothing by lying. He remained mute.

After a moment, Jason said, "You got the federal government to clear your background. That left you without a past at all. Life can't be easy."

Ryan really disliked the fed. It was more than his holier-than-thou attitude, though that was bad enough. The guy was too perfect. His wet clothes weren't muddy or wrinkled. His hair, damp still, looked freshly barbered.

"Life is never easy." He paused a beat. "You charging me with a crime? Because if not, then I'm free to go."

"Go where?" Isaac asked. "It's pouring rain and you're miles from nowhere."

At one time, he had thought that Isaac was his friend.

Guess he'd been wrong about that, too. "Anywhere is better than here."

"I'll need your gun," said Jason. Then he added, "For forensic testing."

What the fed really meant is that he wanted to see if there was evidence to corroborate his story. "It's not my gun. The undersheriff gave it to me."

Holding out his hand, Jason said, "I'll make sure she gets it back when we're done."

He removed the gun from his waistband and slapped the weapon into the other man's open palm. "Anything else?"

Jason shook his head.

"Then, I'm outta here." Ryan jogged down the porch steps.

He was going to regret his decision, he knew it. But he'd be damned before he'd spend another minute at the abandoned farmstead. Shoving his hands in his pockets, he strode past the other collected law-enforcement agents. They were preparing to search the house and gather whatever evidence Decker had left behind.

He walked on. Rain pelted his face. Water rolled down the collar of his shirt. His shoes squelched. With each step, he cursed his decision to come back to Encantador and Mercy in the first place.

The year he'd lived here and run the bar was like a fever dream. All the memories were surrounded in a haze. But he knew life could be good. He wanted it to be good again. At the end of the driveway, he turned to the right.

A set of headlights shone on him from behind, turning his stride into the shadow of a giant. A second later, the shadow passed. From the side of his eye, he could see the large SUV. The window was down, and Isaac leaned on the center console as he drove.

"Can I offer you a lift?" Isaac asked.

"Nah. It's a lovely night for a stroll," he said, knowing full well he was being sarcastic.

"Stop being a smartass and get in the car."

Ryan shook his head.

"I'm trying to be a friend."

He snorted. "Thanks for accusing me of being a criminal again, pal."

"I know you aren't involved with Decker, but Jason doesn't. He would've gotten around to asking you. Trust me, it would've taken a lot longer, and probably he'd put you in custody. I just short-circuited his interrogation."

Ryan stopped. "Am I supposed to thank you?"

Isaac stopped his vehicle. "They found the under-sheriff's car. It's about ten miles from here. Looks like Decker parked the cruiser and stole another car."

"What about Old Blue?"

"He was in the back seat and is doing well. In fact, his barking is what woke up the homeowner." Isaac paused. "I can give you a ride to pick up the dog and then take you back to your truck."

"So I'm not going to be forced to stay?"

"Just get in the car and we can talk. You look too wet and miserable for me to answer any more questions."

"I'm not miserable," he lied, opening the door. He slid into the passenger seat. The back seats were empty. "Where's Michael and the FBI agent with the big mouth?"

Isaac chuckled. "Jason Jones is an acquired taste, that's for sure."

"Acquired tastes," he said, echoing Isaac's words, "are for wines. That guy's a bottle full of vinegar."

Isaac laughed. "I've missed you, man."

He pulled on his seat belt, thankful to be out of the rain and to have a soft leather seat. It was nice to be missed. That was one of the many reasons he wanted to come back to Mercy. "It's good to see you again," he said. What would a good friend do next? Ryan wasn't sure. Instead, he said, "Decker's up to something."

Isaac drove, gripping the steering wheel tighter. "How'd you get this intel?"

After all the talk of friendship, the private-security operative still didn't trust him one hundred percent. "*Intel* is a pretty solid word. Let's call it a hunch on my part."

"Like a gut feeling."

Ryan shrugged and turned to look out the window. He saw nothing but his own reflection. "Something like that."

"What's your gut telling you that he's planning?"

"Honestly, I'm not sure why he's fixated on this town." Although in truth, Ryan was drawn to this area, just like iron to a magnet. "But he wants something here. Revenge, for what happened earlier, maybe."

"Maybe," said Isaac.

Ryan sat without a further word. The drive to the small brick house took less than ten minutes. Kathryn's cruiser was parked in the yard. A collapsible shelter had been set up over the car, presumably to protect any evidence from the weather. Several other vehicles sat on the lawn as well. There was another cruiser from the sheriff's office along with a crime-scene unit's van and several cars from the Texas Rangers.

Isaac parked next to the CSI van. He opened the door and stepped into the rain. Ryan had begun to dry and loathed the idea of getting cold and wet again. The sound of barking came from the house. Old Blue stood on his hind legs and looked out the front window. He couldn't help but smile.

He ran through the storm. A blonde woman opened the door as he approached. "This must be your dog," she said, smiling. "He started making a racket as soon as you pulled into the yard."

Old Blue jogged from the adjacent living room. In the foyer, he dropped to his back and exposed his belly for rubs. "Hey, boy." He bent down to scratch the dog's stomach. "You miss me?"

Old Blue whined.

"I'd take that as a *yes*," said Isaac. Then to the woman, "Thanks for taking care of the dog."

She blew out a long breath, ruffling her bangs. "When I think of the bad that could've happened with Decker Newcombe in front of my house..." she shook her head "...well, I'm just glad he only stole the car."

"We're all relieved that he didn't do anything more," said Ryan.

"I don't know if y'all can comment. But is it true that he killed the bank manager and posted the murder to the internet?" She paused. "I know police can't always talk about open investigations." She looked from Ryan to Isaac and back. Did the woman think he was a cop? He wanted to laugh but kept a neutral expression.

"Sorry," said Ryan, "we really can't comment."

"C'mon," said Isaac, "let's go."

It took several minutes of driving to get to where Ryan had parked. It'd only been a matter of hours since Old Blue had taken off into the dark, but it felt like days. Thankfully, the rain had stopped and taken the oppressive heat with it. Isaac parked next to the truck, and that's when he saw the truth.

"Damn," he groaned. "I left the windows open." He opened the door of his vehicle. Water was pooled on the floor mat. He pressed a hand onto the upholstery and his palm was soaked. "Sitting on these seats will be like lying on a leaky waterbed."

"By tomorrow, they'll be dry."

Isaac was probably right, but Ryan was worried about right now. "It's gonna be a special kind of hell to drive for hours with a soggy butt," he said, trying to make a joke. But even he heard the indignation in his voice.

"I can help you out." Isaac opened the lift gate of his SUV and pulled out two tarps. Both had *Texas Law* stenciled on the back. "Use these for now."

"You have merch for your business now? Nice."

Isaac's chest swelled with pride. "It is nice."

"Brother, I am heading out of town and won't be back."

"Then, keep them. They're yours."

Taking the covers, Ryan tucked them under his arm. "Thanks." The thing was, he really was worried about Kathryn. Isaac was in the loop, so to speak. He might know how she was doing. "Have you gotten an update on the undersheriff?"

Isaac shook his head. "I haven't heard a thing."

"But she's going to be okay, right? Michael said that she was unconscious because of a probable concussion. He also said the wound to her side wasn't fatal."

"You know more than me, man."

So much for an update.

Ryan placed a tarp on the passenger seat and snapped his fingers for Old Blue to get into the vehicle. Now, there really was nothing else keeping him here. His chest ached with disappointment. But did he regret having to leave? Or was he sorry that he'd come in the first place? "If you hear anything about Kathryn…" he began.

"I'll let you know," said Isaac, finishing the request. "And do us both a favor. If the feds call with questions, make sure you answer the phone. It'll be easier on you if you cooperate."

Ryan grunted and slammed the passenger door closed.

Isaac said, "Take care of yourself."

"I always do," said Ryan.

He rounded the front of his truck and opened the driver's door. While spreading out the tarp, he watched Isaac. The operative stood next to the bumper of his own SUV and tapped on his phone's screen. "You are one lucky guy," he called out to Ryan.

"Oh yeah?" He'd had all sorts of luck in his life—most of it was the bad kind. "How's that?"

"I just got a text from Michael. It seems the wound to Kathryn's side has been patched up. She's regained consciousness. And she wants to see you."

Chapter 8

Kathryn lay in a hospital bed. Several pillows were propped behind her head. A monitor was attached to her finger. An IV was stuck in the back of her hand and tubing was taped to her skin. The doctor had given her meds for the pain, and right now, everything was surrounded with a golden halo. Yet, she knew one thing. She had to get out of the bed and back to work. What's more, there was only one person she trusted to help her out.

Now she had to hope that Ryan would come to her aid.

Jason Jones was her first visitor at the hospital. He spent several minutes asking about the incident.

Q: Was it really your idea to walk the perimeter and not Ryan's?

A: Yes.

Q: Did Ryan do or say anything suspicious while you were with him?

A: No.

And then, there was the most important question of all.

Q: In your estimation, was Ryan working with Decker?

The thing was, Kathryn had asked herself the same question more than once. Now she had a definitive answer. "He's not working with Decker." A pain gripped her side and left her breathless. "I'm positive."

A black plastic chair sat next to the wall. The FBI agent moved it next to Kathryn's bed and took a seat. "It's been a long night for everyone, so I have to ask you to clarify. How do you know—for a fact—that Ryan and Decker aren't working together?"

"Easy," she said. A cup sat on her bedside table. She reached for the water and took a sip. "After Decker stabbed me, Ryan wouldn't have bothered to save my life."

"You have a concussion and a nonfatal wound to your side, Undersheriff. I hardly think he gets credit for saving you."

Her heart monitor started to beep as her pulse climbed. "Ryan stopped the bleeding—or slowed it, at least. How long would I have lasted without him?"

The FBI agent shook his head. "I can't answer that."

"Trust me, if he and Decker were working together, then Ryan would also be gone. What's more, I'd be in worse shape than I am right now." She paused. "I need to get a hold of my kids and let them know what happened."

"Your deputy, Todd, reached out to them. They're

aware you were injured and are resting." He held out his cell. "If you want to call them, you can."

Kathryn hadn't expected the simple kindness of a loaned phone from the fed. "Thanks."

She took the phone and placed a quick call to both Morgan and Brock. Neither answered—probably because they didn't recognize the number. She left a voicemail for both. "Hey, it's Mom. You heard I got hurt. I'm in the hospital." Would her kids try to visit her? The last thing she wanted was for them to be on the streets with Decker in the area. "Stay at your friend's, I'll call once I'm home." She handed the phone back to Jason. "Thanks."

He nodded. "I have agents watching the homes where your children are staying."

Kathryn knew that pulling agents off the manhunt was a sacrifice. But knowing that her children were safe was like dropping a huge weight. She nodded her thanks. "Where are we with the investigation?"

"We're still looking for the stolen car."

"Yeah, but Decker's MO is to change vehicles frequently," she said, thinking through what she knew of the criminal's history. "He could've ditched two stolen cars by now and be God knows where."

"We have every law-enforcement officer in the area looking for him. Decker won't get far." After a moment, he asked, "How are you feeling, by the way? What's your prognosis?"

"The doctor thinks I need several days bedrest." *Like that would ever happen.* "Everything will eventually heal."

"I'll be in touch." Jason rose from his seat but didn't move toward the door.

"Anything else?" she asked.

"I was wondering if you'd spoken with Sheriff Parsons."

Letting out a long and slow breath, she tried to stave off her irritation. It didn't work. "I was unconscious for a bit. Then I was kinda busy while the doctor sewed up my side." She didn't bother to keep the snark from her tone. "So, sorry, no. I haven't really had time to make a call."

"My question is really twofold. Has Mooky been briefed on what's happening here, and who's the contact person for your office?"

"As far as I know, Mooky hasn't been contacted. Again, I've been otherwise occupied. You can keep in contact with me."

"You?" he echoed. "But you'll be laid up for a week."

"That's what the doctor said." She didn't bother to add that she disagreed with her assessment. "If anything changes, I'll let you know."

"All right, then. We'll be in touch."

He left, and Kathryn eased back into the pillows. She wanted to sleep. She needed to get out of the hospital. Her eyes drifted closed. When she opened them, Ryan was sitting in the chair next to her bed.

She wanted to speak, but her throat was too dry. She whispered his name. "Ryan."

His eyebrows were drawn together. "Hey. How're you feeling? I was worried about you."

"I'm better," she croaked. "What time is it?"

He pulled a cell phone from his pocket. "Three thirty in the morning."

"How long have you been here?"

He shrugged. "I heard you wanted to see me, but I didn't want to wake you."

She could already tell that the nap had been restorative.

"I appreciate you waiting around." She pointed to the plastic cup that sat on a nearby table. "Can you hand me the water?"

"Sure thing."

He held the cup and guided the straw to her lips. She took several long swallows and lay back in her pillows, breathing hard. "Thanks," she said before adding, "for everything."

He waved away her gratitude. "I'm just glad it worked out in the end."

"I have to ask you two questions. First, you said it yourself, you know Decker. Why'd he come back?"

"Isaac was just asking me the same thing. My best guess—he wants revenge. How that'll look, well, I don't know. But everyone in town needs to be vigilant." He paused. "Look, I'm sorry that Decker found out about Encantador and Mercy because he came looking for me all those months ago." His jaw flexed and released. "Well, I didn't know how it'd work out, and I am sorry. I will give you your wish, though. As soon as I leave the hospital, me and Old Blue will get out of here."

"Stay." The intensity with which she spoke was surprising, even to her. She reached for his wrist. His skin was warm under her palm. For a split second, she recalled being cradled in his arms and knowing she was safe. How long had it been since someone had taken care of Kathryn? She let her hand slip away. "I need you," she said. "I need help, and you're the only one I trust."

She looked up and met his gaze. His eyes were wide. "You need me. Why?"

She pushed herself up to sitting. Her side burned, and she gritted her teeth against the pain. "I need to get out of here. I can't lie around while Decker's on the loose."

"And why do you need me for that?"

"Because the doctor recommends that I stay here until noon. Then she said it'd be a week before I'd be back to work. After that, she wants to put me on light duty." Kathryn refused to be sidelined during the investigation. "I need someone to help me get home."

"I understand that you don't want to listen to the doctor, but is that really best? Your health is important."

"Finding Decker before he kills again is more important. Me being sore because of an injury is an inconvenience." She pointed to the table. A slip of paper lay on it. "Besides, the doctor already left a prescription for pain meds. Todd brought me a change of clothes."

Ryan shook his head. "It doesn't sound like a great idea to me. You should follow the doctor's orders."

"You're one to talk. You don't like to play by the rules."

"Yeah," he said. "But I want to be the good guy and do the right thing."

She tried again. "I can't catch Decker from this bed. And I won't rest if he's still at large."

"I really shouldn't," he began.

"But you will, right?"

"You make it hard to be an honorable man, you know

that?" He gave her a wicked smile. Both his smile and his words warmed her from the inside out. She tried to ignore the sensation, but it was impossible.

"Help me get out of this bed." She carefully swung her legs over the edge of the bed and held out her hand. It was dangerous to trust him. To touch him. Had she been honest when she said she had nobody else to help her?

Yes and no.

Certainly, she could have ordered one of the other deputies to get her out of the hospital and take her home. They would have balked and tried to talk her into staying. Who knows, maybe she would have even listened. Or maybe the truth was far more basic. Maybe she asked for Ryan because she wanted to be in his arms again. She wanted to know once more what it was to feel safe and cared for.

He reached for her hand. She'd come to expect the electric current his touch ignited. This time, discomfort short-circuited her reaction. He pulled her to standing. By the time she was on her feet, her legs shook and cold sweat coated her face and back. She should've taken care with her hospital gown. It gaped in the front and was open in the back. She glanced at Ryan. His gaze was glued to the floor. There was no way he'd caught a peek at anything.

Todd had dropped off the gym bag she kept stowed at work. Inside was a fresh change of clothes. "Hand me that duffel."

"Can you stand on your own?"

She pressed the backs of her legs against the bed. The frame held her steady. "I'm good."

He set the bag on the bed beside her. There was also a plastic bag with her other belongings that had been collected by the hospital. It contained her phone, keys, and such. He picked up the second bag. "I'll carry this for you and stand outside. Yell if you need me."

First, she pulled the IV from her hand and taped a bandage to the puncture mark. Then, she shrugged out of her hospital gown. Her side was covered with a large white compress. The emergency room physician, Dr. McDaniel, had gone over the need to keep it dry for the next few days, which meant no shower or bath. After that, the dressing could be changed.

The thing was, she didn't have time to be weak or wounded or sick.

She carefully donned a fresh set of underwear and bra. She put on a T-shirt, and by the time she was pulling up a loose pair of jogger pants, white dots floated in her vision. There was no way she would be able to get on her socks and shoes.

"Ryan." The single word came out as a wheeze. "Can you help?"

He appeared at her doorway. His shoulders seemed to fill the frame. "Yeah?"

"I hate to ask for this." She picked up a pair of sneakers from the bed. "Can you help me with these? It'll hurt too much to bend down."

"I'm still not sure that you leaving the hospital is the best idea. You look worn-out."

The simple act of dressing had left her exhausted. "I'll rest when I get home."

He shook his head but said, "You got socks?"

She picked up a pair. "Here."

He took them from her. The tips of his fingers grazed her palm. A shiver of desire ran through her, and for a moment she forgot how lousy she felt. He knelt at her feet, and a craving for his touch filled her veins once more.

Carefully, Ryan lifted one foot and set it on his bent knee. "Red toenails," he said. "Nice."

Sure, she felt rotten. Still, she smiled. "I get a pedicure once a month. Kind of silly, if you think about it. Nobody ever sees my feet."

"I'm more than a nobody."

Truer words had never been spoken. He gazed at her with his blue eyes. Her fingers itched with the need to stroke his cheek. She balled her hands into fists and pressed her knuckles into the mattress. "I'm sure you've never been accused of being a nobody."

He watched her for a minute before looking away. He slipped a sock and shoe on one foot then took care of the other. Standing, he dusted his hands on the front of his jeans. "Anything else you need?"

"I'm good." She stood. The floor beneath her tilted, but at least, this time, there were no floating dots. The ground leveled, and she drew in a long breath. "I'm good," she repeated; this time it was closer to the truth.

"Can you walk to the truck? If not, I can grab you a wheelchair."

"If I can't walk to the parking lot, then I have no business leaving the hospital."

"Is this a test?" he asked.

It was and it wasn't. "I'm leaving the hospital no matter what."

He stood at her side. "At least hold onto my arm."

Her fingers dug into his bicep. His muscles were taut. She took one step. Pain radiated from her stomach and wrapped around her back. She drew in a long, slow breath. She exhaled and took another step. And another. By the time they made it to the hallway, her back was damp with sweat.

A nurse's station sat at an intersection of two corridors. The physician, Felicia McDaniel, looked up as she approached. She was the last person Kathryn wanted to see.

The doctor scowled. "What are you doing out of bed? I told you that we were keeping you until noon, at least."

"I'm discharging myself."

"I have to advise against it," the doctor began.

"If it weren't important, I'd stay in bed to recuperate. But with Decker at large…" She wanted to shrug but worried that the slight movement would hurt too much. She finished with, "I just can't."

"Can't or won't?" the doctor challenged.

Kathryn knew the difference. But how could she explain to Felicia that Decker was now her personal problem? She couldn't lie in bed and let other people run the investigation. She held tighter to Ryan's arm. He placed his hand on hers. "I'll take it easy," she said, not sure how she'd keep her promise.

"I can't force you to stay," said the doctor. "But if I could, I would." After pulling a pad of paper from her pocket, she silently wrote on the page. "This is for iron. I don't want you to become anemic. Eat something before you take either this or the pain meds. Got it?" She held up the prescription.

"Got it." Kathryn reached for the piece of paper.

"And you," the doctor said, pointing to Ryan, "make sure she rests when she gets home."

"I'll do my best," he said, patting Kathryn's hand.

The walk through the hospital was slow. Yet, with each step she took, she knew she could get through this. The waiting room was empty. A set of sliding glass doors led to the parking lot. The sky was still dark. The rain had stopped, but clouds filled the sky.

"That's my truck," he said, pointing to a blue and white vehicle two rows back. "I can help you get to the bench. I'll drive to you. It won't take a minute."

If Kathryn sat down, she wasn't sure that she'd be able to stand again. "I've got this," she said. Even she could hear the exhaustion in her voice.

She shuffle-stepped across the pavement. At the truck, he let his arm slip from her grip and opened the passenger door.

Tail a wagging blur, Old Blue stood on the passenger seat. Both seats were covered with dark blue tarps. A white Texas Law logo was stenciled on them in white. "What's up with those?" she asked, pointing to the covers.

"I left the windows open and, of course, it rained. Scoot over, boy, and let her get in." The dog climbed over the console and sat in the driver's seat.

"Thanks, Blue." Kathryn backed up to the truck. The seat was higher than she expected.

"I can lift you up," said Ryan. "That way you won't rip open your stitches or anything like that."

"Thanks."

He stood in front of her. "Hold onto my shoulders."

She did as she was told, and Ryan pulled her close.

Her breasts were pressed against the muscles of his chest. Being this close to him left her dizzy and wanting more. The last thing she needed now was to have her judgment clouded by lust. But in the moment, there was no way she could avoid holding him tight.

He lifted her onto the seat and carefully swung her legs into the car. Standing next to her, he held the seat-belt clip. "I'll wait," he said. "You get settled."

Her side throbbed with each beat of her heart. She concentrated only on her breath. The pain didn't go away, but the sharpest edges seemed to smooth. She reached for the seat belt. "I'm okay."

"Don't twist," said Ryan, his hand still holding the metal clip. "You'll make everything worse. I've got you."

He leaned across her, his torso skimming over hers, and buckled the latch. "All better?"

His lips were close to hers. She could kiss him if she wanted. And she did want to kiss him. Yet, she knew better.

Giving a single nod, she said, "I'm okay."

He rounded to the driver's seat and got behind the wheel. It took only a few minutes to get back to her house. Ryan helped her from the truck and let her hold onto his arm while he walked her to her front door. He still had the bag with her belongings. From inside, he fished out her heavy key ring. "Which one is for the front door?"

"The silver one," she said.

He opened the lock and helped her across the threshold. She stood in her living room and glanced at a clock that hung on the wall. It was almost 4:00 a.m. If she lay down now, she could get several hours of sleep before she had to get up again for the meeting.

"What can I do for you next?"

"Help me get to my bed, and then I'll be okay." Who was Kathryn kidding? She was far from okay. Leaving the hospital had been a mistake, but she wasn't going back now. "My room's the last one on the left."

Then again, he knew that already. She'd seen him peeking in through her window.

Had that only been last night?

She stood at her doorway. Her room looked the same as it did before. Her bed was made. The pile of clean clothes still sat on a chair. But everything was different. Her neighbor was dead. A killer was once again loose in her town. And she was injured. She lifted the clock from her nightstand and set the alarm for eleven o'clock. Setting it back down, she said, "It seems like I haven't been here for a million years."

He steered her toward the bed. "Lie down," he said, as she slowly sat on the mattress. "Get some rest, and everything will be okay."

She settled on top of the covers, and sleep came to claim her. But before it did, she had one final thought. Ryan was wrong. Nothing would be okay—not now and maybe not ever.

Chapter 9

Kathryn woke to the sound of her alarm clock beeping. Her side throbbed and her head ached. Before she opened her eyes, every moment of the night before flashed through her mind.

Finding the mutilated body.

A video of the murder coming to her from the victim's phone.

There was undisputed evidence that Decker Newcombe had returned to terrorize her town. Hell, she'd even been attacked by him personally.

And yet the memory that truly sent her heart racing was when she recalled Ryan holding her in the rain.

Sitting up slowly, she rubbed her gritty eyes.

Where was he now? Certainly, he had left Encantador as soon as she fell into bed. It was all for the best, really. He was a distraction that neither she nor the town needed right now. Carefully, she placed her feet on the floor and stood. The pain wasn't as bad as she expected. And what's more, she could smell the nutty aroma of coffee coming from the kitchen.

She listened for the telltale sounds that one of her kids had come home early. Loud music. Banging dishes. Or the voices of them chatting with a friend on a video call. There was nothing. She walked slowly down the hall that ended at her living room.

The room hadn't changed much in the dozen years she'd lived in the house. A large window looked out onto her front yard and the street beyond. A set of sheer curtains was pulled over the pane, providing privacy while still allowing for light to seep into the room. An *L*-shaped sofa sat beneath the window. There was a coffee table in the middle of the floor. Two chairs stood on the opposite side of the table.

A TV sat on a stand. Pictures of her Morgan and Brock, from round babies to gangly teenagers, hung on the walls.

Old Blue sat on the floor. Tail thumping, he looked up as she approached. Ryan sat on the sofa. His eyes were closed. His head was back, and he snored softly. A half-full cup of coffee sat on the coffee table.

The dog rose. Nose down, he walked toward her. She bent to scratch his head.

"Looks like we all had an eventful night."

Ryan opened his eyes, his gaze darting from one corner of the room to the other. "Sorry," he said, raising his arms over his head. His shirt crept up, exposing his hard abs and a sprinkling of dark hair. It had been years since she'd seen such a fit and virile man. Her throat went dry, and she swallowed. "I dozed off."

"I'm surprised that you're here at all. I thought you were leaving town."

"I was," he said. "I mean, I will. It just didn't seem right to leave you alone in case there was an emergency."

Her cheeks warmed. "That was kind of you."

He rose from the sofa. "I made coffee, I hope you don't mind. Also, Dr. McDaniel called. She got the pharmacy to deliver your prescriptions. I also figured you'd need something for the pain as soon as you woke up. I hope you don't mind."

In a lot of ways, his actions were too personal for someone she barely knew. But in other ways, it was just right. "It seems like I keep thanking you for being so kind."

Taking two steps toward her, he closed the distance between them. "That's not something I hear every day. Or ever, really." He shook his head. "But I am trying. You know, I ask myself, *What would a good person do?*" He gestured to the sofa. "Sit. I'll get you coffee, your pills, a piece of toast."

Before she had a chance to think better of it, she reached for his arm. "Good people help, no matter what. Seems to me like you're a decent guy."

"No," he said with a sad smile. "I'm not."

He took a step back, and her hand slid from his wrist. "Well, it smells like you can make a decent cup of coffee. And in my book, that's enough," she said jokingly.

"And how d'you take your coffee?"

"Black. The way mother nature intended."

He gave her his wicked smile. "Black coffee. You

are definitely a woman after my own heart. Sit. I'll be right back."

She sank into the sofa. Old Blue leaned his head into her thigh, and she scratched him behind the ear. For years, her kids had begged for a dog. She'd never allowed it. She couldn't take care of an animal considering the hours her job required. Any time that was left to her, she dedicated to her kids. Yet, as she petted the dog now, she wondered if she'd made the right decision.

Ryan returned a few minutes later. In one hand, he held a cup of coffee. In the other was a plate with two slices of buttered toast and two pills. He set both on the coffee table in front of her. "The white pill is for the pain. The other is for your iron."

After picking up the two pills, she placed them on her tongue. She swallowed them both with a drink of coffee. The hot liquid burned her throat as the caffeine began to buzz through her system. Maybe she would be able to make it through the day.

The plastic bag from the hospital sat on the coffee table. She picked up a piece of toast and took a bite. While chewing, she reached for the bag and found her phone. She glanced at the screen. "Forty-five missed calls?"

She scrolled through the log. Brock had called and texted dozens of times. Morgan had called and texted as well. Her chest ached with guilt and appreciation. Her kids really did care. But what would have happened to them if things had gone differently last night?

She sent a quick message to the family group chat.

Not sure what you heard, but I'm okay. Home now. We'll talk later.

She also sent another text to Todd.

Can you be at the office to meet with Tessa Wray's family?

He replied: I figured you'd need me, so I'm here already.

Truly, she was lucky to have good coworkers.

She sent him another message.

Thanks. I owe you.

She continued to look through the messages and calls. More folks than just her kids had reached out.

Alicia, from the newspaper, had both called and texted. Caller ID showed several cable-news channels had called as well. Between all the messages from the media, she'd missed an important call. The phone log read, Sheriff Parsons. Certainly, Mooky had heard all about last night. He was probably wondering why she hadn't briefed him already. True, she had her reasons. But right now, they didn't seem so solid. She tried to swallow, but the toast stuck in her throat. "Damn."

"Bad news?" Ryan asked. He picked up his cup from the table and took a sip.

"It's nothing about Decker. It's just I have to make a call." Kathryn pushed up from the sofa. The stitches at her side pulled and she gasped.

Ryan held her elbow, keeping her on her feet. "What is it?"

She gritted her teeth. "I stood up too fast, I guess."

She drew in air through her nose and blew it out of

her mouth. The pain didn't vanish, but it became bearable. "Thanks," she said.

"I've been stabbed by Decker before, too." He let go of her elbow and lifted his shirt. A scar ran across his abdomen. "See?"

Without thinking, she brushed her fingertips over the raised, red line. "Does it hurt?"

"Right now, I can only feel your touch." His words danced on her skin.

She looked up at him. He was watching her. A smile tugged at his lips. "Oh, really?"

"Yeah." The single word came out as a sigh.

Then, his mouth was on hers. She ran her fingers through the hair that covered his abs. That electric charge she'd come to expect sparked to life again. Her side still ached, but pleasure mingled with pain.

In the back of her mind, she knew that kissing him was wrong on so many different levels. Yet, it had been years since she'd been kissed. But in all honesty, she'd never been kissed like this.

What the hell are you doing?

She didn't have an answer and she pushed him away. It was the same instant the door hit the wall with a crack.

Heartbeat thundering, she turned to the sound.

"Mom? What the heck?" Morgan stood on the threshold. She wore flannel shorts and an Encantador High School hoodie. Her dark hair was piled on top of her head in a messy bun. But her eyes were wide. Twin spots of red, like the burn from a coal, colored her cheeks. "I heard you got hurt. I got your message from a strange number. I called your phone, like, a million times. Then, I saw your text, so I rushed home. Now I find you…you…" she spluttered, unable to finish. Her eyes filled with tears.

Damn. She'd messed up. Her chest tightened with guilt and regret. Stepping toward Morgan, she opened her arms. "Oh, honey, I'm so sorry."

Morgan held up her palm. "Don't apologize to me. Don't try to hug me, either."

"Can we at least talk?"

From the floor, Old Blue whined.

Morgan spied the canine. Then, she glared at Kathryn. "A dog?" Her tone dripped with incredulity. "When did we get a dog?"

"He's not our dog, honey. He belongs to Ryan."

"Oh, he's your *friend's* dog. Stellar. Well, since you are obviously fine, I'm going to bed. I was up all night, worried about you."

"Young lady, you cannot talk to me like that." Really, she didn't have the energy for a power struggle. "Why is it always an argument with you?"

Morgan sighed. "I'm not fighting. I'm just stating facts. So unless you need something, good night."

This time, Kathryn let her leave. She sank to the sofa, exhausted once more. She was never able to find a balance with Morgan. Either Kathryn was too strict or too lenient—and neither option suited. Her gaze shifted to where Ryan stood. "Do you have kids?"

He shook his head. "I figured one of me was all the world could handle."

"She was sixteen years old when her dad died. It's a hard age to lose a parent. We wiped out our savings with his cancer treatments, so the life insurance went into a college fund. Maybe if I'd quit working to spend time with them…" She sighed. "Who knows?"

"I might not have kids, but that doesn't mean I can't recognize a loving parent. You're a good mom, Kathryn. That's why your daughter rushed home as soon as she knew you were here. Trust me."

"I don't feel like a good mom, but it's nice to hear you say so." She paused. "I mean, what parent gets caught making out at…" She glanced at her phone for the time. Her stomach dropped. "Oh, crap. Is it really almost eleven thirty? I have to get ready for the town hall." She stood and shoved her phone into her pocket. "I have to change. Then call one of my deputies to give me a ride. I hate pulling an officer off the manhunt." She sighed. She really didn't have any other choice.

Her cruiser had been recovered from the home where Decker had dumped it. The vehicle still had to be processed for evidence. Morgan had certainly driven the family car home. But Kathryn knew she shouldn't be driving with pain meds in her system.

Ryan said, "Take your toast and coffee with you. Then, I can take you to the meeting. After that, Old Blue and I will get out of town."

"I'd appreciate a ride," she said, picking up a slice of toast. While taking a bite, she walked down the hallway. The pain in her side had eased from fiery to a dull ache. Maybe the pain meds really were working. Maybe she really could get through today. And tomorrow. And every day after, until Decker was captured or killed.

Kathryn pushed open the door to her room as her phone began to ring. She didn't have time for a call.

Grinding her teeth together, she pulled the device from her pocket. The caller ID read *Sheriff Parsons*.

Well, this was one call she had to take.

She answered with a swipe. "Sheriff?"

"I'm glad to hear your voice," said Mooky. "Todd called last night. He said you'd been stabbed and were getting stitched up."

She should've known that one of the deputies would reach out to their boss. "Let's just say that it was a long night." She paused a beat. "Today's going to be a long day."

"Long day?" he repeated. "You need to rest, Kathryn. You were injured."

She turned on the Speaker function and set the phone on her dresser. "That makes it sound a lot more serious than it was. The doctor just stitched me up where I was stabbed."

"How many did you get?" he asked.

"Umm, I'm not sure," she lied. It had taken seven stitches for Dr. McDaniel to sew up the wound on her side. "But I'm on meds. I've gotten some rest. I'm ready to answer questions and then get back to work. You can count on me." At least now she was being honest.

"Of course I can count on you," Mooky said. "But you need to reconsider speaking at a town hall. Folks are scared and mad. They're going to take it out on someone, and that someone's going to be you."

"I know." She wanted to sigh but refused to give in to the anguish. "I have a job to do."

"You're dedicated to the department. I respect that. But think on what I said. Jason with the FBI can handle the town hall. You don't need to make things worse for yourself."

"I'm not hiding at home and pretending to be sick."

"It's more than pretending. You were stabbed."

"My mind's made up. Unless you have anything else, I need to get off the phone." She had to make herself look presentable.

"Hold on a second. I'm trying to get a flight back home. So far, looks like Saturday is the best I can do."

Kathryn wasn't sure how she felt about Mooky's return. Was she annoyed that he was cutting his vacation short? Or was she thankful to turn all the responsibilities over to her boss? "I can handle things till you get back."

"I know you can. Take care, and keep me informed."

"Will do," she said before ending the call.

Using the en suite bathroom, Kathryn washed her face and brushed her teeth. She combed all the tangles from her hair and pulled it back into a ponytail. She dressed in a fresh uniform. As she stood in front of the dresser, she checked her reflection. Dark circles ringed her eyes. Her complexion was pale. The shadow of a bruise colored both her cheek and chin, and there was a cut beneath her eye.

Her gaze drifted from her reflection to her hands. All her knuckles were scraped and swollen. For the first time, her wedding band looked out of place. She could feel Ryan's lips on hers. It was crazy to think that anything would ever come from that single kiss.

Still, it was time to leave the past and move into the present. Did she dare look to the future? She pulled the band up her finger. It caught on the knuckle. A zing of pain shot through her hand. She cursed and shook her palm. Well, her wedding band wasn't coming off today.

Without a backward glance, she left her room.

* * *

Encantador High School had been built in the 1970s. The parking lot separated the campus from the frontage road. The two-story structure sat behind a wide lawn. It was the same school Kathryn had attended, where she'd been on both the soccer and track teams at the adjacent sports complex. On a typical Sunday, both the frontage road and parking lot would be empty.

But not today. Cars filled the lot and were lined up on either side of the street. Sunlight winked off windshields, until it looked like a field of diamonds. Media vans had pulled up on the grass. Satellites sat atop the vehicles, like weeds that had grown overnight.

"You can drop me off here," she said, as Ryan pulled into the parking lot. "I can walk."

"What you mean is that with all these people, you don't want to explain why I was your chauffeur." After pulling to the side, he stopped his car.

He was right, but she didn't want to admit as much. Instead, she gave him a weak smile. "Thanks for the ride."

"If you need moral support, I can sneak into the back of the room."

She gave him an exaggerated eye roll. "I doubt you've ever snuck in anywhere."

"You'd be surprised." He paused a beat. "You better get going, unless you want to be late."

The last thing she wanted to be was late to her own town hall. Her fingers grazed the door handle. "You take care of yourself, okay?"

"I'll do my best. And how are you?"

"I'm okay." It was the second time she'd lied that morning.

"I know you'll be fine."

This time, when she reached for the handle, she opened the door. She turned to face Ryan again. She pressed her hand onto his cheek and brushed her lips against his. The kiss was over before it began and still, it stole her breath.

She inhaled and cast a quick glance around the parking lot. What if someone had been watching? It was that moment, Kathryn realized something important. She was entitled to live her own life. The notion left her lightheaded. Or maybe that was from the pain meds.

"I need to get going," she said, her voice a hoarse whisper.

He gave her a wan smile. "I know."

There was nothing else to do or say. Easing out of the seat, she stepped to the pavement. After closing the door, she gave him a small wave. In that moment, she caught her reflection on the side window and stood taller. She didn't know what would happen next, but she was ready.

Chapter 10

A perfect Texas sun, a bright yellow ball, hung in a sky of cornflower blue. Last night's storm had chased away the oppressive heat, but Ryan knew that the break wouldn't last more than a day or two. He'd pulled the tarps off the damp seats and opened both doors of his truck. Soon, the interior would be dry. Until then, he had time to waste.

Leaning against the bumper, he threw a tennis ball across an open field next to the high school. Old Blue gave a happy bark. As the dog chased the ball, he couldn't help but wonder how Kathryn was doing. Certainly, the meeting was standing room only. What's more, he imagined that she was being grilled about last night's murder.

Still, the moment that was top of mind for Ryan was the kiss. Holding Kathryn just felt, well, right. She was the perfect combination of soft and strong. The sound of her sigh might be the sexiest thing he'd ever heard.

Get a grip, Ryan. You've kissed other women before.

In fact, in his life, he'd kissed a lot of other women. But none of them were Kathryn.

Old Blue dropped the ball at Ryan's feet. He picked up the toy and threw it again. The dog raced across the field. In the distance, he could see the baseball diamond. Sun glinted off the top of the dugout. In high school, he'd been the team's pitcher. He wasn't like a lot of the guys—hoping for a chance to play professional baseball. Still, he was the star of the bunch.

Where would he be today if he'd had a different dream?

Hell, he still didn't know what he wanted to do— or become.

Being a criminal was behind him. But legitimacy was a goal he might never reach.

Old Blue brought back the ball again. As he bent to pick it up, his phone pinged with an incoming text. After throwing the ball, he pulled the device from his pocket. Ryan didn't recognize the number. It didn't matter. As soon as he read the message, he knew who'd sent the text. His mouth went dry.

You're going to want to see this. A link was attached.

Ryan tapped the link with his thumb. Old Blue dropped his ball and whined. For once, he ignored his canine companion. The link led to a video.

Decker held a camera at arm's length. A brick wall was at his back. "I'm not sure if anyone in Encantador noticed or not, but y'all need to check the dates. August 31 was the same day Jack the Ripper killed his first victim. That's important because now you know when my next murder will take place. Since I can't stay in Encantador and Mercy anymore, I've gone somewhere else. I'll give you a clue."

The camera aspect changed to show a street lined with brick storefronts. The aspect changed quickly, but he'd seen enough to notice a restaurant on the corner.

Decker's face once more filled the screen. "But I'm not like Jack. I won't hide in the shadows. In fact, the next murder is going to happen live on the internet." He gave a wide smile. "I know that everyone will want to watch. And as far as Ryan Steele... I'll see you in hell."

The screen went black.

For a moment, Ryan stood there, as if frozen in place.

Then, his pulse started to race. He coaxed Old Blue into the truck and left the windows down to allow for fresh air. Without another thought, he ran toward the front doors of the high school. It didn't matter what was happening in that auditorium. Kathryn needed to see this video—and now.

Kathryn had made a serious mistake. She should never have come to the town hall. There was no way she could appear that weak in front of the whole community.

And yet, a headache pounded in her skull. The pain in her side was hard to ignore. The meds she'd taken earlier now churned in her stomach. She prayed that she wouldn't get sick. She should've eaten more than a slice of toast and two sips of coffee, but it was too late to correct her mistake now.

At the back of the room, news crews were filming the meeting. All the seats were full. People stood along the walls. Everyone stared at her. The expressions on their faces said everything. They were mad. They were scared. They blamed her for the predicament. At the same time, they expected her to apprehend the elusive killer.

She'd given a briefing of last night's events. Nobody was satisfied with her explanation.

Her neighbor Joe stood and spoke into a microphone on a stand. "Decker Newcombe is one man. How is it that everyone up there…" He swept his arm, taking in all the law-enforcement officials on the stage. Beyond Kathryn, there was Jason Jones representing the FBI. There were also two members of the Texas Rangers. Lou and Georgiana covered this part of the state. "Can't seem to find one man? You had him cornered in a house last night. How'd he get away?"

How was she supposed to answer that question?

She was the reason he had escaped. She drew in a long breath and exhaled. Leaning toward the microphone, she tried to find the right words.

The back door opened, and Ryan entered the room. His T-shirt was damp with sweat. His breath was ragged as he jogged down the center aisle. "You gotta see this."

She tensed, and her headache throbbed. "Ryan, what're you doing here?"

"No questions." He approached the foot of the stage and held his phone out. "Just watch."

Jason and the Texas Rangers moved in close enough to see the screen. After reading the message, she looked up from the device. "Who sent you this text?"

"Just click on the link."

She pressed the underlined code. A video began to play.

As she watched, a chill ran down her spine. The sweat on her skin turned clammy. She had about a million questions. The first one was "Any idea where he shot the video?"

Ryan shook his head. "No clue."

Georgiana, one of the Rangers, said, "I think that's London. Show the street again."

Kathryn restarted the video an instant before Decker showed the roadside view. She stopped the recording.

"See that?" Georgiana pointed to the screen. "That building on the corner with the green sign. It's the Ten Bells. It's in London—Whitechapel to be precise."

"How do you know that?" Jason asked.

The Ranger shrugged. "I took my wife there for her fortieth birthday a few years back."

"London?" Jason echoed. "What in the hell is Decker doing in London?"

Ryan cursed. "It makes sense, though. He murdered the woman here on the same day as the first Ripper killing. Looks like he's trying to recreate all the Ripper murders. Since Kathryn and I found him outside of town, he split."

"London, as in England?" she asked, trying to connect all the dots. "How would he even get there?"

"Maybe he has cash we don't know about," Ryan suggested. "Or connections."

"I'm going to need your phone for analysis." Jason held out his hand. Ryan gave him the device. "And you're going to need to stay in town for a bit."

Kathryn didn't know what the FBI would find on Ryan's phone. But she did know that she was beyond relieved that the killer was gone.

And Ryan? Well, where he was concerned, her feelings were far more complicated.

Decker brought the bottle of beer to his lips and took a long drink. He smothered a burp with the back of his hand and looked around his temporary home.

From the outside, the warehouse looked like any dilapidated old building. And honestly, it was. But a twenty-foot square had been cleaned. What's more, walls had been erected, separating Decker's temporary home from the rest of the warehouse.

Seraphim had provided everything he needed. There was electricity. Internet access.

His open laptop sat on a card table. Several boxes filled with video equipment had been left for him as well. Aside from the table, there was a chair, a cot, and a small refrigerator/microwave combo. The fridge was well-stocked with water, beer, and microwavable entrées. In short, he'd be fine hiding here for a few days. In fact, the only reason he'd ever need to leave would be to find his next victim.

The computer pinged with an incoming message. Holding the bottle by the neck, he walked to the table and checked the screen. Seraphim had sent him a link to their dark-web chatroom. After dropping into the seat, he typed in the preset combination of letters and numbers. Then, he hit Enter.

The hacker, complete with the plague-doctor mask, appeared on the screen. "You made it to the warehouse."

"I did. This place is nice." It was the closest he'd come to giving a compliment in a long time. "What's on the other side of the wall?"

"Junk," said Seraphim. "You can check it out if you want."

True, he could. A door led to the rest of the warehouse. "I might."

Changing the subject, they continued. "Any video you want to post, you can send to me. Just call to let me know that you have something to upload."

Calling Seraphim would be a problem. "Before leaving, I stashed the phone someplace safe."

As if slapped, the hacker reeled. "You left your phone? Why would you do something stupid like that?"

Stupid. The word pecked on his nerves. For now, he'd ignore the insult. "I have two ways to contact you—this computer and the phone. If both are together and they get lost, I can't reach out."

"But I can find you. I've done it before. I can do it again."

He shook his head. "Not good enough."

"I hope you uploaded the video to the computer first. If not, you'll have to go back and get the phone."

"That's not happening. I left the phone in Mexico before coming here." He found the file with the video and sent it to the hacker. He didn't mention that he'd already sent it to Ryan. There was nothing Ryan could do to stop him anyway. "Now what?"

"Once the video's been shared, I'll create a link to your next…" the hacker searched for the right word "…performance."

Performance. He smiled. "Makes me sound like an artist."

"Oh, but you are an artist. Your medium is death. And the world is your canvas."

Sure, the hacker could be a pain. But the thing was, Seraphim saw into his soul. The hacker understood all the dark needs that controlled his actions. It was why he wanted to be remembered for centuries—just like Jack the Ripper. The first Ripper killing took place on August 31, the same day he'd killed Tessa Wray. Now, he had to find another victim and be ready to livestream the murder by September 8. Already he had an idea for who would be next. "I'll be in touch."

"Before you go, I need to ask you about Anastasia Pierce."

Anastasia "Ana" Pierce. Now there was a name he'd like to forget, and yet, he never had. Picking up his bottle of beer, he took another swallow. "She's none of your concern."

"She's the other person who betrayed you."

Decker stared at the black eyes in the plague mask and said nothing.

"I'm right," squawked Seraphim. "I can tell."

Sweat dampened his back. He took another swig of beer. The alcohol hit his gut like a bomb. "Why do you care who betrayed me?"

"I want to know what makes you tick."

"Makes me *tick*?" he scoffed. "I have to go." He ended the video call before the hacker said anything else.

He drained the last of his beer. He didn't like Seraphim nosing around in his past, especially into something as personal as his relationship with Ana. Damn. He hadn't thought about her in years. Yet, the pain in his chest was the same as it had been on the day he came home to find that she was gone.

Rising from the seat, he pulled another bottle of beer

from the fridge. After twisting off the cap, he took a long swallow. There wasn't enough booze to numb his hurt or blunt his memories. Seraphim had opened a wound that Decker thought was healed.

Ana Pierce. He wondered where she'd ended up—and why she had left him in the first place.

Ryan drove on a road he knew well. It was the route that connected Encantador with the smaller town of Mercy. Kathryn's police cruiser still hadn't been returned to her, so she rode shotgun. Sure, she could've gotten a ride in any of the three vehicles that made up the convoy, but after the town hall broke up, she'd come with Ryan. No questions. No conversation. Honestly, he liked having her with him. And maybe that was a problem. He needed to remind himself that he was little more than a chauffeur for the undersheriff. Once his phone had been analyzed, he'd be told to leave town. This time, he'd have no choice but to go.

Old Blue sat in the passenger seat as well. The dog leaned in to Kathryn as she scratched his side. Tongue lolling, the dog absolutely seemed to be smiling.

Lucky dog.

Ahead, he could see a blinking light hanging across the road.

Finally, he was home. Unbidden, the thought came to him.

The blinker of the first car flashed for a moment before it turned into a parking lot. Ryan followed. For over a year, he'd run a bar, a tattoo parlor, and a motel that occupied the newly renovated space. Sure, the businesses had been a front for an undercover sting operation. But the work he'd put into managing the property and the people had been real.

He'd actually made it as a legitimate businessman. He took care of the people who worked for him. The businesses turned a profit. The clientele was rough, but he'd made friends. Too bad it had been a ruse. The neon signs were gone. The building was now cream with blue trim. There was blue lettering on the door.

Center for Rural Law Enforcement.

By appointment only.

The Center was the best—and closest—place for Ryan's phone to be analyzed.

He noted that the parking lot was freshly paved. The once pitted asphalt was now smooth as ice. Muscle memory took over. He parked, as he had for a year, next to the front door. Yet it was all different. His throat was raw. "It's hard to remember what this place used to look like."

"Is it difficult to be back?"

How had she guessed? Putting the gearshift into Park, he said, "Let's get this over with so me and Old Blue can get on the road."

Michael came out of the front door. He shaded his eyes with a hand. Ryan turned off the ignition and hopped to the ground. The other two vehicles parked as well. One was a sedan, driven by the two Texas Rangers. Isaac drove his SUV and Jason was with the Texas Law operative.

"I can't believe all the changes," he said.

Kathryn and the dog exited from the passenger side of the truck. "Having this facility in the area has really helped the local economy," she said. "Aside from having seven well-paid techs on the payroll, law-enforcement officers come in from all over the state." She nodded toward the gas station across the street. "Stu hired a cook. They now serve breakfast and lunch. Only two different options are on the menu, but the food's pretty good."

Michael picked up where Kathryn left off. "Right now, we only use what was once the bar and tattoo parlor. I'm hoping to partner with more law-enforcement agencies to have offices in the old motel. Kathryn will have a space there soon." He opened the door. "C'mon in. Let me show you around."

"Is it okay if the dog comes in?"

"Sure, but we'll leave him in the forensics lab."

Ryan snapped his fingers, and Old Blue loped across the threshold. Kathryn followed. Next came Jason and Isaac. Lou and Georgiana were the last in line.

What used to be a dark room with a mahogany bar, dance floor, and pool tables was now filled with light. Long lights hung from the ceiling and reflected off the white floors and walls. The lab was filled with tables, microscopes, and a variety of equipment that Ryan couldn't name.

The bar was gone. In its place was a wall of glass, with a pressurized door. On the other side of the wall, in what used to be the tattoo parlor, was a computer lab. It had its own server and three wall-mounted monitors.

The change was remarkable. He hated it. What had happened to his old dive bar? "I like what you've done with the place," he said wryly.

"Let's go into the computer lab," said Michael. "One of the cybersecurity techs has been looking at the video. He's found some things that you'll want to see."

Old Blue settled into a corner, and Ryan knew he'd be fine for a bit. "Lead the way," he said.

A young man with bright red hair and a beard sat in front of a keyboard. "This is Hal," said Michael. "He's my resident computer genius. Since the video of Decker surfaced, he's been looking for evidence that it's real. Hal, you want to show them what you've found?"

"Sure," he said, typing on the keyboard. "The time-line from when Decker attacked the undersheriff to when he shows up in London is tight. But it's not an impossible feat—assuming he got to the Dallas–Fort Worth Airport in time to catch a red-eye to Heathrow. I didn't think he'd travel under his real name, so I didn't worry about looking through the passenger manifest, but I was able to access security video from the DFW Airport. Using facial recognition, I found this." He hit a key, and an image appeared on the middle screen. It was of a solitary man walking through the terminal.

"No question about it," said Ryan. "That's Decker."

"We know he was at the airport," said Jason. "That tells us some things, but not enough."

Hal typed again. "Because of international laws, I can't access the British airport's security cameras. But I was able to pick this up in London." The first screen filled with a social-media post. The caption read *Made it to London!* Two smiling young women posed for a selfie. Yet, he was there, in the background of the pic-ture. "I checked. The two students in the picture were on the flight from Dallas. I'd say that's proof positive. Decker's in merry old England."

"If he left the country," Jason asked, "what does that mean?"

Ryan knew the case was complex. There was still evidence to be collected and witnesses to interview. But if the killer was on a different continent, it meant one thing for certain. Decker was no longer an immediate threat. He might not have stopped the killer, but at least he'd chased him out of town.

Chapter 11

Ryan was supposed to stay in town while his phone was being analyzed. Jason had called it a request, but it was really an order by the FBI. Thankfully, the motel in Encantador had a vacant room. Isaac, from Texas Law, made the arrangements. By 4:15 p.m., he and Old Blue had their key. In the room, the curtains were drawn, and the air conditioner was running. Cool and dark, crossing the threshold was like stepping into a cave.

The motel had a Western theme. It started with the name: the Saddle-Up Inn. There was also a whiskey-barrel fountain near the door to the office. The theme stayed consistent with Western-themed prints on the wall and a sign that hung on the bathroom door, which read *Outhouse*.

Once in the room, he kicked off his shoes. He lay down on the bed and stretched out. Old Blue got onto the bed near his feet and curled into a tight ball. Ryan couldn't remember the last time he'd been so tired. Reaching for the remote control, he turned on the TV and flipped through a few channels. His eyes grew heavy, and he teetered on the edge of oblivion.

A knocking pulled him back to consciousness.

At the foot of the bed, Old Blue lifted his ears.

Ryan stood. Every part of him ached. Walking slowly, he peered through the peephole. Kathryn stood outside. She no longer wore her uniform. Instead, she was dressed in a pair of black yoga pants and gray tank top. The tank top hugged her curves in an alluring way.

True, she looked good—great, really. But why had she come at all?

After unfastening the lock, he pulled the door open. "Hi. I wasn't expecting to see you. How's your side?"

She touched the wound. Beneath the fabric of her shirt, he could see the outline of a large bandage. "It's actually not too bad, which is why I stopped by." She shifted from one foot to the other. "I never thanked you for saving my life."

"Actually, you did." He could still feel the caress of her fingers on his cheek. "And you're welcome."

"Just saying *thank you* doesn't seem like enough. I'd like to invite you over for dinner. It'd give me a chance to fire up the grill and make a few steaks."

Old Blue's tail thumped on the bed.

"Sounds like he'd like to join us," she said, pointing to the dog. "What about it? You want to stop by around six?"

"Blue and I have a policy. We always accept invitations for a steak dinner."

She laughed. "I'll look forward to seeing you both."

He recalled how her daughter had reacted to Old Blue. He didn't want to cause any more problems in the family. "I might leave him here, but I'll accept your invitation."

"How's your room?" she asked. "Got everything you need?"

"The room's great. I even have one of those fancy indoor outhouses," he said, making a joke about the sign on the bathroom door.

She laughed.

He understood that she was just making conversation. The thing was, he was also keenly aware of the bed just a few feet away. Erotic images—his mouth on hers, his hands on her breasts, his hips between her thighs—came to him without warning. His pulse thundered in his ears. Turns out, he wasn't as exhausted as he'd imagined.

"I better get going," said Kathryn. It was like she'd read his mind. Had his expression given away his carnal thoughts? "I was on the way to the grocery store to pick up all the fixin's for tonight."

He rested his hand on the doorknob. "Thanks for the invite."

After closing the door, he walked back to the bed. Just like before, he stretched out on the comforter. But now, it was all different. He couldn't get the images of him and Kathryn, naked and tangled in the sheets, out of his mind.

And what was up with her invitation?

Was she just being friendly? Or was there something else?

Kathryn was undeniably attractive. She was smart. Dedicated to her job, and a good mom. He knew that long-term she'd never want a guy like him. Yet, there was a physical connection between them that was impossible to ignore.

Maybe she wanted to use Ryan for sex.

Honestly, he'd been tempted into bed by lesser women for worse reasons.

Still, the thought of a single night with Kathryn and nothing more left a bad taste in his mouth.

Sitting up, he scrubbed his face. He wasn't sure what he needed next, but he sure as hell wasn't going to find it by lying in bed. Wandering to the bathroom, he turned on the shower to cold. After stripping down, he stepped under the spray. The water revived him, and hopefully, it would wash away his thoughts about Kathryn. But it was going to take more than a cold shower to do that.

Between her children's busy schedules and all her responsibilities at work, Kathryn rarely invited company over for dinner. The clock on the microwave glowed with the time: 5:42. Since the town hall, she'd taken another nap and her second round of pain meds. True, she wasn't feeling perfect, but she was happy to have Ryan coming to dinner.

Standing in the kitchen, she chopped romaine lettuce for the Caesar salad.

"Hey, Mom." Her son, Brock, wandered into the kitchen. Brock had inherited his father's height. At fifteen years old, he was already over six feet tall. He had Kathryn's brown hair and blue eyes but her late husband's features. "What's up with all the food?" Aside from the salad she was preparing, there was corn ready to be roasted on the grill, potato salad, and steaks in marinade. "Are we having a party or something? What's the occasion?"

"It's not a party," she said. "Just one guest. And I suppose that we're celebrating Decker Newcombe finally leaving us alone."

"Plus the fact that he didn't kill you." The account of Decker's escape to England was a top news story. Details of her fight were mentioned, but most of the attention was focused on the promised live murder.

"You're right, he didn't kill me." She scraped the chopped lettuce into a bowl. "So we should probably celebrate that, too."

"I'm glad that you're okay. Can I help with anything?"

His offer surprised and pleased her. "Sure. You want to make some lemonade?"

"Who's our guest? Is Aunt Quinn in town?"

Quinn was her late husband's sister. She called Encantador home but worked all over the country with the Department of the Interior. "I think she's still in DC but should be back next week."

Brock pulled a pitcher out of a cabinet. From another, he found a container of powdered drink mix. "Why're you being so secretive about a dinner guest?" Brock put the pitcher in the sink and started filling it with water. "I'm going to find out who it is once they show up, anyway."

He had a point. "It's the man who helped me last night. Honestly, I'm not sure how things would've turned out if he hadn't been with me."

"You mean that gangster guy is coming over for dinner? What's his name? Something Steele, because his bar was called House of Steele."

"His name is Ryan, and he's not a gangster." Because of the pain meds, the stab wound was more of a dull ache she could ignore. She opened the refrigerator door and took out a bottle of salad dressing. As she pushed the door shut, a zing of pain caught her side. She breathed deeply and the discomfort passed. She said, "How do you know about the bar?"

"I'm not an infant. I can understand when people talk. There were a couple of guys on the football team last year who drove all the way out to Mercy to go to the club. They figured since Ryan was a criminal, he wouldn't care that they were underage."

Maybe she'd underestimated Ryan. "What'd he do?"

"Don't worry, Undersheriff." Brock winked at her to show he was teasing by using her official title. "He threw them out. Said he wouldn't serve booze to kids."

"That's a relief." She paused a beat. "Besides, he's not a criminal. His record was cleared."

"But he did a lot of bad stuff in the past." Brock measured out scoops of lemonade mix and dumped them into the water.

"He did," she agreed. "But he had an arrangement with the government. They forgave all his crimes since he helped them out. He put himself in jeopardy to try to stop Decker. That counts for something."

Silently, Brock stirred the lemonade with a long-handled wooden spoon. After a moment, he said, "To be honest, I'm kinda surprised that you're defending him."

In fact, she was kind of surprised that she was defending him as well. "You've done bad things in your life. What if you wanted to make amends but nobody would give you the chance? See my point?"

"I guess," he grumbled. "I just don't see why he's coming over for dinner."

"Because Mom kissed him." Morgan stood at the back of the kitchen. Her arms were folded across her chest.

"I didn't hear you come in," said Kathryn.

Morgan glared. "Obviously."

Brock had gone pale. "You kissed him?"

Great. Now what was she supposed to say? "It's not like that."

"Yes, it is," Morgan interrupted. "Gawd, they were full on swapping spit. It was so gross that I'll never be able to unsee it."

"You kissed him?" Brock repeated.

Anger flared in her chest. Kathryn could feel a flush climbing from her neck to her face. "Both of you, listen to me. I am an adult and your mother. If I want to kiss someone—which I almost never do—I can. I don't need your editorial, Morgan. Or your permission, Brock."

"But what about Dad?" Brock's face turned from pale to bright red. "I never thought you'd want to replace him."

"Oh, honey. I loved your dad. I still love him. But he's gone, and well, I'd like to start living my life again." True, she was ready to move forward, just not necessarily with Ryan.

She waited for Brock to say something. He didn't.

She reached for his shoulder. He shrugged off her touch.

This was not what she'd planned for the evening. She

should call Ryan and reschedule. Or better yet, the dinner could be canceled altogether.

From the street came the sound of a car door slamming. Ryan had arrived. It was too late to cancel now.

"I have a guest at the house for dinner. Neither of you need to eat with us—but you do have to be polite. Do you understand?"

"Understood," said Morgan. "I'll be in my room."

She left without another word. Kathryn knew that this time next year, her daughter would be in college, and she'd miss her terribly. It made the harsh words sting more than ever.

"What about you, Brock?"

"I'm eating the steak," he said, his tone glum. "I'm starving."

The doorbell chimed. Kathryn wiped her hands on a towel and went to answer it, but Brock blocked her path.

"Hold up, Mom. I'll answer the door. I want to speak to this guy first."

Kathryn was touched that her son wanted to also be her protector—even though she was the undersheriff. "Okay kiddo. I'll finish putting together the salad."

While adding croutons and cheese to the salad, she listened intently to the door being answered.

"Hey," said Brock. "C'mon in. My mom's in the kitchen."

"I forgot to ask if I could bring anything, so I picked up a pie." The sound of Ryan's voice brought a smile to her lips.

"What kind of pie?"

"Apple," said Ryan.

"Nice. Come with me."

Brock's tone was still gloomy, but at least Ryan had passed the first test. Then again, her son liked anyone with food. She poured dressing on the salad and tossed it with tongs.

"Mom, Ryan's here," said Brock, as if she hadn't been eavesdropping the whole time. "He brought pie."

Looking up, she smiled. Yet, she hadn't prepared herself for how nice Ryan looked. He was freshly showered. His hair was still damp and curled at the ends. He wore jeans along with a white button-up shirt. He'd left the shirt untucked, and the top three buttons were undone. A sliver of skin was exposed at his neck. Her throat went dry, and her heart raced. Her side throbbed, but she didn't mind the discomfort. It reminded her that she was alive. "Thanks for coming—and bringing pie. I have ice cream for dessert, so they'll be perfect together." She bumped Brock with her shoulder. "Right?"

He shrugged. "Sure."

"You set the table outside, and I'll get the steaks on the grill," she said to her son. He slunk out the back door with a stack of plates and a handful of silverware. Then to Ryan she said, "You want anything to drink? Beer? Wine? Water? Lemonade?"

"I'll take a lemonade."

Four glasses, already filled with ice, sat on the counter. She poured lemonade into one of them and handed it to Ryan. Then, she picked up the casserole dish with steaks and marinade in one hand and the plate of corn in the other. "You can come with me, if you want."

"Sure thing, but let me take those for you." He reached for the dishes. "You had a rough night and should rest as much as possible."

She wanted to argue—it was instinct alone. Over the years, she'd learned not to ask for favors because of her gender. But Ryan's offer was too nice to ignore. She let him take the dishes. "Thanks."

Brock held the back door open as she approached. "Thanks, honey."

He nodded as she passed. Once she and Ryan were outside, her son went back in. The sun was setting. The awning provided them with shade. Ryan set the corn and steaks on a side table. "Where's Old Blue?" she asked, while igniting the grill.

"I left him in the motel with food, water, and a nature channel on TV. He'll be okay for a while." He took a sip of lemonade. "How're you feeling?"

"Considering everything, it all worked out." She placed the steaks on the grill. They started to sizzle, and the scent of cooking meat filled the air. "Since Decker's out of the country, he's not really my problem anymore, although I won't be happy until he's been caught. I decided to follow the doctor's orders and took next week off from work." It was the closest thing she'd had to a vacation in years.

"I'm surprised you're taking time off at all."

She put corn on the upper rack of the grill and closed the lid. The local law-enforcement community worked well together. Other officials were able to cover the tasks that Kathryn would have taken on personally. But there was more. Even with Decker out of the country, patrols would be increased. Yet, she knew that everyone in town would be more vigilant. "My job's important, sure, but so is my family. I wanted to spend some time at home with my kids. Surviving a serial killer's attack gives you some perspective, you know?"

"Actually, I do."

He was right. He'd survived a run-in with Decker, too. Did that make them kindred spirits? "Have a seat. I'll grab the salads and be right back." Her limbs were heavy. Maybe having Ryan come over for dinner wasn't the best idea. All the same, she wasn't going to send him away.

"You sit. I'll get the salads." She opened her mouth, ready to argue. He held up his hand. "You were nice enough to invite me over and like I said, you've been through a lot in the past 24 hours. At least let me help you out."

"How 'bout we bring everything out together?"

"You bet." He held the door open as Kathryn slipped inside.

"You get those," she said, pointing to the salads on the counter, and he picked up both bowls. "I'll get the lemonade." In the living room, Brock sat on the sofa. She looked at him through the doorway. "Can you grab two glasses and come outside?" she asked. "Dinner's almost ready."

Brock looked up from the couch. "I'm not really hungry anymore."

Was he still upset about Ryan being over?

"Not hungry?" she teased. "I thought you were starved a few minutes ago."

"I was, but I got a text from my coach."

"That doesn't sound good." She paused. Ryan was still standing in the middle of her kitchen with potato salad in one hand and the Caesar in the other. "Grab the glasses from the counter and join us. You can tell me all about the text while you eat. Trust me, you'll feel better with food."

With a sigh, her son rose from the sofa and slumped into the kitchen.

They all returned to the patio. Brock had set the table. Without being asked, he walked over to the grill and flipped the steaks. "Not much longer now," he said, his tone still disconsolate

"I can take care of the food, you know," she teased.

"You sit." He pointed with a set of meat tongs. "And rest."

"I agree with your son," said Ryan. "You have to be tired. Sore."

"You're right." Her side had started to ache and it wasn't time for her next dose of pain meds. Dropping into a chair, she sighed, "Thanks."

Brock grunted and poked at the steaks.

She glanced at her son. "Why don't you tell me about that text you got?"

Brock raised one shoulder before letting it drop. "Coach said he likes me playing tight end. He said I did really good."

"That's great, honey." At the game last week, her son had excelled in the position.

"It's not great if I want to play quarterback again."

Until this year, her son had always been the team's quarterback. It was not just his athletic abilities but his leadership talents as well. As a freshman, his junior varsity team had been undefeated. She knew when he got put on the varsity team, he'd hoped for the QB spot. It broke her heart that he wouldn't be able to play the position he loved. Then again, life didn't always give people what they wanted, and sometimes, important lessons could be found in adversity. She'd save the pep talk for later. Still, she said, "Every player on the field is important."

"Yeah, but I love being QB." He sighed. "Coach says my throw needs work."

She said, "You can work on your throw."

He gave her a side-eye. "Not like it'll help. The guy he has playing is also the pitcher for his church's base-ball team. Because of that, he's got terrific aim."

"I wish I could help you, bud. But I played soccer, not softball." She glanced at Ryan. Using his thumb, he wiped condensation from the side of his glass. "Sorry for all this talk about football. Let's find something we can all talk about. You and I can chat about your throw later. Okay, Brock?"

He shrugged. "Whatever."

Ryan shifted in his seat. "I was the pitcher for my high school's baseball team. It's been a while, but I still remember some of my old tricks for accuracy. If you have a spare ball, I'd be happy to show you."

Brock eyes were bright with excitement. "You'd do that?"

"Sure."

Her son closed the lid to the grill. "Hold on a min-ute. I'll be right back." Brock went inside the house.

Kathryn glanced at Ryan. "Thanks for helping out my son."

"Don't thank me yet. Honestly, I haven't thrown in years." He stood and rolled his shoulders around sev-eral times.

Brock came through the back door. "Here you go," he said, tossing a ball to Ryan. "What do I do first?"

"The first thing—let's warm up." Ryan and her son walked to a spot in the middle of the yard. As they stretched, Kathryn returned to the grill. The steaks were done. The corn was perfect. Using a set of tongs, she set the food on a clean platter.

Still, she watched Ryan and Brock. They were too far away for her to hear their voices, but Ryan was explaining something. Brock nodded and then smiled.

Funny, she'd been worried that the dinner was going to be a disaster.

Tonight was turning out better than she ever could have imagined.

Chapter 12

The sun had set an hour earlier. Kathryn stood in her kitchen and marveled at the clean counters. Brock and Ryan had worked together. The dinner dishes were loaded into the dishwasher, and the leftovers had been placed in the fridge.

After the cleaning was done, Brock went to study in his room. Morgan had yet to emerge. She should really check on her daughter but knew enough to wait until after Ryan left.

"Well, I better get going," Ryan said. "Old Blue's gonna start missing me."

"Speaking of your dog." She held up a plastic container filled with scraps from the steaks. "Does he eat table food?"

"I've had to pull him away from roadkill more than once. That dog'll eat practically anything." He took the offered container. "He'll appreciate you thinking of him. I do, too."

"It's the least I can do since you spent so much time with Brock. Even after one lesson with you, his aim is better."

Leaning against the counter, he stood right beside her. She could reach out and touch him if she wanted. Her side twinged, reminding her of everything she'd been through. "Your son's a good kid," he said. "I was happy to help."

Kathryn didn't hold much stock in gender roles. After all, she did quite well in a field traditionally dominated by men—thank you very much. But she knew that Brock missed having a man around the house. Morgan probably did, too. Though she doubted that her daughter would admit as much.

While looping a dish towel through the handle of the fridge, she said. "I know he enjoyed your company. I did, too. I'm glad I invited you over."

Damn. Why'd she have to be so honest?

"I haven't had such a nice evening for a long while." He gave her that smile and shook his head. "Hell, I can't remember a better night."

"Your life must be pretty boring," she said, kidding.

"Actually, my life's been the opposite of boring. It's the chaos that's worn me down. I don't necessarily want things to be monotonous. But I'd take stable any day."

She looked over her shoulder and regarded Ryan. For the first time, she saw him as a man who lived behind a brick wall. Sure, he'd constructed the wall to hide a lot of his misdeeds. Now, he was more of a prisoner. At the same time, he'd been honest about wanting a place to call home. Was the wall starting to crumble?

She wiped her hands on the towel one last time. "Let me walk you out."

Without comment, they moved through the kitchen and to the front door. Since both kids were in their rooms, nobody had bothered to turn on the lights. The foyer was shrouded in shadows, but she knew the way. Stopping at the door, she rested her hand on the handle. "You got Old Blue's snacks?"

Ryan lifted the container. "Right here."

"Do you have any idea how long it's going to be before you get your phone back?"

"I don't have a clue. It could be as early as tomorrow."

"Looks like this really is goodbye."

"Guess so," he whispered.

The room was quiet and dark. It was like they were the only two people around for miles. For a moment, neither one spoke. Ryan took a step toward her. And then another. She could feel his breath wash over her shoulder.

A bomb of nervous energy exploded in her stomach. Good Lord, Kathryn was a grown woman, not a teenager. Who was she to get anxious over standing next to a man? But he wasn't just any man. It was Ryan who stood next to her. What's more, she wanted him to kiss her. The question was—what did *he* want?

She shifted toward him and reached out in the dark. Her fingertips brushed the back of his hand. He set the container of leftovers on a nearby table. Then, he laced his fingers through hers.

"Kathryn." His voice was a husky whisper. It pierced her heart and her pulse started to race.

"Yes?"

"The last time I kissed you, things didn't go well."

That was an understatement. "They didn't."

"The thing is," he said and pulled her closer, "I'd like to kiss you again."

Her breasts were pressed against his chest. Even in the dark, she could see his pulse thrumming at the base of his neck. "I'd like to kiss you again, too."

He smiled, and her toes began to tingle. "That's all the invitation I need," he said.

He pressed his mouth to hers. She closed her eyes and surrendered to the sensations. In that moment, Kathryn was no longer the undersheriff but only a woman. The kiss with Ryan became her world. Parting her lips, she sighed. He slipped his tongue into her mouth. She was ready to be explored and conquered.

Kathryn reached for his shoulders and pulled him to her. She wound her arms around his neck. And still, he wasn't close enough. He rested his hands on her hips. Using the tips of his fingers, he traced the waistband of her shorts. Her stomach tightened with anticipation. A zing of pain radiated from her side. Breathless, she broke away from the embrace.

"What's wrong?" Even in the dark, she could hear the concern in Ryan's voice. "Oh hell. I tried to be careful. Did I touch your wound?"

He hadn't. His hand was well away from the bandage on her side. "Must be time for my meds." Where she stood, she could see the clock on the microwave. Actually, she should've taken them thirty minutes earlier.

"Let me get you the pills and some water," he offered.

"No." The single word came out with more force than she intended. Kathryn drew in a shaking breath. She could still feel his lips on hers, but her side throbbed with each beat of her heart. She exhaled and tried again. "No, thank you. I'm just going to take my prescription and call it a night."

He lifted the container of leftovers from the table. Then, he opened the door. "You're a hell of a woman, Kathryn Glass." He pressed his lips to her cheek. "Take care."

From the front porch, she watched as he walked to his truck. He opened the driver's door and slipped behind the wheel. He looked at her and waved. After starting the engine, he turned in the middle of the quiet street and drove away.

She closed the door and engaged the lock. Decker might be on the other side of the world, but until he was in custody, she wouldn't feel safe.

Leaning against the door, she pressed her fingertips to her lips, as if her touch could trap the kiss. It really was silly to be so smitten with a man she barely knew. But being around Ryan reminded her of something she'd forgotten. Kathryn was more than a mom and a cop. She was also a woman who had needs of her own.

Her steps were slow as she walked down the hallway to her bedroom. Had it just been just twenty-four hours since she noticed Ryan in her backyard?

It seemed like it all happened weeks ago.

Her meds were stowed in the en suite bathroom. Kathryn took the pills as directed and washed them down with a glass of water. She changed into a large T-shirt for sleeping and returned to her bedroom.

A figure stood at the door.

She started. "Morgan, you scared me. Everything okay?"

"Can I come in?"

"Of course." She pulled back the blankets and slid onto the mattress. "So long as you don't mind me lying down. It's been a long day."

Morgan moved to the bed and lifted the covers. "I'll tuck you in."

Of course she could arrange her own blankets, but the act was kind. She dutifully lay back on the pillow. Morgan took a minute to gather the comforter around her mother. "Just like you did for me and Brock when we were little."

She assumed that Morgan coming in was a bit of a peace offering. "You can lie down with me for a minute—just like I used to do when you were little."

Morgan said, "So long as you don't ask me to read the same picture book over and over."

"Promise." Kathryn placed her hand over her heart.

Then, her daughter stretched out atop the covers. She rested her head on the pillow. "I'm glad you're okay. It really was scary to think that I might lose you, too." Tears swam in her eyes, and she bit her bottom lip. Blinking hard, Morgan continued. "Besides Brock, you're all I have."

"I'm here, honey, and I'm okay."

"You might not always be here. I mean, your job is dangerous."

"Safety is always my top priority. That, and coming

home to you and your brother." She inhaled. Exhaled. "Do you want me to quit my job?"

Morgan shook her head. "You wouldn't be happy."

Her daughter was right. Being undersheriff wasn't just something Kathryn did. It was part of her being. Still, she said nothing.

"I want you to be happy, Mom."

"You're with me. How could I be anything but content?"

Morgan giggled. For an instant, she was a little girl again. "You're slurring your words. I think the pain meds are making you giddy."

"Well," she said and sighed, "they don't hurt."

"You like him, don't you?" Morgan asked.

Kathryn didn't need to ask who her daughter meant by *him*. "Ryan? He's nice."

"Now I know it's the meds." Morgan flopped to her back. "He's not nice. He's too unfriendly to be nice."

"Maybe he's a little serious, but he's been through a lot. It'd make anyone somber. Or maybe it's cautious." Good Lord, Morgan was right. The meds were making her loopy.

"Did you mean what you said to Brock?"

Kathryn pried her eyes open. The thing was, she didn't recall letting her eyelids close to begin with. "It depends. What'd I say?"

"Something about loving Dad but wanting your own future and your own life?"

"Of course I loved you father. I still do."

"No. The other part," said Morgan. Her daughter watched her from the other pillow. She felt the bed undulate, as if she were being carried away on a wave to the edge of oblivion. "Are you ready to start a new chapter in your life?"

Her eyes were so heavy, yet she refused to let them close. "Yes. Maybe. Not tonight, that's for sure."

"I think that's where you're wrong," said Morgan. "I think you did start a new chapter tonight. You've kissed that Ryan guy twice."

Now Kathryn was fully awake. "Twice? I only kissed him once."

"Liar."

She was lying, but she wasn't going to admit anything to Morgan. Unless… "Were you spying on me from the hall?"

"No, Mom." She rolled her eyes. "I have ears. I can hear. You two were talking. Then whispering. Then nothing. Obviously, I can figure out how you were filling the silence."

"Okay, I think we're done."

"Mom, I do want you to be happy. I do know that you like Ryan. Brock likes him—especially since he helped with his throw." She paused. "Maybe he is nice."

"It really doesn't matter." Her eyes burned. She tried to tell herself that it was all fatigue, but she knew that was a lie. Ryan was the first man to spark her interest in years. "He's only in town for another day. Two at the most."

"Then, I'm sorry for you."

"You don't have to worry about me. It's my job to worry about you." She looked at her bedside clock: 9:15 p.m. "You need to finish your homework. You have school in the morning."

"I got all my homework done earlier. If you don't mind, I'll stay here with you until you fall asleep."

"Just like I did when you were little?" She let her eyelids close.

Morgan softly kissed her forehead. "G'night, Mom."

As she fell down, down, down into deep sleep, she had one final thought. Tonight had been something special. Too bad it couldn't last. Out there—somewhere—was Decker Newcombe.

Ryan woke with a start. As his eyes opened, he wasn't sure what was real and what had been a dream Old Blue stood at the end of his bed. Ears up, the dog gave a low growl.

The feds believed that Decker was in England. But what if he was back?

Someone knocked on the door. Then again, Decker wouldn't knock on the door. Besides, it must've been the knocking that had woken him up. "Just a minute," he called out.

He rose from the bed. His legs were heavy. His knees popped, and his shoulder was stiff. He'd thrown the ball with Brock for less than an hour and that was Sunday night. It was Tuesday morning, and he felt like he'd been hit by a truck.

As was his habit, Ryan slept only in his boxer shorts. Yesterday's jeans were draped across a chair. By one of the chair legs sat the container Kathryn had used for the leftover steak. Ryan had used the plastic dish as a food bowl for Old Blue. The dog had licked the container clean.

After stepping into his jeans, Ryan looked through

the peephole. Isaac stood on the sidewalk. He raised his hand, ready to knock again.

Unlatching the locks, he pulled the door open. "You're here early," he said by way of a greeting. "And eager to see me. What's up?"

Isaac pulled a phone from his back pocket. He held up the device. "They're done looking through your cell. I wanted to give it back to you on my way back to San Antonio."

Taking his device, he tapped it against his palm. "And? Did they find anything?"

Isaac said, "As suspected, the text from Decker originated from a cell tower in London. The area's being searched now. So far, nothing's been found."

"Decker's just like a rat. If there's a hole he can sneak out of, he'll find it." He paused. "At least he's not your problem anymore."

"I hate that he got away," Isaac said with an exhale. "The FBI's catching hell that a serial killer hopped on a plane from Dallas to Heathrow."

"Maybe Decker will stick out in England," he said, thinking out loud. "After all, he's an American and not able to blend as easily as he does here."

"Well, I hope you're right."

Old Blue jumped off the bed. He nosed the empty container. The dog needed breakfast first and a walk second. Still, he could wait a minute for both. "What's next for you and the investigation?"

"Last I heard, Jason is heading to London to assist with the investigation. And I'm going back to San Antonio. It's nice of Michael to let me use the Center, but I need my own space to work." He sighed. "What about you?"

"Me and Old Blue are gonna hit the road."

"Where're you headed?"

"To be honest, I don't know. But once I find it, I'll let you know."

Isaac shifted from one foot to the other. "Jason left me with directions for you. If Decker reaches out again."

"I'll let you know that, as well," he said, finishing the anticipated directive.

Isaac extended his palm. "Good to see you again."

Ryan shook the other man's hand. "Good to have been seen," he said, recycling his old joke.

Isaac waved once before walking away.

"Looks like it's just me and you," Ryan said, after closing the door. "How'd you like some food?"

The dog raised his ears and licked his chops.

The bag of kibble he'd purchased the day before sat on a small dresser. He filled up Old Blue's dish. While the dog ate, Ryan donned a clean T-shirt, socks, and shoes. By the time his canine companion had finished his breakfast, he was ready to take the dog for a walk.

The motel was close to Encantador's downtown area. They walked several blocks to the only restaurant that was open. Over Easy served breakfast and lunch. On this Tuesday morning, the crowd was thin. A bicycle rack was pushed up against the wall of the restaurant, and a metal bowl of water had been placed nearby. Ryan wrapped Old Blue's lead around a rung. "I'll be back in a minute." He scratched the top of the dog's head as he passed.

Mae, the owner of Over Easy, stood behind the counter.

She smiled as he entered the restaurant. "Well, look what the cat dragged in. Ryan Steele. I heard you were back in town. What brings you here?"

He liked the warm welcome. "This morning, I'll take a cup of coffee, along with a bacon egg and cheese sandwich. All of it to go."

"Lots of excitement around here," said Mae. "We're famous on the news again."

He wasn't going to comment on the investigation. "So I heard."

"You know anything about it?"

"You know I'm not going to say anything, even if I did."

"Well, I've heard some rumors." She poured coffee into a cup and handed it to Ryan.

Of course, Mae wanted the latest gossip. She served up town news with the same exuberance as her pancakes. Sipping his coffee, he said nothing.

She slipped a piece of paper with his order into the kitchen through a pass-through. "Your sandwich will be ready in a minute."

"Thanks, Mae."

"How long are you planning on staying in town?" she asked.

"Not long. In fact, I'm leaving right after breakfast."

After a few minutes, one of the cooks passed a white paper bag back through the window.

"Looks like your order is ready." Mae retrieved the bag and set it in front of Ryan.

Reaching for his wallet, he asked, "How much do I owe you?"

She shook her head. "It's on the house."

He gave her a wave of thanks and walked out the door. Old Blue stood as he stepped outside. "You ready?"

The dog wagged his tail. They walked back to the motel.

Ryan ate his breakfast while sitting at the small table. As he ate, he knew that Kathryn had been right. There were lots of small towns in the world. He just had to find the right one and make it his home. Popping the last bite into his mouth, he chewed and swallowed. "Well, boy," he said, "once we get packed, we'll find a new place to call home. What d'you say?"

Old Blue nosed the empty, plastic dish and looked up at Ryan.

"You're right." Bending over, he picked up the container from the floor. "We should return this before we leave."

Ryan doubted that Kathryn cared about a cheap tub. But really, that didn't matter. He'd use any excuse just to see her one last time.

Chapter 13

Kathryn rarely had the house all to herself and never at 9:00 a.m. on a weekday. Her kids had left for school ninety minutes earlier. She'd taken the week off from work to recuperate from her run-in with Decker Newcombe. On Monday, she'd slept most of the day. Morgan had made dinner. Brock had cleaned the kitchen. It was Tuesday morning, and she was definitely starting to heal. Now, the day stretched out before her with endless possibilities.

A steaming cup of coffee sat on the coffee table. Since she still couldn't shower, she'd washed off with a damp cloth in the sink. Her hair was pulled back into a ponytail. She wore a pair of sweatpants and a tank top. They were the most comfortable items in her closet.

Yet, Kathryn was determined to do more than rest this week. She was truly ready to move forward in her life.

Sitting on her sofa, she twisted her wedding band around her finger. She gave it a hard tug. The ring slipped from her finger. The skin beneath the band was smooth and white. Eventually the mark would fade. For now, it was a reminder of where she'd been and where she was going.

She set the gold band on the coffee table and picked up the remote. She turned on both the TV and a streaming service. There was a show everyone at work talked about, but she had yet to watch. Shoot, she hadn't picked out a TV program for years. Well, today was the day of new beginnings.

On the street, a car door slammed. The noise was followed by a dog's bark.

She glanced out the window.

Ryan strode up the walkway. The container she'd given him on Sunday night was in his hand. Rising from the sofa, she crossed the room. She opened the door as he approached her stoop.

"Morning." He held up the container. "I wanted to get this back to you."

She stepped outside. The morning air was already sultry and sweat dotted her upper lip. She imagined that the oppressive heat was about to return. But there was more besides the weather that left her warm. Ryan wore jeans and a dark blue T-shirt. Both garments fit him like a second skin and accentuated his muscular chest, flat stomach, and long legs.

"You didn't have to stop by so early. I hope you didn't go out of your way."

"Actually, me and Old Blue are about to leave town."

Disappointment struck her chest. "You must've gotten your phone back."

He nodded. "I did."

"And?"

"I talked to Isaac. The IT people could tell that Decker's text came from England. So they really didn't learn anything new."

"Did Isaac know anything about the investigation?" Kathryn had taken a week off work, but she was still a cop. Decker was still wanted for several murders in her jurisdiction. Bringing him to justice was more than her job—it was her mission.

"He didn't say much of anything." Ryan held up the container. "This is yours, and Old Blue says thanks."

She took the dish from his hand. Without thinking through her actions, she said, "I just sat down with a cup of coffee. You want to join me?"

Ryan turned his face to the sun. "I'd love to, but it's starting to get hot. I can't leave the dog in the car."

"Bring him in," she suggested. "He'll be fine for a few minutes."

"Yeah, but the other day your daughter seemed pretty upset to see him in the house. I don't want to cause an issue."

"Old Blue's not a problem," she said. "Besides, my kids are at school. They won't be home until after football practice ends."

A look flashed across his face.

She'd invited him into her empty home. What's more, they wouldn't be interrupted for hours. Suddenly, there was much more that she wanted to do with her day than binge watch a show on TV.

It brought up two important questions. What did Ryan expect? And what did she want?

She knew the answer to the second question. She wanted Ryan. He'd ignited feelings that she thought had died years ago. It turns out that her libido wasn't dead after all, only buried so deep that she forgotten she had needs at all.

She knew there was something to the timing as well. It was more than simply thinking she was ready to start over. But she'd survived an attack by a serial killer. Somehow, that made life even more precious.

Besides, Ryan was leaving soon. After, she'd never have to see him again…

"Only if you're sure," he said.

She took a moment to consider his words. "Absolutely."

While he got Old Blue out of the truck, she held open the door. As master and dog crossed the threshold, she asked, "How d'you take your coffee?"

"Black is fine."

Old Blue sniffed the edge of the sofa before settling on the floor.

Kathryn let the door close and engaged the lock. "I'll grab you a cup."

He pointed to her television set. The streaming service menu filled the screen. "What're you watching?"

"Nothing, yet." Using the remote, she turned off the power. "Hold on a sec. I'll be right back."

Ryan followed her into the kitchen. She didn't mind. She could feel his eyes on her as she pulled a clean mug from the cabinet and lifted the pot from the coffee maker. "I made this a few minutes ago," she said, while pouring the coffee. "It's fresh."

She handed him the cup. His fingers grazed hers, and he gripped the handle. Their gazes met, and he lifted the coffee to his lips. He watched her over the rim as he took a sip. "It's hot, just like I like it."

Her skin tingled. Was he trying to seduce her over coffee? God, she hoped so. "So, you like things that are hot?" Okay, maybe that wasn't the best line. Seems like flirting was a skill that she'd forgotten.

He didn't mind her cheesy line. Closing the space between them, he reached for her waist. His fingertips grazed her side. "What do I like that's hot?" he repeated the question, never taking his eyes from hers. "I like hot summers, hot pizza, hot coffee, and you."

She laughed. "Are you calling me hot?"

"Of course."

"Nobody's said that to me in years." *Correction, make that decades.*

"That's too bad because you're a beautiful woman. You should have someone tell you every day that you're gorgeous."

"So you say," she said, her tone flirtatious.

"It's not just words. It's true."

"You know what?" She moved closer to Ryan and wrapped her arms around his neck. "We're talking too much."

"We are?" His mouth was next to hers. His words mixed with her breath. "What should I do instead?"

"You should kiss me."

He smiled and placed his lips on hers. His tongue was in her mouth. His hands were on her hips. Then, he gripped her rear. She ran her fingers through his hair and let the strands slip through her fingers. But she wanted more of him, and she wanted it now.

She pressed her hips into him. It didn't matter that they were both fully dressed, she could tell that he was hard. That was fine with her because she was already wet. Her hands traveled from his shoulders to his chest to his abs to the fly of his jeans. She cupped him with her hand, and he moaned. "Oh, Kathryn."

He moved his mouth to her ear and kissed her lobe.

"I like to hear you say my name." She rubbed him through his jeans.

"Kathryn," he growled, "you're driving me wild."

"That's kind of the whole point, isn't it?"

He kissed her harder and slid his hand inside her tank top. His fingers blazed a trail across her skin. His lips were still on hers as he stroked her breast. She hadn't bothered with a bra today, and her nipple hardened under his touch. He moved his fingers to her other breast and rolled her nipple. It was pleasure mixed with pain. She hissed with ecstasy.

"Oh, Kathryn. What do you want now?"

Even in the middle of a lust-fueled fog, she understood the irony. For years, she'd simply avoided sex. But since she'd decided to take Ryan as a lover, any delay was torture. Once more, she asked the question *What did she want?*

The answer was simple. "I want all of you."

He kissed her harder. Lifting her into his arms, he carried her into the living room. Ryan set Kathryn on the sofa. She opened her thighs, and he settled between her legs. The need to have him inside her was powerful and primal. She undid the top button of his jeans. He untied the laces at her waistband, and suddenly her pants were loose. She refused to think too much. Shimmying hips, she worked her pants down until they fell to the floor. She also slipped out of her panties. She spread her legs open further. He finished opening his fly and freed himself.

There was one word in the back of her mind—a word she couldn't ignore. "Condom?"

"Yeah," he said, breathless. "I have one. It's here." He pulled his wallet from his back pocket. He opened a foil packet from it and rolled the condom down his length.

Kathryn watched as he entered her slowly. Then, at the last moment, he drove in hard.

She threw back her head and moaned.

"You like it like that," he said, his breath hot in her ear.

"Yes," she cried out. "Oh God, yes."

He adopted a rhythm. Slow. Slow. Hard.

She wrapped her legs around his waist. He reached between them and found the top of her sex, stroking her. She knew it wouldn't be long before she came.

She pulled him in closer with her legs. "Faster," she panted. God, she was so close to her release. "Faster and harder."

He obliged, driving into her hard and quick, while still rubbing the top of her sex. She cried out with an orgasm. Ryan placed his palm on the cushions behind her. His hips pumped. With a guttural moan, he threw back his head and came.

His breath was ragged. He kissed her shoulder first,

then said, "I was wrong about you being hot. You're a damned inferno."

"That's quite the compliment, considering." She bit her lip, worried that she almost shared too much.

"Considering what?"

She shook her head. "It's nothing." But that wasn't true. "It's personal."

"I can tell that it's a whole lot more than nothing." He lifted her chin, so she had to look him in the eye. "We've gotten to know each other pretty well over the past two days. I hope you know that you can trust me."

He was right. She did trust him. "It's been a while since I've had sex." Longer even than the two years since her husband's death. He'd been so ill at the end that she'd been his caretaker only—not his lover. "I was worried I'd forgotten how."

He placed a noisy kiss on her cheek. "Trust me, you haven't forgotten a thing." He backed up, sliding out of her. "I need to take care of the condom before it gets messy."

"There's a bathroom down the hall. First door on the left."

Her pants and panties lay in a pile on the floor. She bent over to pick them up. The movement left her dizzy. She sat on the sofa and waited for the faintness to pass.

As the sensation abated, she surveyed the living room. The room was just as it had always been. The TV still sat on the stand. Pictures still hung on the wall. As far as she could tell, there were only two differences to her normal living room. First, she was naked from the waist down. And second, her pants and underwear were bunched up in her hand.

Oh, wait. She found a third difference. There was a butt print on the fabric. Even if she cleaned the spot a million times, how was she supposed to just watch TV in here now?

Her side definitely hurt. She dressed slowly. Ryan appeared in the doorway as she was tying the drawstring at her waist.

"How're you doing?"

"Good. Tired." But she was more than weary. She was drained and sated at the same time. "Actually, I think the right word is *spent*."

"C'mon. I'll get you settled on the sofa."

Lying on his side, Old Blue slept on the floor. He opened one eye and regarded them. "He's a good dog," she noted. "It was kind of you to rescue him."

"I know it sounds like a saying that belongs on a bumper sticker or a T-shirt or something, but he's the one who rescued me." He bent over to scratch the dog's belly. "Before I adopted him, I was alone. Sure, I knew people. There were a few I even liked." He gave her a quick smile and stood. "But I never had anyone who counted on me. I never had anyone I needed to care for—not until him, at least."

"After my husband died, I was angry. I felt alone. But I had my kids, and they needed me." Having to take care of her children was the one thing that had helped her get through the days when the grief was a weight that could crush her soul.

"You think that's the key to life? Having someone who needs you, even if they are a dog?"

She thought he might be right. Leaning back into the sofa, she said, "Maybe."

Ryan sat next to her, before reaching for her hand. She slipped her fingers between his. In that moment, she realized there was another key to life as well. It was to find another person who completed you. But the fatigue was starting to take over, and she couldn't find the right words. She closed her eyes and drifted to sleep.

Ryan hadn't meant to doze. Kathryn had fallen asleep holding his hand. He hadn't wanted to risk waking her by getting up. Eventually, he'd faded as well. In their sleep, they'd stretched out on the sofa. Kathryn lay in his arms. From the floor, Old Blue regarded him. The dog thumped his tail on the floor and whined.

Ryan understood what the look meant. Old Blue needed to go outside. But how was he supposed to get off the sofa without waking Kathryn?

The dog whined again, louder this time.

Kathryn's eyelids fluttered open. "Looks like we drifted off."

"I guess so." He sat up. "I need to take Old Blue for a walk."

"What time is it? I'm starving."

Ryan pulled the phone from his pocket. There were no missed calls. No texts, either. He really was a man alone in the world. "It's already two thirty."

"No wonder I'm hungry." She sat up. "You want something for lunch? I have leftover steak and potato salad."

Her offer of a late lunch sounded perfect. Too bad that afterward, he really would have to leave. After leading Old Blue through the kitchen, Ryan let the dog walk around the backyard. When he came back into the house, Kathryn was wiping off the counter.

While putting salad and slices of steak onto two plates, she said, "Let me get some forks." She opened a drawer and grabbed the utensils. "We can sit outside."

He picked up both plates. "Lead the way."

She opened the back door as the front door opened. Brock bounded through the front door. "Mom! Mom! Where are you?"

"I'm in the kitchen." Did he hear a tinge of alarm in her words? Even with Decker half a world away, Ryan imagined that Kathryn was still on high-alert. To be honest, he was, too. "What're you doing home? I thought you had practice."

"I do but I had one of the guys bring me home for a minute. I have huge news." He came into the room and saw Ryan. He smiled. "Oh, hey. I'm glad you're here, too."

The kid's reaction surprised him. "You are?"

"Yeah. After you and I practiced with the baseball on Sunday, I knew my throw was better. I stopped by Coach's classroom during my free period and told him I wanted him to reconsider letting me play QB." Brock drew in a deep breath and continued. "He let me throw for him today at lunch. He liked that I spoke to him and that my accuracy had improved."

"And he made you the quarterback?" she asked.

"Not exactly," Brock admitted. "But he said he'd keep an open mind for Friday night's game."

"Honey." She pulled her son in for a hug. "I'm so proud of you. And you came home between school and practice to tell me. I love it."

The kid let his mother embrace him and then stepped away. "I wanted to tell you. But I also wanted to ask about Ryan." The kid turned to face him. "How long are you staying in town? Because I'd love to work with you more. I mean, if you're available."

Sure, Ryan was planning on leaving soon. But he couldn't say *no* to Brock. "I can stay a couple of days longer." He hoped that there was still a vacancy at the motel.

"Thanks, man." Brock smiled wide again. "I appreciate it." He kissed his mother's cheek. "I'll see you both after practice."

The door slammed, and he knew that Brock was gone.

"You don't have to stay and help him," said Kathryn.

A thought came to him, and it filled his chest with acid. Yet he had to know if he was right. "Are you kicking me out of town again?"

"I just don't want you to feel obligated."

"There's nothing else I'd rather do than help your son," he said, even though his words were a lie. Sure, he liked the fact that the kid wanted his help. But really, he was looking forward to spending more time with Kathryn.

Yet, he knew for every minute he spent with her, leaving once and for all would be that much harder.

Chapter 14

It was Friday at 5:30 p.m. Ryan stood in the kitchen of Kathryn's house. The last week had been one of the best in his life. As had become his habit, he slept at the Saddle-Up Inn. In the morning, he walked Old Blue. They always stopped at Over Easy for breakfast. Then, he and the dog would go to Kathryn's house.

In the morning, he put his construction skills to work: So far, he'd installed a new toilet, fixed a leaking sink, and rewired the garage-door opener. He'd even repaired the back fence where several boards were missing.

But he'd done more than odd jobs around her home. When it got too hot, he came inside. Over the week, he and Kathryn had streamed an entire seven-season TV series set in a postapocalyptic world, complete with zombies and an evil dictator. In the afternoon, they made love in her bedroom and slept in each other's arms.

They prepared dinner together, and he ate with the family. After supper, he coached Brock on his throw. Old Blue always brought the balls back. The kid had secured the QB spot for this week's game, and Ryan had promised to attend.

There were two hours left until kickoff. Honestly, he was a little excited and a lot proud.

It was the exact life that he wanted. Too bad it would be over in the morning. He still wanted to move to Encantador. But what he needed was for Kathryn's invitation to stay. She hadn't said anything, and he wasn't about to beg.

"There you are." Brock came into the kitchen. He wore a red and gold football jersey and shorts. "I have to get to the school for warm-ups, but I figured you could use this." He tossed Ryan a red T-shirt. He opened the garment. In gold lettering were the words *Encantador High School Football.* Brock continued, "It's mine, but I don't wear it much. You can keep it if you want."

To Ryan, it was a treasure. "Thanks, man. I will keep it."

"I figured that you deserved your own shirt. If it weren't for you, I wouldn't be starting as quarterback."

"It's all your hard work," said Ryan. He wasn't the kind to give pep talks, but it seemed like the right thing to say. "I just gave you a few things to think about."

"Well, thanks for all that, anyway."

"There's my two favorite men," said Kathryn. She stood in the doorway of the kitchen, next to her son. She wore a similar T-shirt to the one he'd been given, but the gold lettering said *Encantador High School Football Mom.* Her dark hair fell loose over her shoulder.

She looped her arm through Brock's. "How are you? Excited? Nervous?"

"Both," said her son with a quick laugh. A car horn blared from somewhere on the street. "That's my ride. I'll see you at the game."

Kathryn rose to her tiptoes to place a kiss on her son's cheek. "Go get 'em."

Brock ran from the room. The front door opened and slammed shut, then he was gone.

"What's that?" She pointed to the shirt in his hand.

Holding up the garment so she could see, he said, "Brock gave it to me." He paused. There was so much he wanted to say, but what was the point? By this time tomorrow, he'd be long gone. Instead, he said, "If he keeps working on his throw, he might have a career as a pitcher, too."

"He likes you a lot."

"What about Morgan?" Brock had warmed up to Ryan. But Kathryn's daughter had not.

"Morgan doesn't really like anybody. It's part of being a teenage girl, I think."

"She glares at me whenever I walk into the room. I tried to talk to her the other day, and she actually rolled her eyes and groaned." He shook his head. "I've known some brutal people before in my life. But teenage girls might be the worst."

Kathryn laughed. "Go and change into your shirt. We'll have dinner at the game. The senior class is running the concession stand as a fundraiser for an after-prom party. Morgan is the APP chairperson. So we definitely need to get there early and eat a lot."

Ryan went into Kathryn's bedroom and stripped out of his old shirt.

He pulled on the new one before checking his reflection in a mirror.

"Looks good on you." She stood in the doorway. He hadn't realized that she'd followed him to her room.

"Yeah, it fits pretty well," he said, smoothing his hand down his torso.

She came into the room and stood behind him. Wrapping her arms around his stomach, she leaned her head into his back. "It's hard to believe that the week's already over. I hope you know how much I've appreciated having you around."

Placing his hand on hers, he said, "I've liked being here."

Please, ask me to stay.

She pressed her lips into his back. "It's going to suck saying goodbye."

His chest ached. For the first time in his life, he understood how heartbreak felt. "I guess this really is the end."

She held him tighter. "It sounds so permanent."

Turning to face her, he lifted her chin and gazed into her eyes. "Don't worry. I'm not the kind of guy who gets a fairy-tale ending." He wanted to be with her but knew a cop and ex-con couldn't be together—not permanently anyway.

"Don't say that. You deserve to be happy. You'll find someone."

What about her? Would Kathryn find another man? A shock wave of possessiveness rolled through him. Cupping his hand behind her head, he brought his mouth to hers. The kiss was hard, fierce, and made to be remembered.

Winding her arms around his neck, she sighed. "Oh, Ryan."

"I want you, Kathryn," he said, slipping his hand down the front of her shorts. He worked his fingers into her panties. She was already wet. His dick hardened knowing that she wanted him as much as he wanted her.

"Yes," she said into the kiss. "Take me."

If this was all they had left, then he intended to make it something she'd never forget. Holding onto her hips, he turned her around. They both faced the dresser, and he pushed her shoulders down so she bent at the waist. He worked her shorts over her hips and pulled them down her thighs. They pooled at her feet, and she kicked them away. She took off her panties.

Pulling down his pants, he slipped on one of the condoms he'd kept in his wallet. Using his tip, he traced Kathryn's opening. She gave a sexy little mew. He entered her slowly, watching as he disappeared inside of her.

Over the course of the week, he had learned what she liked and knew how to make her orgasm. While he was deep inside of her, she lifted her hips, taking him in deeper.

"Oh, God, Ryan. Yes."

She tightened around him. He knew that she was close. He moved his hips, driving into her hard. The dresser started rocking, the back corners hitting the wall.

"Ryan," she cried out. "Don't stop."

He could see her reflection in the mirror. A flush crept up her neck and left her cheeks red. Her eyes were closed. His lips were moist. She gripped the dresser's edge. Then, she came. Panting, she relaxed.

He didn't hold back. Focusing only on the sight of him inside of her, he let go. He lay on top of her for a moment, breathing hard, not wanting to let her go. Pulling out, he held onto the edge of the rubber. "I'll be right back."

Hustling to the en suite bath, he closed the door.

Kathryn had to see that they were perfect for each other. More even than the amazing sex, they got along well. Brock and Ryan had bonded over sports. It seemed that Morgan didn't really like most people. So her feelings for him weren't worse than for anyone else.

He had to wonder if there was anything he could do to change Kathryn's mind, especially since she was so determined to say goodbye.

There was no doubt about it, England was in an uproar. A serial killer had been imported from across the pond, specifically the United States. And Yankee Jack, as the press was calling Decker Newcombe, meant to murder someone live on the internet.

Jason Jones had come to the United Kingdom to find the killer.

Sure, the FBI already had an office in London. As far as he could tell, it was being run by capable agents. But Jason was going to personally take care of Decker.

If Newcombe was following the calendar laid out by Jack the Ripper, another murder would take place on Sunday. It was 11:30 p.m. on Friday night. That meant he didn't have much time to find and stop the killer.

The Bureau's London office was in the US Embassy complex at 33 Nine Elms Lane. He sat in an interview room on the fifth floor. The windowless room held a table with four chairs and had room for little more. His palms were wrapped around a paper cup of cold coffee. Across the table sat Tiffany Hoffman and Isabella Kang.

Both girls were students at a large university near Dallas, Texas. They were in England for a semester abroad. What made them interesting—at least to Jason— is that they'd inadvertently captured a photo of New-combe after disembarking from the flight.

It was the same one they'd posted online and part of what proved that Decker was in the UK.

Even though both girls had been interviewed before, he had them brought down to the embassy. He wanted to speak to them personally. Neither were happy.

"You know," said Isabella, tossing her long black hair over her shoulder, "my father's an attorney. He says that you people asking us all these questions is harassment."

He was neither impressed nor intimidated. "Yeah? Well, I went to law school, too. And I have the right to ask my questions."

"If I refuse to say anything?" she challenged.

"Well, then, I'd stop talking to you."

The girl smirked. "That's what I thought."

"But I'd take you back to Texas with me and let you answer my questions there."

The smile slipped from her face. "Oh."

"Just cool it," Tiffany said to her friend, her voice a stage whisper. Then, to Jason, she said, "This has all been wild. I mean, that murderer was on the plane with us. I don't remember seeing him at all."

"Me, either," chimed Isabella. "I mean, the flight was totally packed, but still, he seems kinda hard to miss."

"Yeah, and you want to know something else that's weird?" Tiffany said and didn't wait for an answer. "I don't even remember him standing behind us when we took the selfie. I checked our background and everything because, obviously, I hate having some random person in my pic. Plus, posting some rando on social media is bad manners."

He paused and mulled over what the coed had said. There was something important…something he'd missed. "Say that again."

"It's bad manners on social media…"

"No, not that part. You said you checked your background," he said, clarifying her statement.

"Yeah. Nobody was behind me."

"And you didn't recall seeing him on the flight, either."

The girls looked at each other. Isabella shook her head. "Neither of us did."

"Can I see your phone?" Jason held out his hand.

"Do you have a warrant or something?" asked Isabella.

"Do you want me to get one?" Jason was done playing games with the college students. "Because I can. But it also means you'll be spending all night in this conference room."

Tiffany glared at her friend. "Just chill. We don't have anything to hide. Besides, I want to help." She pulled her phone from the tote bag that was slung over the back of her chair. "Here you go."

"Can you open the photo app for me? And can you find the original picture you took at the airport?"

"I can," said Tiffany. "But I can't."

Jason was getting fed up with the coeds and their attitudes. "What's that supposed to mean?" he snapped.

"It means she can open the photo app," said Isabella, "but she can't show you the original. She took the picture on social media. The photo isn't stored on her phone."

Because of the nature of his job, Jason didn't have any social-media accounts. But he did understand how they worked. What's more, he knew the original photo was in the phone somewhere. He just needed the right person to find it.

At this time of night, most everyone on the FBI's staff was gone. They were either home or out looking for the serial killer. "I'd like to find someone to look at your phone, if that's okay with you."

Tiffany wrote a six-digit number on a slip of paper and handed it to Jason. "That's my passcode."

He took the piece of paper and nodded his thanks. "You two need to hold tight here for a little longer. Can I have something brought to you? Water? A coffee?" Hell, they were in England. "Do you want some tea? I heard the stuff they serve in the embassy is pretty good."

"A tea is fine," said Tiffany.

At the same time, Isabella asked, "How long is *a little longer*?"

"I'll get back to you as soon as I can." He rose to his feet. With his fingers resting on the door handle, he added, "I'll have someone come in and take your order for food or drink."

He walked out of the interview room. At the end of the hall, the duty agent sat at a shared desk. Sherise, a Black woman from Boston, wore an FBI polo shirt along with black slacks. She looked up as Jason approached.

"How's it going?" she asked.

"That depends on if you can help me out or not."

Sherise straightened in her seat. "What do you need?"

"First, can you check on the college girls? Get them food if they're hungry or something to drink. One of them wants a cup of tea. Keep an eye on them, too. I doubt they'll leave the building, but I'd like them to stay."

"Sure, I can. But are they being detained?" Sherise asked, her Boston accent heavy. *Sure* sounded like *Shoer*.

"No, but I have one of their phones. That brings up the next favor. I need someone who knows a thing or two about tech, especially phones and social media."

"All of our IT people have gone home. But..." She drummed her fingers on the desk. A phone sat on the corner of the worktop. Picking up the handset, she said, "Let me check with someone."

Jason listened to one half of the call.

"Hey," said Sherise. "It's me...Yeah, I'm the duty agent this weekend...Are you still here?...Listen, I've got someone in from Texas. They need help with a phone and social media. Can you take a look?" She smiled. "Great, I'll send him down." She hung up the phone and looked back at Jason. "You're in luck. Theo Fowler works with the NSA and is a tech genius. He's on the third floor." She pointed down the hallway. "Take the elevator and he'll meet you when you get off."

Jason followed the directions. On the third floor, a tall man with brown hair and eyes stood next to the bank of elevators.

"You the Texan?" the man asked.

Jason wasn't sure what to expect from a cybersecurity genius. But this guy wasn't it. Aside from being tall—taller than Jason's six feet—the guy had broad shoulders and muscular arms. He wore a polo shirt and ID on a lanyard around his neck.

"You must be Theo Fowler." The two men shook hands. "I'm Jason Jones, from the FBI's San Antonio Field Office."

"Nice to meet you. You got the phone?"

He handed Theo the device, along with the passcode.

"Follow me and tell me what you need." Theo led him down a long, dark hallway. Motion lights clicked on overhead as they passed.

"On Sunday morning, two coeds from the Dallas area took a photograph on an app at an airport in London. They then posted that image to social media. I want to see the original picture."

Theo stopped in front of a door. An electronic lock was attached to the wall. Bending slightly, he tapped the ID on the keypad. A light switched from red to green. He then entered a seven-digit code, and the door clicked as the lock disengaged. "I'm not going to ask about the case," he said, opening the door, "but I might be able to guess."

Of course he'd be able to figure out this was related to the Decker Newcombe investigation. The photo of Decker at the London airport had been blasted by the media all over the world. Besides, why else would a federal agent from Texas be in England? He followed Theo into a computer lab. A single desk lamp at a workstation illuminated the large room. "If you guessed, you'd probably be right."

"Do you have a warrant to search the phone?"

192 Texas Law: Lethal Encounter

"The owner gave consent."

Theo wove his way to the lit desk. He pulled a chair from another terminal. "Have a seat, and I'll take a look."

Theo unlocked the phone. Using a USB cord, he attached the device to a computer. "Here's the trick. How much of the phone's memory is used will determine whether or not we can access the picture."

"How long will that take?"

Theo shook his head. "Not long." He typed on the computer's keyboard. A line of letters and numbers began to fill the monitor. A moment later, a grid of pictures filled the screen. "Let's see what we have," said Theo, while scrolling through the images.

There were pictures of Isabella and Tiffany in front of Parliament. There were photos with the two coeds in the foreground and Buckingham Palace and a Beefeater in the background. There were several pictures of food and even more of drinks. Finally, they came to a series of four pictures. All of them had been taken in the airport's Terminal Five. "Is this what you're looking for?"

Jason sat up taller. "It is."

"Looks like those girls took four pictures in the app before settling on this one to post." Using the mouse, he circled one picture with the cursor.

Jason had seen the picture so many times that it was burned into his brain. But this time, the image was slightly different. His pulse pounded, making him deaf to every sound but the thud of his heartbeat. Decker Newcombe wasn't in the background. "Where are you, you bastard?" he asked the screen. "And how'd you get into the picture to begin with?" He turned to look at Theo. "Is that possible—to insert someone into a social-media post?"

"Possible? Yes. Easy? No."

"Could an image be inserted into a video taken from a public camera? Like one at an airport?" After all, Decker had been seen in security footage at the Dallas–Fort Worth Airport. Those two pictures were the whole reason everyone was looking for the killer in England. But what if both images had been altered?

Energy surged through his veins. Jason rose from his seat and began to pace.

Theo said, "Hacking into a securities video system isn't impossible, but there aren't many people who could do it."

"Could you?"

Theo paused, seeming to consider the question. "I could."

"So it's possible that video might not be legit, either?"

"Yeah, it's possible." Theo paused. "What're you thinking?"

"I'm thinking that Decker Newcombe might not be in England after all."

"If he's not in England, where is he?"

He stopped walking and looked at the NSA agent. "That's really the only question that matters—and honestly, I don't have a clue."

Chapter 15

It was late in the second quarter of the football game at Encantador High School. Only two minutes remained until halftime. EHS was up 13 to 10. So far, Brock had played well as quarterback. He'd run in one touchdown and gotten the team close enough to kick a pair of field goals. Morgan had kept the line moving at the concession stand. For the first time in a long while, Kathryn was content.

Yet, there was more to her happiness than her children's successes.

She and Ryan sat side by side in the stands. She dared not hold his hand—small-town gossip being what it was. But occasionally, his thigh grazed hers, and her skin tingled with the touch.

It seemed like everyone in town had come out for the game. Her neighbor, Joe, sat behind Kathryn. With him were his wife and Gladys, the elderly woman who lived across the road from Kathryn. Another neighbor, Stan Vargasky, and his wife sat nearby. They attended every game since all three of their daughters were on the cheer team. Armando Cruz, the assistant principal, divided his time between patrolling the students' section and sitting with his wife and their twin toddlers.

As the buzzer blared, ending the first half of the game, Joe leaned forward and clapped Ryan on the shoulder. "I've seen you working with Brock this week. His throw has improved a lot. Who knows, with an arm like his, we might be in contention for a state championship."

"The kid works hard, that's for sure," said Ryan.

Joe exhaled. "I didn't get a chance to thank you for everything you've done for the town. Chasing Decker out of hiding. Helping the QB get his pass accurate." He paused. "I might've said some harsh things before, but you're all right in my book."

Kathryn assumed that was the closest thing Ryan would get to an apology. He seemed to know it, too. "I appreciate you saying that."

"If you ever need anything from me, either of you," said Joe, "let me know."

"Go to the concession stand and get your wife and Gladys something to eat. The senior class is raising money for after prom," said Kathryn. The least she could do was send some business to Morgan and her cause.

"I could use something to eat," Ryan said as he stood. She stood as well. "Shall we?"

Kathryn had been coming to games in this stadium for decades. She could probably find her way to the concession stand with her eyes closed. It was tucked into a small building on the outside of the track that surrounded the football field.

A long line of people waiting for concessions snaked around the side of the track. She and Ryan took up their place at the back of the line. "Looks like everyone's hungry," said Ryan.

"It'll be good for the APP committee," she said, hopeful that Morgan would be pleased to have such a successful fundraiser.

"It's not just that there's a lot of people," grumbled a young woman standing in front of them. "The line is moving so slow."

"That's odd." She peered into the concession stand. From where she stood, she could see seven kids behind the counter. Morgan wasn't one of them. Correction. It was more than odd. Where was her daughter? "I'm going to check and see what's going on."

"I'll come with you," Ryan offered. She didn't need his help. But there was no reason to turn him away, either.

As they walked toward the front of the line, it was impossible to miss all the complaining.

"What's taking them so long?"

"This is too much of a wait for popcorn."

"If the school can't run the concession stand right, then they should let spectators bring in their own food."

She shouldered her way to the counter. The vice president of the APP committee stood behind the cash register. "Hi, Courtney," said Kathryn. "You guys look a little understaffed. Where's Morgan?"

Courtney rolled her eyes. "Like I would know. Twenty

minutes ago, she and Elliot took a break." She hooked air quotes around the last word. Then, she checked her watch. "Oh, wait. She's been gone for twenty-four minutes."

Okay, it was time for Kathryn to step in. Morgan might be trying to find her way in the world. But disappearing with a boy when she was supposed to be working was definitely the wrong path. "Any idea where she went?"

Pointing toward the parking lot, Courtney said, "They were going to get something from Elliot's car."

"I'll find her and send them back."

The other girl slumped with relief. "Thanks."

She'd pulled over Elliot more than once and knew he drove a blue sedan. But it might take some time to find his car in the sea of vehicles that filled the parking lot. She started walking toward the lot. Ryan was at her side.

"You don't have to come with me," she said, before warning him. "It might get messy for a few minutes."

"That's okay. I'm good with messy."

As it turns out, Elliot's car was easier to find than she feared. He was parked at the back of the lot. The headlights on his blue sedan were on—as were the high beams. Even with the lights shining in her eyes, she could see the outline of Elliot in the driver's seat.

For a moment, she was angry with her daughter—and herself. She should've used more discipline than understanding. But as she walked closer to the car, she realized an important fact. Elliot was in the driver's seat, but the passenger seat was empty.

"What the heck?"

"What the what?" Ryan asked.

"Where's my daughter?" Her anger morphed to concern, twisting in her gut.

She increased her walk to a trot. Then her trot became a jog. By the time she reached the blue sedan, she was covered in sweat. After looking in the window, she went cold. Elliot was unconscious. Had he not been wearing his seat belt, he would have fallen over. His hair was wet and matted with blood. One eye was swollen and ringed with a bruise. There was a cut to his cheek.

The interior of the car was red with gore.

Morgan wasn't there.

Kathryn swallowed down her rising panic. She opened the driver's door and reached for Elliot's arm. His skin was warm. The pulse at his wrist was surprisingly strong.

"He's alive," she said with relief. To Ryan, she said, "Call 9-1-1."

He stepped away from the vehicle and pulled his phone from his pocket. "I need emergency medical services," he began.

Certainly, dispatch would send EMTs who were already at the game. They'd be here within minutes. She looked inside the car. Morgan's purse lay on the passenger floorboard. Her jacket was in the seat. "What in the hell happened?" Certainly, there were clues in the car as to who'd committed this crime and why. She tried to think like the undersheriff. It was impossible since she was also a mother. Then she asked the question that made this nightmare all too real. "Where's my daughter?"

Elliot groaned. "Morgan. Revenge."

Kathryn knelt next to the open car door. "It's me,

Morgan's mom." She reached for his hand. "You're safe now. We're going to get you to the hospital. They'll patch you up. What happened?"

He held onto her fingers. It was like being trapped in a vise. "I'm so sorry. I tried to protect her. But he was everywhere. Hitting. Kicking. Cutting. He slammed my head into the hood of the car, and I blacked out. The last thing I saw was Morgan being thrown into the trunk of his car."

"Who?" Her pulse raced. "Who attacked you? Who took my daughter?"

"It was him."

"Him who?"

"I can't remember his name."

"Think, damn it," she said, as a wave of grief and fury pushed her under.

Elliot's head drooped to the side. Once again, he slipped from consciousness.

There was nothing more he could give her—not now, at least. No, that wasn't true. He'd said plenty already. The attacker was male. Elliot recognized him. It means that he knew the kidnapper.

A thousand faces flashed through her mind. Of course, she'd arrested rough men over the years. Even now, some might want revenge. But to kidnap her daughter and beat her boyfriend to a pulp?

Nobody made sense.

Did Elliot—or even Morgan—have enemies at school?

Then again, kidnapping someone was difficult. More than getting the victim to go with the perpetrator, they had to control them afterward. How could a lone student hope to pull off such a crime?

Yet, someone had. Her stomach cramped, and she thought she might retch.

Two EMTs sprinted through the parking lot. She waved her arms. "Over here. We have one victim, male, aged eighteen. He's been beaten pretty badly." She stepped away from the car, giving the paramedics room to work.

Ryan stood nearby. He opened his arms, and she stepped into his embrace.

"What's going on?"

Her eyes burned, and her throat was raw. "Honestly," she croaked, "I don't know. Someone attacked Elliot, and they took Morgan." She knew there were video cameras in the high-school parking lot. Several nearby businesses had cameras, too. They could get the footage. And then what? She was having a hard time thinking. Her mind was a tire stuck in the mud. It turned but got her nowhere.

"It'll be okay," Ryan whispered the words into her hair.

Far from being soothing, his sentiment left her pissed. "You don't know that," she snapped. She pushed on his chest, but he held her tighter.

"Undersheriff," one of the EMTs called out, "the patient's awake, and he wants to talk to you."

Elliot had been removed from his vehicle. He was strapped onto a gurney and a blanket covered him to the chest. A white bandage had been placed over the cut to his cheek. He regarded Kathryn with a single eye. "I know who took Morgan."

Her pulse raced, as if she'd just run a marathon. She gasped for air and information. "Who was it?"

"It was him. The guy everyone keeps talking about."

Elliot touched his forehead and screwed his eyes shut. "I can't remember his name, but I'll always remember his eyes. They were ice cold. More than just being blue, there was nothing behind them. Like his soul was empty. You know?"

She did know because she'd seen those eyes before. Until now, she'd tried not to think too much about the attack at the abandoned ranch. But it all came back to her in a frigid rush of memories. As she'd fought with Decker, he'd regarded her with eyes so cold that his gaze burned.

"Was it Decker?" she asked, knowing full well that she shouldn't give any information to the victim of a crime. It tainted their recollections of the event. Yet, she had to know. "Did Decker Newcombe attack you and take my daughter?"

Elliot nodded slowly. "Yeah," he said. "That's him."

"Excuse me, Undersheriff," said one of the EMTs. "We have to get the patient to the hospital."

She stepped away from the stretcher. An ambulance had been driven to the scene. Elliot was wheeled into the back. The doors were closed. With lights strobing, they drove away.

She looked at Ryan. "Decker's taken my daughter."

"That's impossible," he said. "He's in England."

She didn't know how he'd done it. As bad as things were now, they were about to get worse. "If he is back, then it means my daughter is his next victim." How could any of this be happening? Good Lord, this was worse than any nightmare. "He's going to murder her on the internet."

Ryan drew his eyebrows together. "Why would he want Morgan?"

At least she knew the answer to that question. "Elliot said he wants revenge. He must want to get even with me for finding him at the old McCoy ranch."

She'd never felt more lost before in her life. But she refused to give in to the hopelessness. Her daughter was missing but she was the undersheriff. It was her job to find Morgan and bring her home.

She stared at the brightly lit stadium. There was a clawing in her throat. It was ultimate need—she had to find her child and bring her home. "I'm coming for you, Decker. But this time, you won't get away."

Ryan knew that Kathryn's daughter being kidnapped was serious. But he had a hard time believing that Decker had actually taken the girl. There was evidence that Decker was on the other side of an ocean. He might've been able to sneak out of the country once. But he doubted that the killer would be able to get back in.

He was determined to help Kathryn find her daughter. Right now, she wasn't thinking like a cop—only a mom.

It left him with a simple explanation for what happened. Morgan's friend, Elliot, was mistaken.

"I'll call Jason," he said. The FBI needed to know about the kidnapping. But, he also hoped that the special agent would have more proof that Decker was in London. That way, Kathryn wouldn't waste her time looking for someone she'd never find.

Kathryn nodded. "I'll call my deputies and the duo from the Texas Rangers. We also have to see if any of these cameras caught the kidnapping. Get a description of the car. Start looking for witnesses."

He gave her wrist a squeeze and took a few steps away from where she stood. After pulling up the contact information, he placed a call to SA Jones. He answered after the third ring. "Ryan, did you hear from him again?"

Of course the FBI agent was hoping that he'd received another message from Decker. "Sorry," he said. "No."

"Then, I have to call you back. I'm tied up right now."

"You have to give me a minute." Before Jason could refuse, he added, "Kathryn's daughter was kidnapped from a high-school football game."

He cursed. "I'll call my people in San Antonio and have them send a team. But right now, I'm in London."

Ryan wasn't dissuaded. "There was one witness to the kidnapping. He's a friend of the victim's and was beaten. He can't recall everything, but he identified the kidnapper."

"That's good news. It'll help find the undersheriff's daughter and bring her home."

"The kid thinks it was Decker," he said, interrupting. He took another step away from Kathryn and lowered his voice enough that he wouldn't be overheard. "The undersheriff's convinced it's Decker, too. My fear is that after her attack, she's got some posttraumatic stress. She's convinced herself—and the witness—that Decker took her daughter. Since she's the undersheriff, people will listen to her. A lot of time is going to be spent looking for the wrong guy."

He waited for a reply. A moment passed. And a moment more. Had Jason hung up?

Ryan glanced at the screen. A timer continued to count the seconds of their open call. Pressing the phone to his ear, he asked, "You there?"

"I'm here."

"I know that you're busy and all, but if you could talk to Kathryn? Tell her there's no way that Decker took her kid. She'll listen to you." He wasn't sure the last bit was entirely true, but he had no other options.

"I can't do that."

"Damn it, you aren't that much of a coldhearted bastard." Then again, maybe he was. "A young woman is missing. Her mother needs to hear someone talk sense. Otherwise, she's going to go off on some damned wild-goose chase." He looked over his shoulder to make sure Kathryn hadn't overheard his outburst. She hadn't. "Even if this isn't your case, protecting and serving is still part of your credo. All's I'm asking is for you to do your damn job."

"Are you done?" the FBI agent asked.

Ryan grunted. "I guess."

"I can't tell Kathryn that Decker didn't kidnap her daughter because he may not be in England. We have proof that his image was added to a social-media post after it was taken. Same for the video from the Dallas Airport."

Like the first plunge of a roller-coaster, his stomach dropped to his shoes. "Is that even possible?"

"I've been working with a cybersecurity expert from the NSA who happens to be stationed in London. He says it's possible, but not easy. Seems like you were right when you suggested that someone was helping Decker. Any idea who?"

Decker never had friends, other than Ryan. "Not a clue."

"All this time, I've been wondering how the killer got out of the country. Or where he was hidden now. It seems like I have my answer. He never left Texas." Jason paused. Ryan's ears filled with buzzing. The agent continued, "Did the victim say anything else, other than it was Decker who took the girl?"

"He said she was being kidnapped for revenge."

"Revenge?" Jason echoed. "Because Kathryn was first on the scene at his last hiding place?"

His chest felt as if it were being torn in two. He rubbed his breastbone. "That's what she thinks."

"I'll get a flight back to San Antonio as soon as it can be arranged. In the meantime, my people will come to Encantador. I'll contact Isaac, too." He paused. "If Decker did take Kathryn's daughter, he'll post about it soon. And we only have until Sunday to save her life."

Ryan knew that everything Jason said was true. But there were other things he knew to be true as well. Decker was out for revenge. But so was Ryan. He'd do anything to help the woman he...

No. Now wasn't the time to name his feelings. He had to find Morgan and get her back. Then, he needed to face Decker—and finish him.

Chapter 16

The time on Kathryn's phone read 4:17 a.m.

Her daughter had been kidnapped at approximately eight o'clock the previous evening. The game had been suspended, and Brock was staying with friends with a sheriff's deputy guarding the house 24/7. She'd gone home briefly to change into her uniform and get her car.

A statewide manhunt had been launched to find Decker and Morgan. So far, neither had been found. Everyone knew what Decker planned to do next. He was going to livestream Morgan's murder. If she didn't save her daughter in the next twenty hours, it'd be too late.

She sat in the computer lab at the Center. With their supercomputers, the Center was able to set up a secure video call between Kathryn and four others. Isaac Patton was in San Antonio. Jason Jones was on a private jet that had been furnished by the FBI. He was somewhere over the Atlantic Ocean as they spoke. In London was the cybersecurity expert from the NSA, Theo Fowler. It was Theo who confirmed that the images of Decker had been added to photos and videos. Mooky Parsons, the sheriff, was still in Mexico, but he was also on the call. His flight home was in the afternoon, and he was expected back in Encantador around midnight.

Aside from Kathryn, there were three other people in the room. Michael O'Brien, Hal the computer expert, and Ryan. To be honest, there wasn't a reason—official or otherwise—for Ryan to be part of the briefing. But she liked having him with her, so maybe his support was reason enough.

"It looks like Decker used a stolen car to transport Morgan. As per his modus operandi, he took an older-model car without GPS tracking. This is where the car was found." A large screen was filled with a map of the county. A red star marked a section of road that was rarely traveled. Everyone on the call could see the map. She finished her briefing with "From there, the trail goes cold."

Her throat was tight as she tried to swallow down her rage, sorrow, and worry. At her very core, she was terrified of what might happen to her daughter. On the surface, she had to be calm and in control. Otherwise, she'd be pushed out of the investigation, judged to be the emotional mother.

"Do we have anything else?" Jason asked.

Everyone on the video call shook their heads.

"How in the hell does this guy simply disappear?" Isaac asked.

Ryan raised his hand. "Back when we worked to-gether, we figured out how to get away before we ever agreed to committing a crime." He paused. "Decker always had a car that wasn't connected to anyone—especially him—so nobody was looking for it. But it was legally purchased and registered. It'd be parked out of the way. Then, he'd drive to that spot and take off."

The plan was brilliant in its simplicity. And yet... "How does this help us?" she asked.

"Well, there are two things. First, he'd have to have a car near where he left the stolen vehicle. There's no way for him to transport Morgan without another ride," Ryan said.

Hearing her daughter's name was an arrow to her heart.

"Which means what?" she asked, her voice hoarse.

"My guess is that he's always had another car hidden for transport—even after he left the abandoned farm-house with your cruiser." Ryan paused. "Where was the final car found last week?"

After stealing her cruiser, he'd taken four other ve-hicles.

"I can show you right now." Hal tapped on the key-board. He created another star, this one blue, and placed it where the final stolen car was found.

"I'll be damned," said Isaac. "The cars were left close to one another."

He was right. Each car had been abandoned on a county route. The roads ran parallel to each other for three or four miles before veering off in different di-rections. The spots were separated by two miles of hill country and nothing else.

"Any idea what's in between those roads?" Jason asked. "Perhaps he's hiding somewhere between those two spots."

Kathryn knew the whole county better than anyone other than Mooky. "I can't think of an old house in that area. And there's definitely not someplace where he'd be able to set up internet access."

"There's no dwelling around for miles," Mooky confirmed. "Although there's a trail from one county route to the other. Sometimes people go out there to hike and ride mountain bikes and such."

"It'd be easy for Decker to leave a car on one road and walk to the other," said Ryan.

"Yes, it would," Mooky confirmed. "Folks do it all the time."

Folding his hands together, Ryan leaned his elbows on the table. Narrowing his eyes, he stared at the map. "I know he's close. But where?"

Nobody had an answer to that question.

After a moment, he spoke again. "Decker's somewhere on the southern road."

"That's decisive. What makes you say that?" Isaac asked.

"Decker and I used to meticulously plan his jobs. Like I said, we also knew how he planned to escape. If it were me, I'd tell him not to be on the road for long with a victim. I bet he drove straight from the kidnapping to where he left his getaway car. Then, he drove to wherever he's keeping Morgan."

"You're assuming a lot," said Isaac. "Decker's been known to steal three or even four cars while getting away."

"That's true. But he's not trying to get away. He's trying to transport Morgan. Getting her out of one car and into another is the hardest part of a kidnapping. An unexpected motorist could drive by and see the exchange. Morgan might land a lucky punch in a fight. Basically, one simple thing could go wrong and the victim could escape. He wouldn't expose himself to that same risk time and again."

As Kathryn listened to Ryan's explanation, she had two opposite thoughts. First, it was no wonder that Decker had gotten away with so much and for so long. But she was a sworn law-enforcement officer. It didn't matter what Ryan's rap sheet said after helping the feds. He was still a criminal.

Second, she really did care about him. How had she let herself fall so hard and so fast?

Good Lord, now was not the time to worry about her feelings.

Isaac said, "I assume that CSI looked for tire prints."

"They found only one set of tracks. Those belonged to the stolen vehicle we recovered," she said. But she was willing to try anything if it meant finding a clue to her daughter's whereabouts. "But we can widen the search and look again in the daylight."

"I think that'd be best," said Mooky. "What else do we know?"

"Morgan wasn't taken at random," said Ryan. "He chose her."

"You mean he took my daughter to get even with me."

A look flashed in his eyes. It was gone as soon as it appeared. But what had it been? Sadness? Misery? Regret? It was all of that and more. Well, Kathryn didn't want his sympathies. She pinned him with a razor-sharp glare, daring him to say more.

"At the moment, motive doesn't concern us," said Jason. "We all know what Decker plans to do. What we need is a plan to find and stop him."

"I want to know how he is getting around so easily. And who's adding his image to pictures and videos? It seems like the killer has made some talented and well-moneyed friends," said Isaac.

"Theo has some theories as to who might be helping Decker," said Jason.

The cybersecurity expert had been silent through the exchange. He now sat taller in the seat and leaned forward. "Being able to add images after something's been posted—or to hack into a security system and add video—takes a special kind of talent. It's a skill set even the best cyber people don't usually have. I made a list of everyone who might have those capabilities. Then, I looked at the images for an electronic fingerprint of sorts."

Her head swam. "Did you find anything?"

"I did," said Theo. "But it's not good news. Years ago, the NSA hired a young hacker, who went by the name of Seraphim, to try to get past our latest firewalls. They were more than competent and found several ways to breach our security. That job led to another and then another. After a few years, Seraphim had gained our trust." He paused. "It was all misplaced. In the end, they stole government secrets and sold them to our enemies."

Isaac asked, "You think Seraphim is helping Decker?"

Theo nodded.

"Can that help us find my daughter before…?" She

knew what Decker planned to do to Morgan. It's just that she refused to say the words.

Theo shook his head.

"Why not? You said they'd left an electronic fingerprint."

"Just like a physical fingerprint, you can only find it after it's been left—not before. And nobody knows Seraphim's real identity, or where they are now."

"I have a question," asked Michael. "What does a hacker who sells state secrets have in common with a guy like Decker?"

"Seraphim wanted to cause a global incident. According to them, there should be a new world order. I imagine that Decker is a part of the plan to sow chaos," Theo said.

"Where does that leave us?" Frustration burned a hole from the inside of her chest. "We've got nothing and no way to find Decker—or save my daughter." Even she heard the anguish in her voice.

"We've got clues to follow," said Ryan.

Sure, he was trying to make her feel better. But she wasn't in the mood to be soothed.

"It's my daughter who's stuck with that monster," she snapped.

Her mind was a jumble of thoughts. It was impossible to even think straight.

Theo said, "I might not be able to find Seraphim. I can use info from the NSA's satellites. I'll upload all images for the past two weeks. I can't guarantee that we'll find anything, but we might get lucky."

Is that what it had come to? She was now relying

on luck. Well, she supposed that she'd take anything. "Yeah," she said, suddenly exhausted. "Thanks."

She checked the time. It was almost 5:00 a.m. She rose from her seat. Her whole body ached. Exhaustion pulled her toward a deep, dark void. But if she allowed herself to slip into the blackness, she'd never find her way back to the light. "The sun will be up in an hour. I'll head over to where we found the car. Maybe we'll find something if we increase the search parameters."

Ryan stood as well. "I'll go with you."

"Hey, guys," said Hal. "Wait up. Something just got posted that you'll want to see."

One of the large monitors on the wall winked to life. Morgan's tear-stained face filled the screen. She was gagged, and her arms were bound behind her with rope. The same rope was tied to her feet, and a noose was looped around her neck. If Morgan moved at all, the ropes tightened, and she'd get choked.

Staring at the face of her child, a wave of shock rolled over Kathryn. Balling her hands into fists, she focused on her breath, on the sound of her own pulse, on Morgan's face.

With her daughter's image still filling the screen, Decker's voice came from off-camera. "This is what you've all been waiting for. You know what surprised me—although maybe it shouldn't—is how many of you people have already accessed the link. There are almost a million of you sick bastards out there. That's why I decided to go live a little early. Just so you could see what terrified really looks like."

The screen went black.

"He's not logged into the internet anymore," said Hal. Then to Theo, he said, "Were you able to track him?"

Theo shook his head. "I didn't get a lock on the location, but I'll see what was left behind in the broadcast."

As the IT specialists talked, speaking a language that was all but foreign to her, Morgan's face was burned into her brain, her heart, her soul. Kathryn's hands started to tremble. The walls in the small room closed in on her from all sides. "I need some air."

Without looking back, she marched from the room. The computer lab led to the forensics lab. From there, she pushed open the front door and stepped outside. The sky was black, and the air sizzled with heat. She walked to the edge of the sidewalk. Her legs refused to hold her any longer, and she sank onto the curb.

"Hey."

She looked over her shoulder. Ryan stood behind her.

"Hey," she said, her voice a whisper.

"I wasn't sure what you wanted. I decided to come out in case you need some company."

The last thing she wanted was to be alone. "I just couldn't think with everyone around." She pressed her palms into the concrete curb. The rough surface bit into her flesh. "I should get back inside."

Ryan sat beside her. "You can take a minute, if you need one." He paused. "There's no playbook for how a parent should handle something like this."

"Do you think I should step away from the investigation?" It was a question she'd asked herself more than once. "Can I really be the acting sheriff and the victim's parent?"

Ryan exhaled. "What do you think is best?"

"If Mooky were here, I'd let him be in charge." Admitting that she'd turn the case over to the sheriff left her hollow. At the same time, she'd gain nothing with bravado or false confidence. "I can't be an impartial law-enforcement officer when my child's life is at stake." Then again, she could use the agony to make her stronger. Or would she be crushed by the weight of hopelessness? She raked her fingers through her hair. "I don't know what to do."

"Back when I lived here before, there were a lot of late nights at the bar. It was part of the job. I didn't mind because it meant I got to see this." He pointed across the desert. In the distance, a thin line of gold ran across the horizon.

"Is this where you tell me that if the sun can rise every morning, I can rise from this adversity, too?"

He raised his brow. "I'd never say something like that. Just watch."

She stared across the desert. The sky brightened, turning orange and pink.

It was hard to appreciate the glory of a sunrise. Still, she said, "Beautiful."

"I hope it made you feel better."

"It did, a little, at least."

"Glad I could help." His phone trilled with an incoming call. He pulled the cell from his pocket. "It's Isaac. Mind if I take it?"

A flicker of hope came to life in her chest. He might have news about Morgan. "Go ahead."

After swiping the call open, he pressed the device to his ear. "Any news?"

Ryan hadn't turned on his Speaker function. It didn't

matter as she could hear Isaac's voice. "No news on my end." He paused. "I liked the way you thought in the meeting."

"Liked the way I thought?" Ryan echoed. "I just outlined how Decker and I used to commit crimes."

"You know how the NSA hired the hacker to find the weaknesses in their security system? It got me thinking. You have a unique perspective that'd be invaluable to Texas Law."

"Because I'm good at committing crimes, I'd be good at solving them?" Ryan asked.

"You'd be even better at preventing them, but yeah." Isaac cleared his throat. "Back when we were undercover, we didn't like each other much. Still, we worked well together. Basically, I'm offering you a job."

Ryan glanced at Kathryn. "Can we talk about this later?"

"Let me tell you one final thing," said Isaac. "It wouldn't be in San Antonio. I'm going to open a satellite office in Mercy. Texas Law will take one of the office spaces that Michael's trying to fill. Promise me that you'll consider it, at least."

"Yeah. Sure. I promise."

"Call me if you hear anything new."

"Will do," said Ryan, before ending the call.

Filling her lungs with air, she held her breath until she found the fine line of pain. She exhaled. "That worked out well for you."

"You heard that Isaac offered me a job," he said, slipping the phone into the pocket of his jeans.

"It sounds exactly like what you wanted." She didn't

have the bandwidth for any more emotions. "Congrat-ulations."

"I thought you wanted me to leave town." He waved away his words, as if erasing writing from a whiteboard. "I have one priority. To find Morgan before anything bad happens to her."

"Bad things have already happened," she said. And then, "I think you should take the job."

He reached for her hand. She laced her fingers through his. On the eastern horizon, crimson and vermilion filled the sky. It was a new day. Right now, she couldn't think about anything other than saving her daughter. And yet she'd heard everything that Ryan said during the meeting. It was more than knowing how Decker thought—he had the mind of a criminal as well. She couldn't keep the acid from her veins. The only reason Decker knew about her community was because of Ryan.

She rose quickly, wobbling as she stood. "It's you."

"What about me?"

"You know what I mean," she said. "You helped Decker become the monster he is today."

Guilt was etched into each line of his face. "You're right."

How had she been so naive? So stupid? From the be-ginning, she'd known that Ryan was no good. But she'd been blinded by lust and hope and the tingling in her stomach every time he looked in her direction. Walk-ing backward, she said, "You stay away from me, you hear? I don't ever want to see you again. I don't ever want to speak to you again."

Turning her back on Ryan, she strode toward her cruiser. Sure, she'd given him a ride to the Center. But she sure as hell wasn't giving him a ride back to town. Wrenching the door open, she slid into the driver's seat. Every cell of her body vibrated with hate and rage as she started the engine and backed out of the parking space.

She hated Decker for all the pain he had caused. She also hated Ryan for making her community a target of the killer. But mostly, she hated herself. It was more than the fact that she should've sent Ryan away but hadn't.

She hated herself because after everything, she still wanted him at her side.

Chapter 17

Sitting on the curb, Ryan watched the taillights of Kathryn's car as she drove away. He knew that Kathryn was right. He had created Decker.

Yet, he hated that his past caused a split between them. It left him with an interesting question.

What should he do next?

He could go back to the motel, get his dog and his gear, then leave. He imagined that few people would be sorry to see him go.

If he left now, he'd never be able to look in the mirror without loathing his reflection. He couldn't abandon Kathryn and her daughter now.

But she'd been clear. She hated him. She never wanted to see him again. It made helping her difficult. No, it made it impossible.

Rising from the curb, he knew what he needed to do.

His legs were stiff as he walked to the Center and opened the door. Standing next to one of the lab tables, Michael looked up as he entered the building.

"Hey," he said. "Any chance you can give me a ride back to the motel in Encantador?"

"Sure." He paused. "I thought you rode with the undersheriff."

"I did," he said simply. He didn't owe the doctor an explanation. "She had to leave."

"Uh, okay. Give me a minute to shut everything down. Then we can go."

He nodded. "I'll wait outside." Pushing open the door, he stepped into the parking lot and drew in a deep breath. He'd stood in this exact place countless times. The last of the stars were disappearing from the night sky and the horizon had started to brighten. The landscape was as familiar to him as his own face.

He knew what he had to do. Pulling the phone from his pocket, he placed a call.

Isaac answered after the second ring. "Hey, is there an update?"

"I was thinking about that job offer." Straightening his shoulders, Ryan was certain of his decision. "I've made up my mind."

Kathryn drove without seeing anything other than the endless line of asphalt. Sure, she was furious. The question was: What should she do now?

She pulled onto the shoulder of the road. A cloud of dust surrounded her car. Holding tight to the steering wheel, she wiped her face with her shoulder. Only then did she realize that she'd been crying. She had to get her emotions under control. Sobbing wouldn't bring her closer to finding Morgan.

Then again, there was someone who might be able to help.

She'd left him sitting in the parking lot of the Center. What's worse, she'd told Ryan that she never wanted to speak to him again. Or see him. She wouldn't blame him if he never wanted to talk to her, either.

Yet, for Morgan, she had to call a truce and ask for his help.

She inhaled a deep breath and counted to ten. After exhaling, she turned the car around in the middle of the road. Within minutes, she was back at the Center. She'd hoped to find Ryan still sitting on the curb. All the same, she wasn't surprised that he wasn't there.

A single car was parked in the lot. Lights from inside shone through the front door. She let herself into the building. The forensics lab was spacious and filled with light. One look around the room told her all she needed to know.

Ryan was gone.

She tried to draw a deep breath. This time, her chest was too tight.

Hal was still in the IT lab. He looked up as she approached the glass wall that separated the two labs.

Rising to his feet, he met her at the door. "Can I help you with something?"

"I was looking for Ryan," she said.

"He left with Dr. O'Brien. They haven't been gone long—only a few minutes."

"Any idea where they were going?"

Hal shook his head. "The doctor said something about dropping Ryan off at the motel."

Kathryn tried to smile but the expression hurt her face. "If you hear from Ryan or Michael, ask them to give me a call."

"Will do." After letting the door between them shut, Hal gave her a small wave.

She hurried out to the parking lot. After slipping behind the steering wheel and starting the engine, she turned on the emergency lights atop her cruiser. She drove toward Encantador and watched the speedometer climb to seventy miles per hour, eighty. She settled in at ninety miles per hour. Scanning the road, she hoped that she'd catch sight of Michael O'Brien's sleek blue car.

There was nothing.

A sign on the side of the road read *Welcome to Encantador. A Nice Place to Live.*

After letting her foot off the accelerator, she turned off the strobing light. She drove down the quiet and deserted street. It took her a few minutes to get to the motel. Letting her car idle, she stopped in front of the building. A dozen rooms stretched out in a row. Several cars filled the parking lot. Ryan's truck was gone.

So, he had finally listened to her and left town.

Well, after everything, she didn't blame him.

Yet, a hard ball of regret stuck in her throat.

The car used to kidnap Morgan had been found twenty miles outside of town. She headed straight to the location. By the time she arrived, the sun had fully crested the horizon. Pulling onto the shoulder, she parked on the opposite side of the pavement. Last night, a team of forensic investigators had scoured the area, looking for clues. Was there something they'd missed?

Ryan thought so.

She hoped he was right.

Turning off the ignition, she opened her door. Heat rolled over her in a wave. The desert spread out in all directions, and the silence was complete. There was no breeze to stir the hair on her neck. No call of a bird, circling its prey. It was like Kathryn was completely alone in the world.

In some ways, she was.

She refused to feel anything. It was the only way she'd survive.

Slipping on a pair of sunglasses, she crossed the road. A small marker still sat next to where a set of tire tracks had been found. Using an electronic database, investigators were able to prove they belonged to the stolen car. Kneeling, she picked up the slip of paper.

She heard a deep bark and looked toward the noise. That's when she saw him. Tail a wagging blur, Old Blue ran toward Kathryn.

"Hey, boy." She ruffled the fur on his back. "What're you doing here? Where's Ryan?"

The dog looked over his shoulder. Clad in the same Encantador High School Football T-shirt from the night before, Ryan sprinted up the side of a gully. "Old Blue," he called. His gaze landed on hers, and he skidded to a halt.

Her mouth went dry. Despite the circumstances, she wanted to smile.

The dog dropped to his haunches.

"You know, I can give you a ticket for not keeping your dog on a leash," she said, standing up.

He glared. "Is that supposed to be a joke or something?"

"Well, I guess it's not a very funny joke."

He shrugged. "It's kinda funny. There's something I want to show you." Without another word, he turned and walked down the hill.

The dog barked and ran after his master.

She jogged, trying to keep pace with Ryan. "Where are we going?"

"I found something," he said, without looking over his shoulder.

His truck was parked at the bottom of the ridge. No wonder she'd thought she was all alone. He'd walked fifty yards beyond his bumper and knelt. "I found these. They're tire tracks."

She stood next to him. A set of ridges had been formed from the ground.

True, he'd found a set of tracks. But were they from Decker's vehicle?

She didn't dare to hope these tracks were a link in the chain of clues. "I can take a picture of this and get it to SICAR." SICAR stood for *Shoeprint Image Capture and Retrieval*. It was a database where thousands of tread imprints—for tires and shoes both—were stored. "If they can do an analysis from a photo, we might get a brand or type of tire."

Otherwise, it was back to old-fashioned policing. The CSI team would come out to the location. A cast would be made of the tire print and then submitted physically.

Really, it'd be a waste of time. Morgan would be dead before the plaster was done drying.

The ground seemed to tilt. Kathryn focused only on her breath. Once the vertigo passed, she pulled her phone from her pocket. After opening the camera app, she focused on the ridges again and snapped several pictures. "Hopefully, these are good enough to find a manufacturer's match."

Ryan stood. "That's it? I thought you'd be happy."

"Right now, I can't feel anything." She didn't want to discuss her emotional state anymore. "What're you doing out here anyway? Aside from looking for tire tracks, I mean."

Standing, he dusted his hands together. "Me? I'm working."

That was news. "Oh?"

"I decided to take the position with Texas Law," he said.

Her heart skipped a beat. "I guess you'll be staying in town."

He shook his head. "Not necessarily. You were right when you said that I created Decker. He's my mess and I intend to clean up. After that…" He shrugged, using the gesture as some sort of answer.

She shouldn't care. Yet the sour taste of disappointment coated her tongue. "Listen, about what I said earlier—"

He held up his palms. "Don't apologize."

That's exactly what she'd planned to do. Now she was left with nothing to say.

He continued. "You should be furious with me. I'm furious with myself."

"I'm not angry with you—not anymore, at least." She took a step toward him. God, she wanted to lean in to his chest. To feel his arms around her. To listen to the soothing sound of his heart.

"I promise you," he said, closing the distance between them. "I will find Morgan."

She nodded. "Can we just move forward from here?"

"I'd like that," he said.

She blew out a long breath. "Well, I need to text the tire tracks to Hal. Come with me if you want."

"I'm with you," he said, "all the way."

She wondered about his choice of words. Were they meant to buoy her sprits or was there more? She couldn't let herself think about that now. Finding her daughter was the only thing that mattered.

Decker had installed a countdown app on his computer. He sat in the dark warehouse and stared at the screen.

Twelve hours and twenty-three minutes remained until midnight.

Then he'd livestream the murder and secure his place in history. For all eternity, Decker would be the world's most famous killer. The girl he'd kidnapped, Morgan Glass, lay nearby and cried quietly. He hadn't thought about what it was like to spend hours with a victim. But her constant weeping was getting under his skin.

He needed to do something and soon, or else he was going to explode. If he killed her now, all his work and planning would come to nothing.

His computer pinged. It was a message from Seraphim. After clicking the link, he entered the preset password. The hacker's plague-doctor mask filled the screen. "Everything's going as planned. The authorities are trying to find the origin of your latest post, but I've added so many layers to the encryption it will take an army of IT specialists a year of working to find you."

Decker didn't believe in luck. But the day that Seraphim reached out had certainly been fortunate. "How many people are signed up to see my…performance?"

"Right now, over two million people have gotten access," the hacker squawked. "I've implanted tracking on all their devices. I'm not surprised that there are so many people willing to watch a live murder. After all, society is a cesspool. What shocks me is how easily they gave me access to their computers."

Like he'd been sucker punched, Decker's stomach clenched. He finally understood. "This murder has nothing to do with making me famous or causing the world to burn. It's all about you gaining access to people's computers."

"It's not just their computers I want, but everyone keeps their life on their devices. It gives me a window into their soul. I'm sure there are a quiet a few people who would pay to keep their secrets hidden."

For the most part, he had a low opinion of humanity. It kept him from being disillusioned. Yet, he was disappointed. "Money," he spat. "This is all about money."

Seraphim waved away his concern. "You are about to make history. Soon, you'll be immortal."

He knew the hacker was playing to his vanity. But he didn't mind. Still, he said, "I don't like being lied to."

"I don't blame you. Which is why I have a gift for you."

A gift? "Yeah? What?"

"I did a little digging into Ana Pierce."

"I told you that she doesn't matter." He leaned toward the screen and glared into the dead eyes in the mask. "I also told you to leave my past alone."

Seraphim held up their hands in surrender. "Then, I won't tell you what I found. Forget I ever mentioned anything."

Their words were bait. He refused to walk into the trap. Yet, he sighed. "What'd you find out about Ana?"

"She has a son. His name is Seth."

He didn't want to care. He shrugged. "I figured she'd get married eventually and have a kid. Back when we were together, she wanted children."

"She's not married," said Seraphim. "She's never been married."

Who was he to judge? "So?"

"Do you know her son's age?"

He really didn't want to play games with the hacker. Then again, anything was better than listening to the girl cry. "How could I? Until a minute ago, I didn't even know that she had a kid."

"The child turned eleven years old on his last birthday. It was in May."

The hacker had his attention now. That was eleven years and eight months after Ana ended the relationship. The math would be right for the child to be Decker's son. "So?"

"You don't fool me," said Seraphim. "I can tell that you're wondering the same thing I did. You want to know if Seth Pierce is your child."

Decker's throat was suddenly dry. Without a word,

he rose from the seat and walked to the small refrigerator. From it, he pulled out a bottle of beer. He returned to the computer desk and twisted off the cap. After taking a long drink, he let the alcohol buzz through his blood. "Congratulations, you can add *mind reader* to your résumé. There's no way to know for sure if that kid is mine—or not."

The hacker tapped their keyboard. The ridiculous mask disappeared. In its place was an electronic copy of a birth certificate for Seth James Pierce. Scanning the document, he found what he wanted.

Name of father: Newcombe, Decker.

He didn't trust anyone completely, Seraphim included. Sure, there was a birth certificate. But the document might not even be real.

But what if it was?

Crap. It meant he was a dad.

With all the other women, he'd taken extra precautions. But Ana had been different. At the time, he wouldn't have minded if they'd made a baby together.

"You know," said Seraphim, their squeaking voice pulling Decker from his thoughts. "She was difficult to find—even for me."

He stared at the screen and said nothing.

"Don't you want to know all about your ex-girlfriend's life? Don't you want to know about your son?"

Taking a drink of beer, he exhaled. "Not really. What Ana did with her life is her own business—not mine."

It was then that he realized the crying had stopped. He looked at the girl. Even in the dimly lit warehouse, he could tell she was watching him. Looking back at the screen, he ended the video call without a word.

The girl's eyes were on him, tickling his skin. He rubbed the back of his neck. "What?"

She said nothing.

He looked back at her.

Oh yeah, he'd left her gagged.

"I know you heard everything the hacker said. I don't care what you see or hear. You know what's going to happen to you next. You'll have no choice but to take my secrets to the grave with you." He glanced back at her. Despite the fact that she was hog-tied, she shrugged. He mimicked her gesture. "What's that supposed to mean?"

She wasn't going to answer him. She couldn't. But if she could, what would she say? He was intrigued. Rising from his seat, he crossed the floor. Kneeling in front of the girl, he said, "I'm going to take this gag from your mouth. If you scream, there's nobody around to hear you except for me. You'll annoy me. Then I'll give everyone a preview of what's going to happen next." He pointed to the camera. "I'll tie you to a chair and cut out your tongue. Got it?"

Wide-eyed, she nodded.

After loosening the knot just enough, he pulled the gag from her mouth.

She gasped for air. "Thanks."

"Thanks?" he scoffed. "What're you thanking me for?"

She worked pressed her lips together and then opened her mouth wide, probably to ease some of her soreness. "I don't know. Only it's more comfortable without that rag in my mouth."

"Well, don't get used to it." He paused. "You heard that freak on the computer."

"About you having a son?"

"Yeah."

"First of all, what's up with their voice? That screeching is obnoxious." She drew in a long breath. "Talk about annoying."

"Agreed," said Decker. "But what d'you think? Are they lying about the kid?"

"Honestly, I'm not sure. It's hard to guess because you can hear their words but not their actual voice. Ya know." She shifted her hands and feet, trying to find a comfortable position.

Decker loosened the knot that kept her arms and legs tied together. It gave the girl another inch of room.

She relaxed a bit. "I do know one thing. You're lying. You care about having a kid. And you care a lot."

Decker's jaw tightened. "What makes you say that?"

"I saw the way you got tense when you heard the news. Your shoulders pinched together. You sat up taller. Your voice held an edge."

Had he reacted that much?

"You're pretty good at reading people."

"Not really." She made a face. "I'm just really good at lying."

Her answer surprised him. He gave a bark of a laugh. "The undersheriff's daughter is a liar. Who knew?"

"Everyone but my mom." A single tear leaked from the corner of her eye. It snaked down the side of her face until it was lost in her hair.

"Why you gotta lie to your mom?"

"I don't have to lie to her." She exhaled. The sound was filled with a lot of sorrow for a teenager. "I just do."

Now Decker was truly curious. "About what?"

"My friend Elliot and I smoke weed. Not all the time, but enough. She's smelled it on us before, and I told her skunks live under his deck."

He laughed again. "And she believed that bull?"

"I guess. Or she's too busy with her work or my brother, Brock the Perfect, to care."

Decker sat on the floor next to the girl. "What makes your brother so perfect?"

"First of all, he's athletic. All the girls think he's cute. He works hard in school, and he's always happy. It's like having a damn golden retriever for a brother. Everyone wants to say *hi* and pet him."

He laughed again. "Kid, you're funny."

"My name is Morgan," she said. "Not *kid*."

"Seems like you're funny and brave. Not many people have the courage to correct me."

"I guess in some ways, I'm my mom's daughter. She's brave, too." She paused. "You wonder what your kid's like? Do you think he's like you?"

"You mean a killer?"

"That wasn't what I meant, but it's a good question. I was more wondering if he looked like you. Or sounded like you." A lock of hair slipped into her mouth. She spit it out. "Everybody says I sound just like my mom. It's weird."

"Until just a few minutes ago, I didn't even know I was a father. Not that I entirely believe Seraphim's story. I really haven't had any time to think about Seth at all," said Decker.

"What're you going to do?" she said.

It was a question he'd eventually have to answer. But for now, he said, "I don't know."

Morgan exhaled. "You don't have to do this. You don't have to kill me." The last two words came out as a squeak. "You're a father now. You know how precious life can be. You can drop me off somewhere and I won't tell anyone where you took me." Her eyes darted around the small room "Besides, I don't even know where we are."

Did Decker regret kidnapping Morgan? Maybe a little. But now, the world was waiting for her death. He couldn't walk away from this murder. "I get what you're trying to do," he said. Other victims had done it before. "You're trying to appeal to my sense of humanity. It's not going to work." With a shake of his head, he shoved the gag back into her mouth. "I'm not a decent man. In fact, I don't even have a soul."

Chapter 18

Kathryn pulled into a parking place in front of the Center. It was already 1:12 p.m., which meant that Morgan had ten hours and forty-eight minutes to live.

Ryan parked his truck next to her police vehicle. When he opened his door, Old Blue scrambled over his master and bounded into the parking lot. Ryan followed.

She watched it all yet remained frozen in her seat. Ryan knocked on the passenger window. She lowered the window, and a cloud of hot air rolled over her.

"You okay?" he asked.

She wasn't sure that she'd ever be okay again. "I'm just giving myself a moment."

"This is a lot to deal with. Take all the time you need."

The word *time* stuck a chord. With each second that passed, with each beat of her heart, time was being wasted. If she wanted to save Morgan—and for her, there was nothing else—she had to act.

She turned off her engine. Without a word, she walked from her car to the front door of the Center. She entered the facility. The air inside was cool and dry. It was only as perspiration dried on her skin that Kathryn realized she'd been sweating.

Ryan and Old Blue followed. The dog found a corner and lay down.

Hal sat at a keyboard in the computer lab. All three wall-mounted monitors were divided into six screens each. Each screen was filled with different aerial images. Some were of streets in downtown Encantador. Some were of deserted roads around the county. There was even an image of Kathryn's home.

They entered the lab, and Hal looked up.

He gestured to the monitors. "The guy from the NSA was able to get these images. I've been going through them, looking for something out of place. So far, nothing."

"We have pictures of tire tracks taken not far from where the car used to kidnap Morgan was found," said Ryan.

"We can do a manufacturers' search," said Hal. He tapped on his keyboard, and a desktop monitor winked to life. "You got those pictures?"

"I'll send them to you in an email." She found the photos in her camera roll and attached them to a message. She hit Send, the email leaving her phone with a whoosh.

In the other room, Old Blue started to bark.

What had gotten the dog so riled? Gooseflesh covered her arms. Fingers trembling, she unfastened the snap on her holster.

Ryan shot her a worried expression. "I'll see what's going on."

He opened the door between the two labs. At the same time, Stu, the gas-station owner, opened the outside door. The old man held a pizza box in both hands. "Whoa, boy," he said as the dog's barking continued.

"Come," Ryan commanded. Old Blue trotted to his owner's side and sat.

Stu held the box higher. "I saw all the cars and thought y'all might want something to eat."

The scent of pizza sauce and melted cheese wafted into the computer lab. Kathryn's mouth started to water, and her stomach rumbled. When had she eaten last? Was it the hot dog she'd had before the football game? It must've been.

"That's kind of you." Ryan reached for his wallet.

"No charge," said Stu, pushing the box forward. "I just want to help. And Ryan, it's good to see you again. Stop by and say hello now that you're back in town."

Ryan took the pizza box. "I'm not sure how long I'll be staying. But it's good to see you. Thanks again for the pizza."

Stu let himself out.

She hurried to the door between the labs. After pushing the door open, she stepped back to let Ryan pass.

"Man, I'm starved." Hal rose from his seat. He moved a stack of papers from the end of a conference table. "You can set the box there. Doc O'Brien keeps plates in his office."

Ryan lifted the lid of the box and fragrant steam filled the room. "I don't need a plate."

"Neither do I." She grabbed a piece from the pie and took a bite. The cheese burned the inside of her mouth, but she didn't care. Everyone ate silently and with relish. It was then she realized that a whole team of people—many of whom she didn't even know—were looking for Morgan. People, like Stu with his pizza, were willing to help the cause.

They all felt as worried and helpless as Kathryn.

Gratitude and guilt swept over her like a gale. She swallowed the final bite. "How long will it take to run a search of the tire imprints?"

Hal lifted another slice of pizza from the box. "Let me check." While chewing on a bite, he returned to the workstation. Using the mouse, he rewoke a monitor. "We're in luck. They were able to identify the tires." He read off the name of a manufacturer. "It looks like they're from an eighteen-inch wheel and haven't been made in the last six years. It also looks like the vehicle is probably a minivan."

Kathryn had driven a minivan when her kids were small. Most of her parent friends had as well. Their popularity had waned, replaced now by small SUVs. But that didn't mean that an older minivan was a rarity. In fact, it was the kind of car that people would look at once and forget they ever saw.

"I can send out an APB on a late model minivan." It wasn't much. What's more, it was going to end up with a lot of inconvenienced drivers and busy law-enforcement officers. Right now, she didn't care. "Any way we can narrow down which types of vehicles, to only look for the one that uses these tires?"

Hal typed in a search. "Looks like they're aftermarket, so they never went on anything new."

"Well, I'll send out the APB anyway." The slice of pizza sat in her gut like a rock. Perhaps eating wasn't such a great idea after all.

"Then again, if that van belongs to Decker, I doubt he's driving it around," said Ryan. "My guess, or what I'd counsel him to do, is to park somewhere that it wouldn't be seen."

He was right. If Decker didn't have the minivan on the street, there'd be no way to identify him by the car. Almost certainly, he was holed up somewhere with Morgan. She choked down a sob. "As a police officer, hearing those insights is invaluable. As a mom," she said and shook her head, "not so much."

"I don't mean to upset you," said Ryan. "But there is some good news."

Unlikely. "What's that?"

"Decker's driven the minivan before. We have images to look through. All we have to do is match the two."

Hal rose from his seat and returned to the table to grab another slice of pizza, "I can add search parameters to the images. The computer can look for us."

"How long will that take?" she pressed.

Hal took a bite and seemed to consider while he chewed. "Not long," he said, speaking around his food. "An hour."

To her, it seemed like an eternity. "Let's assume that we find a possible vehicle for Decker. What then?"

"Then, we figure out what comes next," said Ryan.

His tone was soothing, but his words didn't help her feel any better. Because with each second that passed, her daughter came closer to losing the ultimate game.

During the hour that the computer searched through satellite images, Ryan had taken Old Blue for a walk and purchased a bag of dog food at the gas station across the road. He spent a few minutes visiting with Stu. By the time he returned to the Center, it was after 2:00 p.m.

Less than ten hours remained, and they were no closer to finding Morgan.

For her part, Kathryn had called in the APB. An Amber Alert had also been issued. In less than sixty minutes, over two hundred and seventy-five minivans had been pulled over and searched. So far, none were associated with Morgan's kidnapping.

In the cyber lab, there was a running tally on the computer screen.

Report 96% complete.

Report 97% complete.

Report 100% complete.

Click here to view your report.

"Guys," said Hal, "it's in."

"What does it say?" Kathryn sat in a chair and rolled across the floor to sit next to Hal.

The computer generated a convenient spreadsheet

with a description of the vehicle. The date, time, and place it was picked up by a satellite were listed. There was also a link to the image.

In the week before the kidnapping, a minivan had been picked up by an NSA satellite ninety-five times.

Ryan dropped into a chair. "How do we organize all of this?"

"Hal, you're going to set Ryan and me up with monitors," said Kathryn. "Then, it's just old-fashioned police work. We're all going to look at each of the entries."

"I can do that," said the cyber tech. "What are we looking for?"

"First," said Kathryn, "we find out if the vehicle uses the same size tire. If the tire isn't right, we can dismiss the entry. Then, we look for discrepancies."

"Like what?" Hal asked.

"Like if a car and the license plate don't match. Or if the car is reported as stolen," said Ryan.

Kathryn leaned in to him, knocking her shoulder against his. "You'd be a pretty good cop."

Sure, he had skills. It's just that he'd gained them through dubious means. He gave a quick smile. "I just spent a lot of years avoiding cops is all."

"Kathryn, you take that computer. And Ryan, you go over there." Hal pointed to different workstations as he spoke. "I'm sending everyone the report and the ability to access the DMV's website. When you've checked out an entry, click it. That way, it'll get highlighted as finished."

Ryan rose from his seat and moved to his assigned station. Going through the list of cars was tedious work. After looking at ten entries, he'd found nothing. His neck was sore. His head hurt. And his back was tight. He stood, stretched, and checked the time: 3:17 p.m.

Less than nine hours left.

A sour taste filled his mouth.

"How's everyone doing?"

Kathryn leaned back in her chair and rubbed her eyes. "I've got nothing but…"

"But what?"

"But I can't stop because there's nothing else to do. We know Decker has my daughter. We know what he plans to do to her and when. What we don't know is where she's being held. If we could find his car, then we'd come closer to finding him. Finding them." She cursed. "I've been at this for over an hour, and only cleared nine entries. How 'bout you two?"

"I've gone through nine entries as well," said Hal.

"Ten," said Ryan.

She sighed, "That's not even a third of the list. There's got to be a more efficient way."

He considered her words for a minute. "We all agree that Morgan isn't a random victim. Decker chose her. It means that he was waiting for her at the game. But more than that, he knew she'd be there. How? Easy, he'd been following her all week." His pulse raced, leaving him jittery. "Hal, can you find all of the times that a minivan is near Kathryn's home?"

"Sure can." He typed and the spreadsheet appeared on one of the wall monitors. Seventeen entries were highlighted with a new color.

"Let's go through these together," he suggested. "That way Kathryn can let us know if the vehicle is legit or suspicious."

Kathryn rose from her seat. "Good plan. What have you got for us, Hal?"

The computer tech said, "The first minivan on the list is a blue 2012 van—"

"That belongs to Gladys, my neighbor," said Kathryn, interrupting.

"Are you sure?" Hal asked.

"I'm positive. She rarely drives and leaves her car behind my driveway all the time. I almost hit her side panel twice a week, at least."

Hal marked the entry as checked. "Next one," he said. "On Tuesday, this car that was parked down the street from your house, Undersheriff. The paint is dark gray or faded black."

The image of a darker van appeared on another screen.

Kathryn drew her eyebrows together. "I've never seen that car before. What's the license plate?"

Hal tapped on the computer. "The tags aren't visible in this picture."

"Does that car use the same tires as the tracks we found?" Ryan drew in a deep breath, trying not to get too excited.

Hal's chairs sat on rollers. He wheeled himself to another workstation. He brought up the list of cars that used the same sized tires. "It's a match."

He wanted to smile, but he kept his expression neutral. "You can alter your APB and Amber Alert," he said to Kathryn.

She flicked her fingers toward the screen. "Assuming this is Decker's car, we aren't any closer to finding him or my daughter. If he's hidden the car, no cop will run across him on the road." She paused. "In the end, it won't matter."

Her pain and anguish squeezed his chest, making it hard to breathe. "We'll find her. I swear." Even as he spoke, he knew full well it was a promise he might not be able to keep.

But he knew the killer. He'd personally helped plan dozens of crimes. If he were working with Decker, what would he do? "His comfort zone is the middle of nowhere. Is there any way we can expand the satellite search, say, twenty miles outside of town? But we need to search with purpose. Where else could he hide?"

"You mean another place like the abandoned farmhouse where he was hiding last time," Kathryn suggested.

"Exactly," said Ryan.

"There are a handful of abandoned houses in the county," said Kathryn. "The railroad used to have a line that ran through the northern part of the county. There are some buildings near the depot. But nobody has used those since the railway left the area in the fifties."

"Do you want to get a real-time image? Because if you do, then that's going to require a call to the FBI or the NSA or some other federal agency," said Hal.

Decker wouldn't just leave his car parked outside. "Let's see what we have from Tuesday. That's the same day the minivan was seen parked down the block from Kathryn's house. If it was Decker, he drove to and from somewhere."

"There's a farm off the interstate," said Kathryn. "The family moved out about five years ago." She gave Hal an address.

After a moment, he found the correct coordinates for the images. A dilapidated home, surrounded by crumbling outbuildings, filled the screen.

Kathryn sighed. "The property was flooded about three years ago." She bit her bottom lip. "There's another farm near that one." She pointed to the screen. "But there was a fire. The family took the insurance money and left. I'm not sure what's there beyond the foundation."

"We won't worry about looking at that property right now." Ryan was intrigued by what she'd said about an old railroad. He bet that Decker would be interested, too. "Can you bring up an image for the depot?"

The cyber tech typed on the keyboard, and after a few clicks, the image changed to an aerial view of three buildings in the middle of the desert. Weeds grew around the train tracks. Surprisingly, the metal structures still stood. Yet, there was no evidence that anyone was using the property now—nor that anyone had been there in years.

Disappointment burned in his chest. He'd been so sure. "Is this the only satellite image the NSA sent?"

"Let me see." Hal typed some more. "I have two more. The first one was taken on Friday morning, and the other is from a week ago, Sunday at four in the morning."

The two images replaced the first, splitting the screen down the middle.

To Ryan, there was no difference between the images, save for the direction of the sun. But the one taken in the early hours of Sunday was different. The area was dark, the buildings nothing more than outlines in the night.

He tried to recall where he was at 4:00 a.m. on Sunday. It didn't take long for the memories to surface. He'd just brought Kathryn home from the hospital. She was sleeping. He and Old Blue were on guard.

On the other hand, Decker had stolen several cars throughout the night. The last stolen car had been found by four. But if Decker was staying at the old depot, would he have made it back?

He looked back at the screen. Was there a clue in the photo?

"Just show us the night image," he said.

The large screen was filled with the murky picture.

"What're you looking for?" Kathryn asked.

"I'm not sure." He scanned the picture, inch by inch. "There." He pointed. His pulse jumped. "A light's coming from the largest building."

"Where?" Rising from her seat, Kathryn stood at his side. "I don't see anything."

"Look at the left side of the building, on the ground."

Everyone went quiet as they looked for what he saw.

"I guess." Hal's tone made it clear. The computer tech was unconvinced. "But all these buildings are made of metal. It could be a reflection from the moon."

Kathryn shook her head. "There was no moon that night. Saturday night we had the big storm. The clouds didn't clear until after sunrise." She swallowed and looked at Ryan. "I have to go and check out the old depot. Are you coming?"

He was going with her. Turning to Hal, he asked, "Can Old Blue hang out with you?"

"Your dog can stay here as long as you need." Hal's voice quavered. "But are you sure this is a good idea?"

She said, "I'm not sitting around and waiting." Her eyes were moist. She shook her head. "I'm not waiting when I could be doing something to save my daughter."

Ryan had to remember that Kathryn wasn't just the undersheriff but also a scared mom. The way she'd held it together was admirable.

"Are you coming?" She pinned him with her stare.

"You know I'd follow you anywhere," he said, his tone light-hearted even though his words were deadly serious. "Even to the gates of hell."

She nodded once and walked to the door. Following her, he realized how apt his sentiment had been. Decker was as close as anyone was to being the devil. That meant his lair could be nothing other than a fiery pit of damnation.

Chapter 19

The adage *You can't get there from here* was true of the old depot. During the Second World War, the railroad had built a spur near Encantador for transporting cattle to the Fort Worth stockyard and then on to feed the troops. After the war, the depot and tracks were abandoned. As was the infrastructure that served the site.

Yet, Kathryn knew where the road leading to the depot was. Correction. She *basically* knew where the road had been laid. Gripping the steering wheel, she stared out the side window. "It's around here somewhere," she said, half speaking to Ryan, half talking to herself.

"We might have an easier time getting out of the car to look," Ryan suggested.

He had a point. She pulled onto the shoulder, parked, and slipped the keys into the breast pocket of her uniform. Ryan had already stepped from the car. He stared out across the horizon.

Low clouds filled the sky and promised another storm. So far, the fat gray rain clouds had only trapped the heat closer to the ground.

"See anything?" she asked, coming to stand at his side.

"Maybe." He pointed into the scrub. "What's that?"

It took her a minute to find the spot. There was a path where the weeds didn't grow as high. "It might be a road. Let's check it out."

Together, they trudged over the rocky ground. Kneeling, Ryan picked up a flat rock. To her, it was unremarkable—just a stone covered in red dust.

"Asphalt," he said, breaking a piece from the edge. The inside was black tar and smaller stones.

How had she missed that clue? "We should get the car," she said.

Ryan didn't move. "How far out is the depot?"

Kathryn shrugged. "Less than two miles."

"We should go on foot." He turned to her. "Decker won't hear us coming. Then, what happened before won't happen again."

She touched the wound in her side. After Morgan was kidnapped, she'd forgotten all about being stabbed. "I've got water and binoculars in my trunk. Plus a little extra."

Turning, she walked back to her cruiser. The pull to find her daughter was strong. But she was going to be prepared this time. The first thing she did was place a call to Hal. He'd been coordinating all the other arms of law enforcement. "We've found the road," she told him. "We're going to walk. I'll be in touch if we find anything."

"And remind him to feed Old Blue," Ryan called out.

"Tell Ryan that he has already been fed, walked, and is perfectly happy," said Hal before she could relay the message.

"Will do." She ended the call.

"What'd he say?" Ryan asked.

"Old Blue is fine," she reassured him. Using the key fob, she unlatched all the locks. She opened the trunk and pulled out a prepacked bag. She unzipped the main compartment and checked the contents. Binoculars. Matches. A first-aid kit. Four quarts of water. A box of extra ammo for her gun. After rezipping the backpack, she slipped her arms into shoulder straps and tightened the sternum strap across her chest.

"I can carry that, you know." He added quickly, "And it's not a sexist thing. I'm trying to be considerate. You're still healing from a stab wound."

"I've got the bag because there's something else that I want you to carry." She took the key ring from her pocket and found the correct key. Lying in the bottom of the trunk was a long metal box. She unlocked it and lifted the lid.

"Whoa," said Ryan as he caught a glimpse of the Benelli M4 Super 90. It was the same weapon used by Navy SEALs. "That's quite a gun."

"Have you ever fired one before?"

"Not that exact type."

"Do you think you can?"

He shrugged.

"Then, it's yours."

Ryan lifted the gun from the case. Also tucked into the foam were four shells. He slid them into the stock, before pulling back on the slide to rack them all. "If we run into Decker, I'll be ready."

"Good. Let's go."

The broken road was easy to follow. A breeze began to blow, making the trek into the desert less oppressive. The sun stayed behind the clouds, but in the distance, she could see a wink of glass. "I think the depot's just ahead."

"You got those binoculars?" Ryan asked.

"Sure do." After dropping the backpack to the ground, she opened the main compartment. First thing, she handed Ryan a bottle of water. She also took one for herself and opened the cap. Neither one would be able to save Morgan if they suffered from heatstroke. "Stay hydrated."

He finished half in one swallow. "Thanks. I needed that."

She drank all the water in her bottle and stowed the empty in her bag. Then, she found the binoculars. Looking through the eye cups, she found the old depot. The buildings came into focus. The larger building of the three stood in the middle. It was surrounded by broken pavement, and a tree had the temerity to break through the blacktop and grow.

Certainly, there were no signs of life. She handed Ryan the binoculars. "I don't see anything, but you can take a look."

He raised the ocular lenses to his eyes and studied the scene. "I say we keep going. It's less than a quarter mile away."

The clock was ticking; she could feel each lost second as a beat of her heart. If Morgan wasn't being held in the old cattle warehouse, hiking there and back would be a waste of time. But what if she was? She'd never be able to live with herself, knowing that she'd been close but had turned around.

"Okay, let's go," she said.

She and Ryan walked without speaking. The wind blew, drying the sweat from the back of her neck. The only sounds were the wind and the crunch of their footfalls on the broken road.

Coming to a halt, Ryan whispered, "Do you hear that?"

She stood without moving or breathing. "All I hear is the breeze."

"It sounds like humming."

She strained to listen. "I don't..." Her words faded as she realized that a whir mixed with the wind. "What's making that noise?"

"I think it's a generator."

He was right. It was the sound of a far-off engine. Her heart skipped a beat. "We've found the son of a bitch." The wound at her side ached, a reminder of past mistakes. Well, this time she'd handle things differently. This time, when she called for backup, Kathryn would wait for help to arrive. Pulling the cell from her pocket, she opened the phone app. There were no bars.

"Damn. I don't have a signal." She turned to Ryan. "What about you?"

He glanced at his own device. "Nada. Let's head back and make a call as soon as we get coverage."

Kathryn took one step and stopped. She'd seen something. But what?

She turned and scanned the ground. Then, she found what had caught her eye.

"Ryan," she said, choking out his name, "look." She pointed with a shaking finger at what she'd found.

Hidden at the base of a rock was a small camera. The Record light glowed green. There was no way they could return to the car or even wait for backup. "If we want to save Morgan, we have to go now."

There were few mementos Decker felt were valuable enough to keep. But a metal lighter that belonged to his grandfather was one. If family lore was to be believed, his grandpa had taken the lighter from an enemy combatant during a battle in Southeast Asia. The silver case bore the scars of time and war. Decker's grandfather had passed the lighter on to Decker's dad. Then, the lighter became his on the day his father went to jail for killing a teller during a bank robbery.

For the first time, he considered passing the light on to the next generation. If Seraphim was telling the truth and Seth was actually his son, that is.

Lying on the bed, he turned the spark wheel. A small fire sprang to life. Watching the dancing flame, he was transfixed. He released the fork lever, and the fire died.

Morgan still lay on the floor. She no longer sobbed. He wondered if she'd fallen asleep. He glanced in her direction. Her eyes were open, her gaze glassy.

He checked the time.

It was 5:47 p.m. Only six hours and change left.

The computer pinged with an incoming message.

After tucking the lighter into his pocket, he rolled off the cot. As he crossed the room, he could feel Morgan's eyes on him. He sat at the desk and jiggled the mouse to wake the monitor. As he expected, Seraphim had sent an encrypted link. After clicking on it, he entered the password.

The plague-doctor beak appeared. But the eyes behind the mask were wild. "You've been found," the hacker squawked.

He sat up straight. "By who?"

"The undersheriff and your former friend."

A million thoughts swarmed his mind. He wanted to know how they'd found him. And if he was surrounded. He'd never give up. But what was he supposed to do with Morgan? "Are you sure?"

"I just got an alert from one of the perimeter cameras. This is what it recorded."

The image on his monitor changed. The plague doctor was gone. In its place was a grainy recording of two people. Ryan lifted the camera from the ground. He stared into the lens. There was no sound, but his lips moved. Then, the video became a jumble of images. Sky. Rocks. Dirt.

Ryan had obviously thrown the camera. It crashed into the ground, and the screen went black.

Seraphim reappeared on the monitor. "I've been able to do an aerial search. There's only two of them. They're on foot. Backup hasn't been called."

In the corner, Morgan started to struggle against her bonds. Certainly, she'd heard that her mom was close. She screamed into the gag. Decker looked back at the computer. A new plan was already forming. "Start the live feed."

"It's not midnight yet," said Seraphim. "If you kill the girl now, you won't be following the dates of the Autumn of Terror."

"Who cares about that?" After tonight, nobody would remember Jack the Ripper: Decker Newcombe alone would be the most famous killer in the world. He didn't have long before Ryan and the undersheriff would be at his door. Morgan had to be dead before they arrived. Then, the real performance would begin. "Give me two minutes to set up the camera and the light."

Seraphim said nothing.

"You know I'm right. This is the only way."

They exhaled. "You'll be live in two minutes."

Decker moved quickly, collecting everything he needed. The chair. His knife. He unplugged the camera from the charger. Then, he grabbed the ring light on a stand. But even as he created his set, he still saw Ryan's face as he looked into the camera. True, the video hadn't come with sound. But it'd been easy to read the other man's lips.

"I'm coming for you, you bastard. This time, you won't get away."

From fifty yards out, the setup was obvious to Ryan. The generator was stored in one of the two smaller buildings. A long brown cord ran to the building that had once been the cattle warehouse and stockyard. A large bay door had rusted in spots, and light shone through the chinks in the metal. A satellite dish was hung under one of the eaves.

Ryan knelt behind a large rock. Kathryn was at his side. He could feel the pull of a mother to save her child. "I want to rush in there and grab Morgan and hold her to me," she said, her voice a whisper. "But I won't. Please tell me you have a plan."

"Decker plans to kill Morgan on the internet."

Kathryn squeezed her eyes shut, as if trying to block out the horrible truth. "I know."

"What if we stopped him from broadcasting?" It'd be only a temporary distraction, but it might be enough to save Morgan. "You turn off that generator, and his power supply is gone. I'll go in through the bay door and introduce him to this." He lifted his M4. "Then you'll come around from the back."

"Will it work?" She looked at him. There was so much hope and trust in her gaze that his chest ached.

Her question echoed in his soul.

Would his plan work? There was a lot that could go wrong. Hell, he didn't even know if Morgan was still alive. Or if Decker was still in the warehouse.

Holding the gun with one hand, he stroked her cheek. "It will work." He paused a beat. "You ready?"

She nodded once. "I am."

He started to stand.

Gripping his arm, she pulled him down at her side. "I—" Kathryn placed her lips on his, the kiss frantic, then broke from the embrace "—I'll see you on the other side." She sprinted toward the outbuilding and disappeared inside.

Moving as quickly and quietly as possible, he ran to the side of the warehouse. Pressing his back into the wall, he sidestepped to the large bay door. After years of weather and neglect, the door and wall no longer met. Peering through the seam, he could see only a sliver of the room. Yet, he'd witnessed enough for his blood to turn cold.

Sweat dripped down Decker's back, and his breathing came in short gasps. It had been a struggle to place Morgan in the chair. Despite the fact that she was tied up, she'd fought him at every step.

The light shone on her red and tear-stained face. The camera was on. Everything was being streamed online.

Turning, he faced the camera. "I know y'all were expecting to see this later tonight. But sometimes plans change. This is one of those times." He held his hunting knife. Using the blade to point to Morgan, he continued. "I'd also planned on giving you more of a show with her. But she got lucky and gets to die quick. Don't you turn off your computer when I'm done with her. After is when the real fun will start."

One quick flick of the blade across her throat and Morgan would be no more. He stood behind the chair and gripped her chin in one hand. She thrashed in the seat, sending the chair toppling to the side.

"Damn it," he growled.

After righting the chair, he pulled Morgan's hair until her head was pinned to the back of the seat. Holding the knife in front of her eye, he asked, "How much pain do you want?"

Then there was a pop. The overhead lights went dark. The ring light was no longer on. *What the hell?*

The bay door rolled upward. A wedge of light spilled across the floor. A man's shadow stretched into the warehouse, and Decker didn't need to see a face to know who it was. "Ryan."

"Let her go," said Ryan.

"You know I'm not going to do that." He pressed the knife into the soft flesh under her chin. The skin opened and wept blood. There was a boom and a flash of light. The scent of gunpowder filled the room. The gunshot had punched a hole through the ceiling. A circle of daylight shone on the floor. With the stock tucked into his shoulder, Ryan stared down the barrel of a shotgun. "Take that as a warning. Don't move or the next round goes through you."

He didn't doubt Ryan's sincerity. It's just that the old Ryan would've blown a hole through Decker's middle already. His old compatriot really had changed. Lifting his hands, he feigned surrender.

Holding the shotgun with one hand, Ryan kept the weapon pointed in Decker's direction. With the other hand, he worked on the knots that bound Morgan to the chair.

Decker knew this was the best chance. He lunged forward and reached for the gun, making it impossible for Ryan to aim. Sure, he was strong—but Ryan was stronger. He wrenched the gun away. Then, Ryan brought barrel down on his skull, holding the gun with both hands. The pain was blinding and the blow knocked Decker off his feet.

Before he could pull the trigger, Decker scrambled to his hands and knees. It was all about survival. Pushing past the roaring pain in his head, he ran for the door that led to the dark corners of the warehouse.

* * *

Once Kathryn turned off the generator, she ran from the outbuilding to the warehouse. The report of gunfire exploded in the silence. All at once, she thought of every bad thing that might've happened. Her eyes stung. She blinked hard, refusing to cry. Drawing her own weapon, she sprinted the rest of the way. The bay door was open, and she looked inside.

A bloodstain covered the floor. Morgan was tied to a chair. Ryan stood behind her daughter and worked at the knots.

Blood ran down her daughter's neck.

"Oh my God, what happened? Is she all right?" Morgan met her mother's eyes.

She holstered her gun and ran to Morgan's side.

"Decker cut her, but the wound's not deep," said Ryan.

Pulling the gag from her mouth, she kissed her daughter's cheek. "I can't believe we found you." Until that moment, she hadn't admitted the truth to herself: she hadn't believed the story would have a happy ending.

"Mom, I'm so happy to see you! I thought…" she swallowed as tears gathered in her lashes "…I thought I'd never see you again."

"We're here now, and you're safe. That's all that matters," she said to Morgan. Then to Ryan, she asked, "Where is he?"

Raising his chin toward the back of the warehouse, he said, "There, somewhere."

Through the open door, she could make out stalls and pens that at one time had been used to hold cattle. Machinery—a tractor missing a wheel, a sharp-edged tiller, and who knew what else—had also been stored in the warehouse and forgotten.

"I'm going after him," he said.

"No way." Her heart slammed into her chest. "Come with me. We found Morgan. We can get out of here, the three of us, together."

"How long do you think it'll take for Decker to disappear? But he won't be gone forever. He'll come back." He shook his head. "I have to stop him."

She couldn't imagine leaving without Ryan at her side. "No."

"Once she's free, you both get out of here," he said. "Head back to the car, and call for backup."

"I'm not leaving you."

Placing a fierce kiss on her lips, he stopped whatever else she had to say. "Just go."

Standing taller, he walked into the shadows. For a moment, she could make out his outline in the darkness, and then even that was gone. Working on the knot that held Morgan to the chair, she feared she had just seen Ryan for the last time.

Chapter 20

Decker stumbled through the darkness. His head throbbed with each beat of his heart. Somehow, he'd made it into a narrow corridor. On his right, oil drums had been stacked into a wall. On his left was a long line of enclosures, meant to hold a cow or two. His vision was blurry. He tried to focus on something. But what? He heard footsteps coming up from behind. Ducking into a stall, he crouched in the corner.

In the dim light, he watched Ryan as he passed. His gait was slow. He held the gun with both hands across his body. Then, he stopped and took a step back.

Touching a wooden beam, Ryan examined his fingers. Brows drawn, he searched the darkness. His gaze never landed on Decker. After wiping his fingers on his jeans, he walked on.

His best guess was that Ryan had found his blood.

Must've been that he brushed against the post, while staggering into the pen. It also meant he was leaving a blood trail—one that was easy for Ryan to follow.

If Decker wanted to get away, he had to staunch his wound. He sat for a moment and then scanned his surroundings. An old blanket lay in the corner. He picked it up. Rodent droppings and dust scattered into the stale air. The fabric was filthy and threadbare. But he didn't have any other choices. He pressed the cloth onto his scalp. A bolt of pain shot all the way from his skull to his toes.

The taste of rot coated his tongue. He swallowed down the urge to vomit and instead quietly spit onto the ground. He focused on his breath and after a moment, the pain lessened enough that he could think.

Ryan's arrival had ruined everything.

Had he really been smacked down during a livestream? Well, he hadn't done himself any favors by running away. He could only imagine the memes.

Grinding his teeth, Decker knew there was only one path to redemption. And that it ended with Ryan in a grave.

Kathryn dropped her backpack to the floor. The only light in the warehouse came in through the open bay door and the hole in the ceiling. It wasn't much, but a little was all she needed. After unzipping the top, she searched for her emergency knife. She cut the rope holding Morgan onto the chair. Without the bonds, her daughter slumped to the floor.

"Crap. That hurt," Morgan said.

"I'm so sorry."

"Just get me out of here." She could hear the panic rising in her daughter's voice.

Morgan's anxiety left her own pulse racing.

She didn't know where Decker had gone or if he'd come back. She had to get her daughter out of the warehouse and to safety. Nothing else mattered. Yet, she realized that Ryan mattered to her as well.

Slipping her shoulder under her daughter's arm, she pulled Morgan to her feet.

"Mom," she cried, "I can't walk."

"Are you hurt?" A protective fury filled her veins. "What did he do to you?"

Morgan was heavy in her arms. "He didn't do anything to me, but my legs won't work."

"You've lost feeling from being tied up for so long. But I've got you."

Blood still seeped from the wound under her daughter's chin. "Let me see that cut."

Morgan lifted her chin and grimaced.

Ryan had been right—the wound wasn't deep. But still she needed care. Setting Morgan on the ground, Kathryn looked in her backpack. She found a large bandage. After placing the sterile pad over the cut, she pressed the adhesive into place.

"Better?" She slid her shoulder under Morgan's arm. After lifting both her child and the backpack, they hobbled to the door.

Outside, the sky was dark as dusk. Dirt and bits of gravel skittered along the ground, blown by the wind. They were far from safe, but at least Kathryn could breathe. She reached into her backpack and found some water. "Here," she said handing the bottle to her daughter. "Drink this."

Morgan took the drink and clumsily opened the lid. Lifting it to her lips, she swallowed half the water. The rest washed over her shirt. "Thanks," she said, gasping.

Kathryn wanted to hold her daughter forever and ever. But she knew that if Morgan could stand on her own, it'd be best. Not only could they move faster but she'd be able to keep her weapon out and at the ready.

With one hand on her daughter's side, she stepped away. Morgan swayed and started to fall. Diving forward, she caught her daughter before she hit the ground. There was no way they could make it back to the road on foot.

Kathryn turned and looked at the warehouse. The bay door was open in a silent scream. Ryan was in there, somewhere. He could carry Morgan. But waiting left them both exposed.

Right now, she needed to think like a cop.

"What do you remember of your kidnapping?" she asked her daughter. "Do you recall the car Decker used to bring you here?"

"I was pretty terrified so everything's a blur." Morgan's eyes filled with tears. "But it was a dark-colored minivan."

So the search had turned up the correct vehicle. "Where is it now?"

Morgan shook her head. "I don't know."

The car hadn't been parked in the outbuilding with the generator. She hadn't seen it in the warehouse, either. That left them with one building to search. "Come with me," she said.

Even with Kathryn's arm under her shoulder, Morgan stumbled as she tried to walk. Finally, they made their way to the last building. The door was off its hinges, but inside was what she'd hoped to find. The car. The driver's-side door was unlocked. She pulled it open. "Get inside." She ushered Morgan into the vehicle. "Do you see any keys?"

Morgan flipped both visors open. Nothing. The cup holders and console were both empty. There was nothing in the glove box.

It was too much to hope that Decker would have left the keys in the vehicle. "Did you ever see a set of keys?"

Morgan shook her head. "Never."

Decker might have the keys with him. But if he didn't, they must be back in the warehouse. She knew what she had to do next, and her mouth went dry.

"I want you to stay in this car," she ordered. "Keep the doors locked. Even if Decker shows up and he has the key, you don't let him in. If you see him at all, use the horn. I'll come running."

"I can't be by myself again." Morgan gulped down a sob. "I don't want you to go."

Her chest ached. Pulling her daughter in for a tight hug, she whispered into her hair, "I know I'm asking a lot of you. But I need you to keep being brave. Can you do that?"

She blew out a breath. "I can."

After shoving the backpack into Morgan's chest, she said, "Keep this with you. There's more water. Drink it."

"Mom." Morgan's tone stopped her. "I love you. Be safe."

"I love you, too." Kathryn slammed the car door shut. "Lock these doors."

Morgan obeyed. With a click, she engaged the automatic lock.

Kathryn drew her firearm. With a final glance at her daughter, she ran toward the warehouse. Each footfall brought her closer to the unknown and her heartbeat thundered. She wondered about Ryan. She also wondered about Decker. If the killer was still alive, she'd be walking into an ambush. It didn't matter—she had to go back.

Walking through the warehouse, Ryan searched for the blood trail he'd been following. Somehow, somewhere, in the darkness, he'd lost the path.

The last time he'd seen a trace of blood had been near the pens. Turning, he retraced his steps. He found the stall. A smear of blood still stained the wood. He stepped inside. With his eyes adjusted to the darkness, he could clearly see drops of blood on the floor.

So Decker had been here. But where had he gone?

He had to find Newcombe before he escaped again. Or, worse yet, caught up with Kathryn and her daughter. Backing out of the pen, he inhaled deeply. The stench of old motor grease hung in the air.

From above came a metallic screech. Ryan only had a moment to look up. An oil drum somersaulted down. The metal rim hit his back, knocking him over. He only had a second to curl into a ball before the next container landed on top of him.

A thick liquid oozed over his shoulders. The stench burned his eyes and his lungs with each breath. The oil drums rolled to the side, clanging against each other as they came to rest. Eyes watering, he looked up.

Decker stood just a few feet away. "I may be destined for hell. But I'm sending you there first."

He held a metal lighter. Using his thumb, he rolled the spark wheel. Ryan didn't have time to think—only to react. Using the butt-end of his shotgun, he swung out with his weapon. The comb caught Decker's ankles. The momentum swept him off his feet.

The killer landed on his back at the same moment a flame caught on the lighter. The fire spread along the ground. Scrambling to stand, Ryan jumped back before the flames could ignite his clothes or hair. Aiming his gun, Ryan pulled the trigger. Then, everything happened in slow motion.

There was a boom. A flash of fire erupted from the muzzle. The stock slammed into his chest as the stench of gunpowder rolled toward the ceiling.

But Decker had been ready. The killer charged forward. He reached for the barrel, pulling it to the side. He screamed as the hot muzzle burned his palm. The shot scattered, punching holes into a stack of old oil drums. Sludge began to slide down the sides and pool onto the ground.

Decker still held onto the gun. Ryan kicked out, aiming for his chin. He missed, but his boot connected with the killer's shoulder. It knocked him down. Scrambling to his knees, Ryan rose to his feet.

Decker lay on his back. Flames danced along the ground.

Before the killer could lift his palms in surrender, Ryan pulled the trigger.

Click.

Damnit. The gun had jammed. Decker smiled and dove forward, reaching for Ryan's leg. Flipping the gun around, Ryan shoved the firearm down, hitting Decker in the head with the butt-end of the gun. The blow left the killer dazed. Ryan would have reveled in his success. But that's when the first flames caught the leg of his pants and started to climb.

Kathryn found the car keys on the desk. She gripped the ring tight in her palm, the metal teeth of the keys biting her flesh. She sprinted for the door. A single blast of gunfire erupted from the darkness.

She froze as her breath caught in her chest.

She didn't know who'd fired the gun. Or who'd been the target.

Could she really leave without Ryan?

Her stomach twisted into a knot. But she shoved the keys deep into her pocket. At least now Decker wouldn't be able to unlock the minivan doors. Weapon in hand, she rushed toward the sound of the gunfire.

Smoke hung in the air. It burned her eyes and her lungs. What had caught on fire?

"Ryan?" While yelling out made her an easy target, she had to find him. "Ryan! Can you hear me?"

He didn't answer. Using her sleeve to shield her nose and mouth, she ventured farther into the warehouse. Flames danced along the floor. The railing of an old indoor corral was alight. Sparks rose in the air. She took a step. Then another. And another. A wave of heat crashed down on her. She looked up: flames raced along the ceiling.

She couldn't stay in the building much longer. But she couldn't leave without him, either.

"Ryan!" she called out. "Where are you?"

An oil drum rolled along the floor.

She turned and that's when she saw them. In the middle of the inferno were Decker and Ryan. Both men were on their feet. Ryan's pants smoldered, and blisters covered his arms. Swinging out, the killer struck Ryan on the cheek. She felt his pain as her own. Despite the waves of heat that obscured her vision, she could see the determination in each man's eyes. And she knew this was going to be a fight to the death.

Ryan refused to lose. Gripping the butt-end, he lifted his weapon high. He brought down the firearm at the same moment that Decker charged.

The killer grabbed him around the middle and the two tumbled back. The gun skittered from his grip. Decker slammed his fist into Ryan's face. He shook off the blow and reached for the other man's wrist. He squeezed hard.

Decker screamed and reeled back.

Flames were everywhere. If Ryan wanted to escape, he had to go now. Otherwise, he'd be trapped in the inferno. But what kind of life would he lead if he let Decker get away again? He couldn't let the killer go free and hurt someone else that he loved. Kathryn's face flashed in his mind.

Then he saw her. For a split second, he thought she was a mirage in the blaze.

Kathryn stood only yards away. What the hell was

she doing? He wanted her to be safe. Not in this burning building with him.

He'd turned his attention to her for only a moment, but a moment was all it took. Decker scrambled to the gun. He brought the barrel up. It caught Ryan under the chin, and the blow knocked him off his feet.

Shaking his head, Ryan tried to stand. Decker slammed the butt into his back. It knocked him to the ground. Decker hit him again. And again. His side filled with a searing pain, and one of his ribs snapped. Rolling to his back, Ryan looked up.

Standing over him, Decker held the gun above his head. The hems of his pants had caught fire. He didn't seem to notice the flames. He sneered, "Looks like I was right. We are going to die, but you're going to hell first."

Tensing, he braced for the blow.

Kathryn couldn't let Decker shoot Ryan. But she couldn't risk causing an explosion by firing her own gun, either. Rushing through the flames, she brought her firearm down on the back of the killer's head. He dropped to his knees, then fell, face first to the ground.

Later, she'd wrestle with any emotions that might arise for attacking a man from the back. For now, she had to get Ryan and then get out.

Dodging the flames, she ran to Ryan. "Come with me." She slipped her arm behind his back. The stab wound to her side pulled and she sucked in a quick breath. Ignoring all pain aside, she said, "We have to get out of here while we can."

He sat up and cursed. "I think my ribs are broken."

She'd heard the crack. He might be right. "Let's get you out of here."

He stood slowly and took a step. Then, he stopped. "We can't leave him."

Oh yes, they could. For all his sins, Decker deserved to burn. "He kidnapped my daughter. I can't even count the number of people he's killed."

"Somewhere I heard that good people help—no matter what," he said, giving her a wan smile.

At least he had his sense of humor. Then again, she knew he was right. "I hate to have my words quoted back at me."

The path between the flames was narrower than before. But Decker was easy to reach. He lay on the floor, unconscious and surrounded by a pool of blood. She tried to find some sympathy for the man. It was impossible. "Help me get him to his feet."

Ryan grimaced as he bent down to lift Decker's head and neck. They hefted him to his feet. Yet, there was one more thing for her to do. She jammed her gun into Decker's side. "If he so much as twitches," she said, "I'm going to blow a hole in his side."

Decker's head hung forward. She wasn't sure if he'd heard her or not.

They made their way toward the door. Once outside, she exhaled sharply. "Drop him here."

She let Decker slip from her arms. Ryan dropped him as well. He landed on the ground in a heap. She held out her gun to Ryan. He took the firearm. His fingers grazed the back of her hand. An electric charge danced along her skin. She wondered if she'd always be excited by his touch. Lord, she hoped so.

She said, "You watch him. I'm going to get Morgan and the car."

"What's that?" He pointed toward the broken road.

A cloud of dust rose on the horizon. She stared for a moment. Then, she could see red and blue lights in the haze. Her knees went weak with relief. "That's backup. I wonder how they knew."

"Must be that Hal saw the livestream and told them where we were."

He was probably right, but really, it didn't matter. She placed a kiss on Ryan's cheek. "I need to get my girl."

After running to the outbuilding, she got her daughter from her hiding place in the minivan. An explosion came from the warehouse. The ground shook and flames shot out of the open door. Oily smoke wafted into the air. It mixed with the dust until the air was filled with noxious fog. Breathing hurt. Her eyes watered. But at least it was over.

Decker wouldn't get away this time.

Her daughter would get the care—both physical and emotional—she would need to heal.

That left Kathryn with one important question. What was next for her and Ryan?

Three state police officers led the caravan of law enforcement. They parked their cars around Decker's prone form.

One of the troopers placed the killer in handcuffs. "There's an ambulance on the way," he said. "Does anyone else need care?"

They should all be seen by a medical professional. "Ryan has burns, and my daughter's having trouble walking. There's a cut under her chin, too," she added, although the trooper could see the bandage.

Ryan said to Kathryn, "Make sure Morgan gets seen first. I'll be okay."

The ambulance stopped. One of the troopers helped Morgan to the waiting EMTs.

"You should go with your daughter," he said.

"I will. But first I want to make sure you're okay." She took his hand in hers. Turning his palm up, she gently traced his raw skin. "Does it hurt?"

"Not when you touch me."

She smiled. "What happens now?"

"I thought you'd be the expert in that. I assume Decker will be charged with a ton of crimes. Then, there will be a trial. But he'll go to jail for the rest of his life." He paused. "Right?"

His assessment was correct. "That's not what I'm asking. What's next with you?"

After pulling her to him, Ryan wrapped his arms around her waist. "That depends, Undersheriff. Are you telling me again to leave town?" He gave her a grin, and she knew he was teasing.

"I'd like you to stay." He was now employed by Texas Law. More than once, Ryan had proved he was a man who had changed. And wasn't it change she was looking for as well? Who knew what the future might hold for them? "We can start with right now and see what the next chapter holds."

Ryan placed his lips on hers. Despite the chaos, they were the only two people in the world. "I'll start with having you for now. But don't be surprised if we find our own happily ever after."

Epilogue

Two weeks later

It was Sunday evening, and the shadows were starting to lengthen as Ryan parked his truck next to the curb. He turned off the ignition. Old Blue sat in the passenger seat and looked out the window, his tail thumping like a bass drum. He knew how the dog felt, just seeing Kathryn's house surrounded him in a halo of warmth. He supposed it was happiness.

Yet, the latest report buzzed through his system like a caffeine high. He'd thought about texting Kathryn with the news but had decided to tell her in person.

In the two weeks since Morgan was kidnapped and Decker was arrested, a lot had happened in his life. First, he'd spent several days recuperating from a broken rib and a concussion. Kathryn had invited him to stay with her—an invitation he'd accepted. His presence in the home meant that Brock had to give up his room and sleep on the sofa, so Ryan had stayed only as long as necessary.

He'd used the recovery time to find a place to live. Turned out that Mae owned the whole building where her restaurant was located. The floors above Over Easy had been renovated to apartments and Ryan was able to rent one that was fully furnished. For now, it suited his needs. And in the morning, he'd start his new job as an operative for Texas Law.

Opening the door, he got out slowly from the truck and stepped to the pavement. Old Blue followed.

Across the street, Gladys sat on her porch. "Nice night," she called out.

He waved to the woman. "It definitely is."

"Enjoy your evening. Smells like there's chicken on the grill."

She was right—the scent of spices and smoke hung in the air. "How's the light above your sink? Is it still working?" He'd done more than just rest and find an apartment over the last two weeks. He'd also helped Gladys with some work around her house. Brock had helped. The kid enjoyed learning about home maintenance.

"The light's perfect, as is the sink in the bathroom, and the pictures you hung. Thank you."

He waved as he started up the walk. "Happy to help. You have my number if you need anything else."

"That's a dangerous offer to make. My driveway needs to be resealed."

He laughed, hoping she was joking. Although, in

truth, he'd reseal her driveway if that was what she needed. He might have a job now, but he'd discovered that he liked being useful. He liked being of help to people.

It helped make up for the past. For the unforgivable things he'd done.

The front door opened as he approached. Morgan stood on the threshold. "I heard you yelling down the street."

"Hello to you, too," he said. "How was your weekend?"

Morgan had gone to San Antonio to see Elliot, who was getting PT after the Decker Newcombe attack. She leaned over and scratched Old Blue behind the ears. "Elliot's ready to come home. His doctor says he should be released by next weekend."

He nodded. "Sounds like good news."

"It is. We're both lucky to be alive." She paused. "All of us are lucky, really."

"How're you?"

She snorted. "I wasn't even hurt." The cut to her chin had turned into a red line. She touched the scar. "Not unless you count this."

"Not all injuries can be seen, you know."

"Yeah, that's what my therapist says. But they don't really know what it's like to survive Decker, do they?"

She was right. "Still, talking will help." He paused. "You know, your mom has some experience with Decker. Me, too. You can talk with me anytime."

Folding her arms tight across her chest, Morgan pressed her lips together. Damn. He'd said the wrong thing. Talking to Morgan was the equivalent of walking through a minefield. He'd gotten too confident and had accidentally stumbled onto a land mine.

Sighing, she let her arms drop to her sides. "Maybe."

Maybe? He'd take that as a win.

"Mom and Brock are outside. You can hang out with them. I'm making my world-famous brownies."

"World-famous? That sounds pretty good."

"It is." Morgan slapped her thigh, trying to call Old Blue to her. "Who's a good boy? You want to come into the kitchen with me?"

Old Blue trotted over to Morgan.

Ryan grinned. "It's nice of you to notice that I'm a good boy, but I should really go and see your mom first."

"Not funny," she said. "I was talking to the dog."

"Be honest, it was a little funny."

Without turning around, she held up her thumb and forefinger, measuring a small space.

Yeah, he'd definitely take that as a win.

On the back patio, Brock was at the grill. Kathryn was sitting at the table, sipping a glass of lemonade. She looked up and smiled as he stepped out of the house. "There you are." She held out her hand to him. "I was starting to wonder when you'd get here."

He laced his fingers through hers. They fit together perfectly. "I had to take a call." He'd wait until they were alone to discuss what was said. To Brock, he said, "The chicken smells good."

"Thanks. I need lots of protein to keep playing QB." He looked past Ryan. "Where's your dog?"

"Old Blue is learning how to make the best brownies in the world."

"Morgan really likes having the dog around," Kathryn said. She filled a glass with lemonade and handed it to Ryan. "She might even be warming up to you, too."

"That'd be nice." He took the glass before sitting down.

"So, you start your job tomorrow…" Kathryn began.

"I do. Me and Old Blue will open the Mercy branch of Texas Law."

"I'm glad you'll be around. You'll get to see the whole football season," Brock said while turning off the grill. "The chicken's done. I need to get a clean platter. Be right back."

Ryan waited until the kid was inside before speaking. "About that call. Isaac told me Decker's going to be transported." Since being arrested, Decker had been at the San Antonio Medical Center, treated for a severe concussion and burns to his legs. He'd been guarded around the clock. During the same time, a complaint had been issued by Mooky for all five murders that occurred in Encantador and Mercy over the past year. The complaint had gone to a grand jury, who'd heard the case. They found there to be enough evidence to charge Decker with multiple counts of first-degree murder, and likely several second-degree as well. He'd been deemed healthy enough to come back to Encantador and be charged for his crimes. A trial would happen sometime in the future. And until then, he'd be kept in a regional jail. Kathryn knew all the ins and outs of law enforcement, so he didn't need to explain anything to her. Yet, she needed the particulars. "He's coming back for a hearing early next week."

She cursed. "He's just going to stand in front of a judge and hear the charges against him. The judge will ask how he pleads. Then he'll plead not guilty. Why in the hell does he need to be here? He can have a virtual hearing."

"Yeah, but since he won't get bail, he's going to be housed in the jail in Laredo until his case goes to court. He has a right to be close to his attorney to get a fair trial."

"You don't have to tell me all about the criminal justice system," she snapped. Kathryn held up her palms. "Sorry, I just hate to tell Morgan that he'll be in town again. Right now, she seems strong. Who knows what this news will do to her?"

He didn't blame her for worrying. She was a mom. Wanting what was best for her kids was her job. Kneeling next to Kathryn, he took both of her hands in his. Looking up at her, he said, "Decker's finally been caught. He won't get away this time."

She pinned him in place with her gaze. "You promise me?"

He knew to never make assurances with Decker. Still, he said, "I promise."

The door leading from the house opened. The evening was filled with a shrill scream. "Ohmigod! Brock, come quick. He's proposing."

"What? Wait. No." Ryan rose quickly. He understood how Morgan would get the wrong idea. "I'm not proposing. We were just having a serious chat."

"False alarm," she called to her brother, before going back into the kitchen and letting the door slam in her wake.

Kathryn held her hand in front of her face, hiding a smile. As soon as they were alone, she laughed. "It's not funny," she said, "but it is."

He chuckled, too. Placing a hand on his chest, he said, "That got my pulse racing. Who'd think that we'd ever, you know, get married."

She stood and walked to him. "It's not the worst idea in the world. I mean, not today or anything. But maybe. Sometime."

Ryan was always quick with a comeback or a joke, but she'd left him speechless. Actually, he did know what to say. Reaching for her hand, he pulled her to him. "I never thought you wanted us to be a permanent thing. You are a cop. I'm an ex-con. The two don't usually mix."

Wrapping her arms around his neck, she pulled him closer. "You and I are good together," she said. "The past doesn't matter."

"At all?"

"Here's what I know. You're a good man. You've proved that time and again. And besides…" She sighed and shook her head.

His interest was piqued. "Besides, what?" he coaxed.

He could look into her blue eyes forever. "I love you," she said.

Ryan's pulse started to race again. "I love you, too."

"It's settled, then." She placed her lips on his. "We are both starting over."

"To starting over," he echoed. But with Kathryn, there was more. "You are my second chance. Every time I hold you, I know where I am."

"Oh yeah? Where's that?" she asked.

"With you, I'm finally home."

* * * * *